FLOWERSHOP ASSASSINS

Bye Baby
So Pathetic
Raging Ranger

RAGING RANGER
Louise Collins
Copyright © 2022
Cover Design:
https://www.booksandmoods.com/
Edited by:
https://www.karenmeeusediting.com/

Chapter One

Ranger's heart bled.

He shoved open the door to Blooming Bloomers and collapsed on the nearest seat. His forehead met the table with a bang. His dramatic display only earned him silence. Not enough. Not nearly enough. He lifted his head and dropped it again. And again. One more time with extra force.

"Ow."

"Christ, Ranger," Yates hissed. "You want to give yourself a concussion, do it somewhere else."

Ranger inwardly rolled his eyes. Yates wasn't getting it at all. He'd have to spell it out to him. "You're supposed to ask what's wrong."

"Am I?"

"Yes."

"Well, I don't give a shit."

Ranger didn't lift his head but pointed in Yates's direction, knowing he wasn't alone. He was never alone, not like Ranger, which was the problem.

"Dylan?"

Dylan sighed. "Yes, Ranger?"

"You…you ask me."

"What's wrong?"

Ranger dragged his face off the table and twisted in his seat. Dylan's brow had crumpled in an expression close to pity, but Yates stood next to him with his arms folded, glaring.

"He wasn't there yesterday…again. I can't find him."

Every date Ranger had been on, the stranger had been there in the background, drinking at the bar, smirking under his breath. He was there so often Ranger had dissolved him into a piece of furniture, all until that faithful night when life put their fists on a collision course.

It had been beautiful.

Or at least he thought it had been.

Ranger had punched him.

He'd punched Ranger.

1

The next part had been confusing. Red Fog. Spinning lights. Soaked clothes.

Then they'd scowled at each other across the A&E waiting room.

Talk about a match made in heaven.

Yates huffed. "You've seen him once."

Ranger shook his head. "I've seen him lots of times, but that was the first time we interacted. The first time I looked him in the eye and felt a gooey, warm feeling."

"Maybe you'd pissed yourself?"

"No. It was love at first sight... Not first exactly, but love at first prolonged eye contact. That's practically the same."

"It's bullshit."

"*Date for Success* magazine ran a poll, and one out of three readers said they have experienced love at first sight."

"Those readers still buy that magazine; doesn't that tell you something?"

"It's full of lots of useful tips?"

Yates locked his jaw. "Look, you not seeing him is for the best."

"Is it, though?"

"Yes. There's something about him that left me uneasy." He hummed. "He looked like a goddamn psychopath."

"You look like a psychopath."

Yates puffed out his chest, expanding to maximum height and thickness. One press of Dylan's small hand on his pec, and he deflated.

"Will nobody ever love me?"

Yates grunted. "Get out of my shop."

"Can't you see he's hurting?" Dylan said.

Ranger nodded. "I am hurting. I am."

Yates pinched the bridge of his nose. "Dylan, please don't encourage him."

"I feel like... I feel like Romeo." Ranger clutched his chest. It was a slow bleed, but still a bleed. His heart longed to love. "I feel like I'm dying on the inside. I'm so full of love, but the world is keeping me from my Juliet."

"Have you ever read *Romeo and Juliet*?" Dylan asked.

"Why would I put the subtitles on?"

"No, I meant... Never mind."

Yates clutched his head. "Romeo never punched his Juliet in the face. Maybe that's the reason he's avoiding you."

"What if something has happened to him?"

"Something other than having his nose broken?"

"Yeah. What if…what if he's drunk some sleeping potion, and I'm supposed to find him and go crazy with despair?"

Yates groaned. "Stop watching romance movies on Netflix."

"It's too late. I've moved on to tragedies."

Ranger reached for a rose, but Dylan slapped his hand. Ranger bobbed his mouth open and closed in shock, throwing Yates a horrified expression. "Did you see what he just did?"

"What?" Yates asked from the counter.

"Freckles slapped me."

"Did he?" The smile he aimed at Dylan wasn't manic; it was filthy. Dylan wasn't facing him, but he blushed like he knew.

"I'll have to give him a reward later."

"You two aren't helping my aching heart. You're poking at it. Tormenting it."

"Do you want my advice?" Dylan asked.

Ranger dropped to his knees, begging for it. "Yes, please."

"Forget about him and go on another date. There's someone out there who's perfect for you."

"Do you really believe that?"

"Course I do." He glanced at Yates. "Isn't there?"

Yate frowned. "Huh?"

"There's a guy out there perfect for Ranger, isn't there?"

"I don't know."

Ranger slumped. "You're making me feel really good, bestest bitch of mine."

Yates grunted. "Forget the date part and get yourself laid."

"Get myself laid?"

"That's what I said."

Ranger hummed and got to his feet. He flashed a glance at the bakery across the street. Stud Muffins, appropriately named by the look of the brothers who ran the place. "So what you're saying is I need to get laid, but what I'm hearing is I should go over there and ask those two for a threesome."

Yates frowned, looked, then grew three shades redder. Two of the brothers from the bakery were standing on the pavement outside, taking in an order.

"Stay away from all of them."

"All of them? How many are there?"

"Four."

Ranger counted his sightings with the brothers out on his fingers. "One. Two. Three. I've only seen three."

"There's four. Now leave it at that."

"Twins." Ranger snapped his fingers. "It's got to be twins, right? It's always twins."

"No twins, four brothers, one doesn't work there. Now stop digging before I kill you with the shovel."

Ranger lifted his hands. "Okay, okay, I'll stay away from them." He sighed. "The guy from the hospital was hot though, right?"

Yates shrugged. "If death glares get you going, there's not much beating him."

Dylan scrunched up his face and turned around. Yates pursed his lips and tutted. His whole face softened when he looked at Dylan.

"Your death glares are just pathetic. So pathetic."

Dylan went back to Yates, who all but mauled him with a kiss.

"Guys, come on. This is a flower shop, not a porno set."

Yates didn't pull his mouth from Dylan's. He spoke against his lips while waving Ranger out. "Turn the sign to closed on the way out."

Dylan whipped his head back. "No, leave it on open."

"Kinky motherfucker," Yates growled, going in for seconds.

Ranger grimaced at the smacking sounds and the rustling clothes. He met his limit when Yates, not Dylan, let loose a needy moan and a plant pot crashed to the floor.

"Right. I can tell when I'm not wanted, or needed…"

He waited for them to stop, but they didn't. Yates had lifted Dylan onto one of the display tables, and they rubbed up against each other fast enough to start a fire.

Ranger pushed off from the counter. "I'm off to drown my sorrows elsewhere. Later, bitches."

They didn't reply. Too engrossed in each other's mouths. Ranger was happy for them. Of course he was, but he couldn't help the bitterness too. His closest mates, Yates and Donnie, had both found love when they hadn't even been looking.

He had a few hours left before he needed to pick up Blade and Scope from the dog sitter, so he strolled with no destination in mind and ended up in The Archer pub, like always. The place he brought all his dates. The place he'd met Mr. Right and punched him in the face. The place he'd visited every Friday night since, just in case he showed up.

He breathed in the scent of the place. Smoke, dust, and leather. The lights were kept low, and the floorboards creaked as he stepped across them.

Ranger slipped onto a stool and thudded his head on the bar. A heavy hand patted him between the shoulder blades.

"It might never happen."

Ranger tore his face off the bar and looked at Vince. "Yeah, that's the problem."

Vince pressed his lips into a sympathetic smile. His forehead creased, wrinkles appeared around his eyes, and Ranger gazed up at him with a sigh. *If only Vince was gay.* He was older than Ranger, sure, but the silver hair and the white scruff of his beard looked hot.

"No date again tonight?"

Ranger shook his head. "I think I've got to face it. I'm unlovable."

"Don't say that, of course, you aren't. So what? You've had a few bad dates…"

"A few? I've been on"—he counted them out on his fingers—"twenty."

"Have faith in number twenty-one."

Ranger gestured to the circular table behind him. His dating table. "I don't suppose I can interest you in a date?"

"I told you before if I were gay, it'd be a yes."

"Aren't you even a touch curious?"

Vince snorted, reaching for a glass under the counter. "I think if I was, you'd know by now."

"If I find out you've gotten curious with another guy, I'll kill you."

He was only half-serious. Or half not serious. Depending on whether you were a half glass full or empty kind of person. Vince just smiled and swore across his heart. "I promise it'll be you I experiment with."

He got Ranger his pint, then shuttled to the other end of the bar to serve someone else. The door swung open, sending in a spear of outside light. Ranger hissed and tugged his shades off his T-shirt. He blinked back the burn and slipped them on. Vince looked over and hurried down the bar.

"I swear I'll get the hose like last time if you misbehave."

The hose?

Ranger twisted on his stool, and there he was. Or the shadowy figure of him, at least. The light from outside leaked around his huge body, putting him in perfect silhouette.

He sighed, a long deep sigh, then turned around, and left.

"No, wait." Ranger tripped over the edge of his stool in his eagerness. "Wait!"

He flung open the door and found the stranger leaning against the wall of the pub, lighting up a cigarette. Faint purple bruises lined his eyes. Ranger suspected those were his doing, but the tape had been removed from his nose. His hands were hard-looking and bruised, not Ranger's doing, but something else. The stranger had fighting hands and fighting biceps. He was built to punch and block.

"Hey."

The strange looked him up and down, then tilted his chin in acknowledgment.

The gold hoop piercing in his eyebrow dazzled in the sun. He wore a white-vest top like the last time Ranger had seen him, but this one was free of blood. It hung lower, flashing his pectoral muscles and smooth skin. Ranger swallowed the saliva in his mouth before he drowned himself and took a step closer.

"Your nose is looking better."

The stranger frowned and blew a cloud of smoke in Ranger's direction. "It's crooked."

"It's not noticeable. You have a lovely nose."

You have a lovely nose?

Had he actually just said that? What an absolute idiot. He slapped his face at the prickle of anger forming. It wasn't the time to get lost in the haze. The stranger watched him as he rubbed away his headache, softening it back to a manageable level.

"What about my nose is lovely?"

"Huh?"

The stranger tipped his chin up. His lips crept up in a mocking smile. "You said I have a lovely nose. I want to know how it's lovely."

"It's long."

The stranger's eyebrows shot up. "Long? I've got a long nose?"

"I mean short and not too narrow."

"Not too narrow?"

Ranger swept his hands through his sweaty hair. The stranger was mocking him, and it was starting to make him mad. A dull pain grew behind his eyes, and a blush tinged his cheeks. "Look, it's perfectly proportional to the rest of your features. It suits your face, okay?"

"Okay." He leaned back against the wall, stretching out his body. Ranger couldn't help but look at him, big and beautiful, with giant, hard nipples. *Wait, what?* He slipped his shades into his hair to get a better look. The stranger had oddly shaped nipples.

Ranger glanced at the man's face when he chuckled. Without Ranger needing to ask, he curled his fingers into his vest top and eased it down a little bit more. Both his nipples were pierced with gold studs. Ranger lost all control of his tongue. It rubbed the top of his mouth in a frenzy, and he couldn't seem to swallow hard enough to clear all the drool.

The stranger rearranged his vest and looked away, doing his best to block out Ranger while he finished the rest of his cigarette.

"Are they…are they extra sensitive?"

The man smirked. "Oh yeah, especially when they're being sucked."

Ranger closed his eyes for a second to fight off a wave of dizziness. "Who…who sucks them?"

"Whoever I've taken home for the night."

Ranger scratched the back of his head. It was damp with sweat. He couldn't stop shifting from foot to foot. "And is that usually a man or a woman?"

"Usually a woman."

Ranger took a step back. "Right."

"I said usually."

"*Right.*"

"No date tonight?"

"No date."

"That's a shame. I always enjoy listening to you make a fool of yourself."

Ranger recoiled, running the words around in his head again. "That's not very nice."

"I'm not a nice guy, and don't pretend to be." The stranger dropped his cigarette and stamped it out. "I just want to go for a quiet drink and not deal with you or anyone else for that matter."

"I'm just going for a quiet drink too. Maybe we can sit at a table—"

"No."

"Maybe we can sit next to each other at the bar."

"No."

"With an empty stool between us?"

The stranger smirked. "Make it two empty stools, and we have a deal."

Ranger darted over to the pub and opened the door. "What's your name?"

He hesitated for a moment. "Troy."

"I'm Ranger."

Troy strolled past, leaving Ranger with a lungful of smoke and spicy aftershave. He pulsed his nose like a bloodhound, drawing in the scent in case he ever had to pick it out in a line-up. Vince had his arms folded and watched them intently as they came in with a healthy distance between them.

"No blood, I'm surprised."

Troy glanced at Ranger's pint on the bar, then moved two stools along and sat down. "We came to a truce."

"Good. I can't ban my best customers."

"It was all just a misunderstanding the first time anyway."

Troy attached his fierce frown to Ranger. "Was it?"

"Yeah…"

Truth be told, he struggled to remember what had happened. He'd been on a date. His date had disappeared into the bathroom. Him and Troy exchanged punches. Then he'd come to, staring up at the ceiling with Vince spraying him with a hose.

Vince got Troy a drink but stayed by him at the bar, glancing between them. Ranger gave up on waiting for him to leave and leaned as close as he could to Troy while keeping his arse on the stool.

Ranger cleared his throat. "Do you believe in love at first sight? Or should I walk by again?"

Vince sucked in a huge breath until his eyes verged on popping out.

"I didn't hear that," Troy muttered.

Ranger shrugged. "I can say it again?"

"No, I meant, I'm going to pretend I didn't hear it."

"Okay, so…I don't really know how to go about it, so I'm just gonna come out with it. Will you go on a date with me?"

Troy lowered his drink without taking a sip. All cocky bravado vanished from his face, and he blinked, once, twice, three times. Each time he blinked, he looked more unsure until he blurted in a shrill voice, "What?"

His eyes whipped back and forth as they searched Ranger's for an answer.

"I know I broke your nose, and you broke my ribs, but you said outside sometimes you're interested in guys, so I was wondering if you'd go on a date with me?"

It wasn't rocket science, but Troy was looking at Ranger like it was. His lips bobbed open and closed, and he turned to Vince for help.

Vince laughed awkwardly. "Ranger, I don't think Troy's number twenty-one."

He shrugged. "I don't know until I try, right? Troy?"

"What is it you expect me to say?"

"I'm hoping you'll say yes."

Troy shook his head and huffed at his beer. Whatever wall Ranger had knocked down with his bluntness had come straight back up. "The answer is obviously a no. I'm just thinking of what curse to go with it. No fucking way."

"Why?"

"I'm not interested, that's why."

"Oh, right… You're taken?"

Troy shook his head. "No."

"I'm not your type?"

"It's not that—"

"I'm a pretty adaptable guy."

"Look," Troy growled, slamming his fist on the bar. "You don't want to date me."

"I do—"

"No, Ranger, you don't. I told you. I'm not—I'm the bad guy."

"Let me be the judge of that."

Troy bunched his lips together and tilted his head as he studied Ranger, who was still smiling, still giddy knowing he'd found him. He no longer had to think of them as Ranger and the Stranger, but Ranger and Troy.

"Let's run through what happened a few weeks ago, shall we?"

"What?"

"You heard me."

Ranger grabbed his pint. He concentrated on the cold against his palm. "That's not necessary."

"Oh, I think it is. You were on a date, and as usual, it was going dreadfully." Troy chuckled, lounging back against the bar, body on display again. "Funny as usual."

"How was it funny?"

"You asked him about his first experience of trying hummus…unless that was some kind of code."

Interesting conversation starters are key to a good date.

"No, I was interested. Hummus. It's different, right?"

Troy glared at him. "Oh Jesus, you're serious. Anyway, the date was a disaster."

Ranger couldn't help but curl toward the bar, facing away from him. "It wasn't…"

"The guy looked terrified of you. Everyone except for you knew it was going bad."

Ranger looked over at Vince, who'd shrunk away, shaking his head at Troy. "If you've settled your differences, there's no need to mention—"

Troy brought his hand up, and Vince fell silent.

"No, I think there is. I think he needs a refresher if he's mad enough to ask me on a date."

"Troy..." Vince warned.

"So we all knew your date was a disaster. We were whispering about it. The guy goes into the bathroom and escapes through the window. You sat there grinning like everything was fine, probably thinking about a pot of hummus in your fridge or something."

Ranger couldn't feel the cool against his hand anymore. Even when he tipped the beer into his mouth, he couldn't feel it. There was nothing but heat sweeping through his body. Not a nice heat, but an untamable fire. An inferno that left nothing behind and accumulated in his head.

"Troy—"

"Shut it, Vince. We were gathered around the bar, taking bets on how long it would take for you to notice. Twenty minutes as it turns out, just like I'd predicted. You asked where your date had gone, and I burst out laughing...then you hit me."

"You were lucky I didn't do more."

The words came out of Ranger's numb mouth. His whole body had lost sensation. Nothing left but the inferno that encroached on his vision and the headache beating inside like a drum. Red bled into his line of sight, foggy and stifling. The beginning of a blackout. He closed his eyes to avoid it.

"What was that?"

Ranger smirked. A dark smirk he didn't like the sound or feel of. It twisted his face into something ugly. "You're lucky I didn't kill you."

"Come on, guys," Vince mumbled. "You said you had a truce. Let's not ruin it."

"Did you make a bet too?" Ranger asked. Still not opening his eyes. He took a deep breath and let it go slowly. When Vince didn't answer, he forced his eyes open and looked at him. Everything had a pink hue. The pain in his head left him squinting. He patted his jeans, relieved to hear the crinkle of foil from a paracetamol packet.

Vince dabbed his brow with a beer mat. "I... It wasn't like Troy's making it sound. It wasn't malicious."

"He bet forty-five minutes. He thought you'd be sitting there all night like a dog."

Ranger could do it. He could hold on to his temper. "Right…"

He could clear the red from his vision with just his willpower. He could.

The glass exploded in his hand, showering the bar. His pain receptors didn't register it, nor did his skin pick up on the blood flowing from his palm. It didn't feel like his blood, or his hand, or his arm.

Vince cursed but didn't come any closer. Even Troy's easy smile faded as he eyed Ranger's bloody hand. Ranger turned it over and tutted at the shards of glass sticking out.

"I'm sorry, Vince."

He began pulling them out, leaving a pile of red glass on the bar. The fog of rage cleared. The inferno became muffled, and he let out a relieved sigh at the first sting of pain that wasn't in his head. His hand burned, but it distracted from everything else.

"I didn't mean to make a mess." He leaned over the bar. "Have you got a dustpan and brush or a cloth or something?"

Vince didn't move. His jaw hung open, and his eyes bulged from his face. Troy snapped out of his shock quickest. He pushed his untouched pint away and got to his feet.

"Come on, I'll…I'll give you a ride to the hospital."

"No. I've got it." Ranger slipped off his stool and clutched his hand to his chest.

"Ranger…"

"Yes?" He smiled at Troy, but he didn't smile back. He looked stricken and sunk his teeth into his bottom lip as he watched blood drip from Ranger's arm. Neither Troy nor Vince spoke, but Ranger smiled at them to show them everything was okay, everything was fine.

"So, I better go sort this."

Blood ran in a long dark line from his palm, ruining his T-shirt, but he preferred the sting and mess to blacking out in a rage. He'd controlled it. That was the one saving grace that lit up his face with a smile.

Ranger had controlled himself on the brink of losing it.

He shoved open the door to The Archer and left. He needed to call Anna and warn her he'd be late picking up the dogs—

"Ranger!"

Troy's voice stopped him in his tracks. He didn't turn to face him but looked over his shoulder instead. "What is it?"

"I…I told you I wasn't a nice person."

Ranger looked down at his hand and the long trail of blood snaking down his forearm.

"I don't think I used to be either."

He couldn't remember anything from before he'd been shot in the head, but he had a gut feeling he'd not been a nice man. The sneers and snarls that picked and pulled at his face were muscle memory, expressions he'd once used a lot but no longer wanted. He wanted to smile. Even Yates smiled when he looked at Dylan. Everyone looked nicer when they smiled a true smile. Everyone looked happier when they were in love and someone loved them back.

Troy came up behind him. "What?"

"I said I don't think I used to be a nice person either. But I'm trying to be one now."

"Why?" Troy whispered.

"Because I want to be happy, and I want to make someone happy too."

Troy scuffed his shoe against the pavement. "You serious?"

"Yup."

He carried on walking with a small smile on his lips.

Proud of himself for not killing anyone.

CHAPTER TWO

Ranger stepped into the flower shop with his hand cradled against his chest. Yates ignored him, but Dylan gaped, stumbling off his chair. He offered it to Ranger.

"Sit."

"Thank you, Dylan!"

"He's hurt. Ranger's hurt."

Yates grunted, not looking up from his phone.

"Yates!"

"If he's not currently dying, he can wait."

"What the hell happened?" Dylan asked.

"Oh, what this?"

The nurse had given him a choice of either a nude bandage or a luminous green. Of course, he'd picked green. He lifted his hand, high enough for Yates to see, but he didn't look over from the counter, too busy frowning at his phone.

"Ranger?"

He gave up on getting Yates's attention and put his hand on the table. "Held a glass a bit too hard."

"Ouch."

"That better not be your shooting hand."

Ranger narrowed his eyes at Yates. "So you did notice then?"

"It's practically glowing. I saw it when you were walking by the shop."

"Thanks for your concern."

"Can you still shoot?"

"I could shoot with my feet if I needed to."

Yates cocked his head. "I'll put that on your list of skills."

"Hey," Dylan said, patting his arm. "Does it hurt?"

"Not really, just a prickle. I think I hurt my pride more than my hand. That'll be slower to heal, but never mind."

Dylan eyed him. "What happened to your pride?"

"I found the guy I'd been searching for."

"*The one.*"

"Fucking Christ," Yates muttered behind them.

Ranger ignored him and kept going.

"His name is Troy. And I remember why I punched him in the first place. He laughed at me because my date did a runner out of the toilet window…again." He rubbed his chin. "Maybe I should ask Vince to lock it. What do you think?"

Dylan blinked at him. "I think Troy's an arsehole."

"He's got sexy nipples, though."

"Pierced?" Yates shouted.

"Yep."

"Nice."

Ranger fluttered his tongue on the roof of his mouth just thinking about them. Dylan threw a glare back at Yates, then softened his look for Ranger. "How many dates have you been on?"

"It's got to be twenty. Apparently, the locals make bets on me and how long it'll take me to notice I've been ditched."

"How…" Dylan shook his head. "How can you be so calm about this?"

"If I'm not calm, I'll be angry." Ranger squeezed his eyes shut. "And I try so hard not to be angry."

The pain persisted, always, but he could handle that amount and function like everyone else.

"But they're humiliating you."

Ranger shrugged. "Why are you bothered?"

"Because you don't deserve that, Ranger!"

"Look, Yates isn't bothered…"

His voice trailed off when he glanced at the counter. Yates watched with his arms crossed and a face of thunder. Even with the distance, Ranger could see his nostrils flaring as he struggled to contain himself.

"What pub is this?"

Ranger chuckled. "I don't need you to fight my battles."

"Tell me the address. I'll torch the place for treating you like that."

"Seriously, Yates, if this was a battle I wanted to be fought, everyone would be dead and you'd be trying to smuggle me out of the country."

Yates slumped. "If you're sure."

"I'm sure. Besides, I think you should stay away from fires. For your eyebrows' sake…"

Yates went back to tapping away on his phone.

"What are you doing?" Ranger asked.

"Sending Donnie some last details for his hit."

"Where's he going?"

"Scotland."

"Did you know Scotland's national animal is a unicorn?"

Yates wasn't listening, and Dylan was glaring at the table while his eyebrows twitched.

"Well, I thought it was a fun fact," Ranger said to himself.

"Right," Dylan said, opening up his rucksack. He started loading his books back into it. Then his pens, pencils, and notepad. Determination was written across his face, but Ranger didn't understand the look or why Dylan was beating his rucksack to death.

He finished and dropped it on the floor.

Ranger frowned. "Is that supposed to mean something?"

"It means we're gonna get back at those arseholes."

Yates groaned. "Dylan, your assignment is due on Friday."

"This is more important."

"No, it's not."

"Yes, it is."

"It isn't," Ranger said, smiling at Dylan but intrigued nonetheless. Dylan placed his phone on the table so Ranger could see it. His eyes shone with excitement, and Ranger found his own heart started to thump, not that he had a clue why.

"We'll get back at them rom-com style."

"I like it. I like it a lot. What do you mean?"

"We're gonna hire an escort, and you're gonna have an amazing date, make that arsehole Troy jealous, and show them you are lovable."

"Lovable for a fee," Yates muttered.

"Lovable full stop," Dylan said. He looked up at Ranger. "What do you say?"

"I've got nothing to lose and potentially everything to gain. Maybe I'll hire a high-end, classy escort, and we'll slowly fall in love, and at some point, I'll climb up his fire escape with an umbrella and a bunch of roses."

"That better be a euphemism," Yates muttered.

Dylan shook his head. "It's the ending of *Pretty Woman*."

"Christ, Ranger," Yates growled. "Quit it with the romance movies."

"They give me hope."

Dylan hummed. "I was thinking more like *The Wedding Date* where the lead hires a hot guy to make her ex jealous and want her back."

"Oh." Ranger drummed his hands on the table. "I like the sound of that. What happens in the end?"

"The lead and the escort end up together."

"Okay. It's a win-win either way. Let's find me an escort."

Dylan grinned and began searching the web for an escorting service. Ranger let him take charge and scroll through the men like they were searching for one in a magazine. Ranger said yes to every guy, but Dylan wasn't happy with any of his choices.

"He needs to have the wow factor," Dylan explained. "The stop and stare for a bit without realizing effect."

"You really should be doing your assignment."

Ranger tipped back in his chair and stared at Yates. "Since when did you turn into such a dad? Huh?"

Dylan snorted. "Sometimes I call him daddy. He likes that."

"Really?"

Yates groaned. "You two are insufferable together. I'm going into the office. If anyone comes, let me know."

"He's blatantly going to jerk off."

"Do you think so?" Dylan asked.

"Yeah."

He slid the phone in front of Ranger and slipped off his seat. "You keep looking, and I'll…I'll be back in a second."

"I think you should give Yates more credit than that."

"Keep looking."

An escort to make Troy jealous and show the whole pub someone could last a date with him. Ranger nodded to himself. Yeah, that could work.

It was nice to have Dylan's perspective rather than just Yates's, who would've happily petrol bombed the pub in revenge.

****

Ranger stepped into The Archer wearing his tightest white T-shirt and his smartest black jeans. He hooked his sunglasses over the neck of his T-shirt and gave Vince a dazzling grin.

It wasn't returned. Vince scratched the back of his head while averting his gaze. "Ranger, I'm sorry about last week."

Ranger waved the apology away. "There's no need. It's me that should say sorry. I made a mess of your bar and broke your glass."

"How's the hand?"

"Getting better."

"Here," Vince said, pulling a pint. "This one's on the house."

"You sure?"

Vince nodded and gestured Ranger closer. "About what Troy said." His brow creased, and he shook his head. "We were messing about—no, that's not right. We're a bunch of arseholes, okay?"

"Okay." Ranger sipped his beer, then stared into Vince's eyes. He winked. "Always remember I fuck arseholes."

Vince recoiled. "Right…err."

"How do I look?" Ranger said, stepping back from the bar. He gestured to himself, his hair, his face. Looking good on the outside could make you feel good on the inside. Ranger had read that in a magazine; so far it hadn't worked. The magazine didn't take into account constant buzzing pain, but still, he was trying.

"You look great," Vince said.

"Thanks. I'm meeting someone here. Date number twenty-one." Ranger grinned. A big joyous grin that sucked Vince into grinning back.

"That's great, Ranger. I'm rooting for you."

"Thanks." He took his pint and sat down at his favored circular table with his eyes fixed to the door. Vince watched him with a pained expression, pretending to clean the bar.

"He hasn't stood me up," Ranger said.

That had happened a few times, and Vince always winced on his behalf. Ranger let it go. He couldn't let things like that get to him because if he did…

The door opened, and his date stepped inside. Scott had been more than happy to offer his services to make someone jealous. Shorter and slimmer than Ranger with bright blue eyes and chin-length wavy hair. He stroked it back with his fingers, flashing his sharp jaw, and when he smiled, his eyes popped, and dimples appeared, and the heavens probably opened outside. Ranger's eyes watered at his beauty.

Dylan had wholeheartedly agreed to Ranger's choice, leaving Yates in a possessive grump.

Scott stepped up to the table and offered his hand out to Ranger.

"So, I'm Scott."

Ranger knew that.

"Nice to meet you. I'm Ranger."

Scott knew that too.

"This isn't where you're sitting, is it?"

Ranger looked at the table. "What's wrong with it?"

"It's a bit exposed." Scott looked about, then pointed to a table in the corner of the pub with a padded bench to sit on rather than separate chairs. "That one is perfect. Trust me."

He hiked his eyebrow up, flashing Ranger a look that said he knew what he was doing. Ranger conceded, grabbed his pint, and moved into the corner. Vince exchanged small talk with Scott while getting him his drink. Next thing Ranger knew, he was sliding along the bench, sitting with his thigh glued to Ranger's.

Scott sipped his beer, then smiled.

"Why the table in the corner?"

"It's snug, cozy, and I can put my hand here." He demonstrated, placing his hand on Ranger's thigh and squeezing. "A more intimate touch, also to speak directly to each other we have to twist our bodies, turn into each other. It's the beginning of a kiss that doesn't happen, but it *could*, at any moment. That's the point."

"I see."

"There's sexiness in subtlety. I could sit on your lap and kiss you senseless, but no one would believe that. They'd look over and think either I was after a one-night stand or they'd suspect this wasn't a real date." Scott brushed back his hair again. His soft curls drifted forward again, and Ranger got a whiff of his shampoo. He didn't just look good but smelled it too. "We need the guy you're after to believe this is a real date. He needs to think he sees chemistry."

Scott grinned, flashing cute dimples.

"You could be a model." Ranger shook his head. "No, you *should* be a model."

"Thank you, Ranger. You look like you could crush a man's skull with one hand."

"I could, you know."

Scott snorted, shuffling closer. "So, is he here yet?"

"Not yet."

"Every time that door opens, I know you'll be tempted to look who came through, but you must not. Understand?"

"I understand."

"He doesn't exist, but I do. The only places your eyes should look are into my eyes, at my mouth, your drink, and occasionally, if you need a breather from the intensity, the table. Understand?"

"Yes."

Scott nodded, then brushed his hair back with both hands. Not long enough to tie up, it drifted forward again.

"Your hair looks really soft."

"I'll let you touch it when I kiss you goodbye."

Ranger swallowed. "Kiss me?"

"But it won't be in here, it'll be outside before I climb into a taxi. If we've put on a good performance, he'll follow. He'll be watching."

The air in the room shifted. Ranger picked out Troy's slow steps. His boots clunked on the wooden floor. The leather stool squeaked as he sat down. Ranger swore he heard the small thud as Troy rested his elbow on the bar.

"I don't even need to ask if that's him." Scott chuckled lightly. "You've gone stiff as a board."

"Sorry."

Scott squeezed Ranger's thigh. "Relax for me."

It took effort, but Ranger forced his muscles to soften.

"I'm not gonna look at him either. If I look over at him, it'll be as if I've already been warned about him. Instead, I'm gonna look into your eyes, Ranger."

He did, softly. Ranger looked back.

"You told me I should be a model earlier."

Ranger widened his eyes. "Without a doubt."

"Why do you think that?"

"Have you looked in a mirror?"

Scott chuckled and pressed into Ranger's side. He backed away again, had a gulp of his beer, then leaned against Ranger. "But why exactly? Look at me and tell me."

Ranger licked his lips. "Your eyes are insanely beautiful."

"In what way?"

"The color."

"Give me more, Ranger."

Ranger studied Scott's eyes. "They're blue, but not an overwhelming blue. They're not the deep blue of the ocean. They're the blue of the ocean that meets the sand. You know the bit. It looks cool, but it's not. It's warm. You swim in that bit. There's no danger. There's nothing unknown lurking. It's bright, and clear, and perfect."

"Well done. Is there anything else nice about my face?"

"All of it."

Scott raised his eyebrows. "Specifics."

Ranger swallowed the lump in his throat and dropped his focus to Scott's lips. "You've got a pretty pink mouth."

"Have I?"

"Yes, it looks cushiony, padded." Ranger scrunched up his face and shook his head. He'd never been put on the spot before to describe someone's mouth. His cheeks were glowing, but not from anger. He directed a breathless laugh at his lap.

"You're making me blush."

"I know," Scott whispered. "You don't look like the kind of guy that blushes easily."

"I don't. I get angry, I don't blush."

He took a sip of beer, but it didn't help his flaming face.

"Blushing looks a lot different than anger."

"How?" Ranger asked.

"Well, for one, you're trying your hardest not to smile right now, and you're ducking your chin, not lifting it in challenge. Anger is red pigments in your skin, puffing you up, making you look threatening, but a blush equals vulnerability. It's about letting your guard down, and that's attractive." Scott laid his hand on Ranger's thigh and kept it there. "Now tell me without looking, what is it about the man at the bar that you find attractive?"

Ranger didn't glance over. "He's rugged and rough around the edges with an obvious chip on his shoulder."

"These all sound like reasons to avoid him."

"He's got nipple piercings."

"Ouch."

Ranger laughed. "I find them sexy. He sits with confidence. He's muscular and strong and tall, and I think...I think he's unhappy."

"Unhappy? Why do you think that?"

"I don't know. I get a vibe from him, an angry one. It reminds me of me, I think."

"I'm sitting with you, and I'm not getting any bad vibes. It's quite the opposite, actually."

"I see rage and spitefulness in his eyes. I can't explain it." Ranger lowered his gaze to the table. "I feel like I used to be like that. I feel like he's me or a me that once existed."

Scott hummed and grabbed his pint. He took a sip. "Why do you keep talking like there's two of you?"

"I used to be different. Or so my friends tell me. I used to be crueler, more aggressive, intimidating. I don't think I was a nice person." Ranger tried to shift away, but Scott came with him until they were pressed in the corner together. "I got shot in the head, and I can't remember much about before. I get these vibes and these prickles, and I know it's easier to get angry than it is to feel happy. It's easier to snarl than it is to smile."

"You're always smiling."

Ranger spluttered out a laugh. "It's a conscious thing. I try really hard."

So hard.

"Why?"

"I don't want people to think I look like a horrible person. I mean, my job's not exactly nice, but I'm not horrible. I know I'm not, but it's hard to be a good person when your own brain tells you that you're not. When you know there's something ugly in your head. I'm either happy Ranger or raging Ranger, and I know which one I prefer."

"Like Jekyll and Hyde."

Ranger frowned. "What's that?"

"It's a book."

"Is it on Netflix?"

Scott laughed, patting Ranger's leg. "It might be. How long have you been single?"

"Literally, for as long as I can remember, but according to my mates, I wasn't a relationship kinda guy."

"But you are now?"

Ranger nodded. "I want it all. The love, the sex, the ups and downs, the petty arguments, the make-up cuddles. Even the mundane things like making a grocery list for the week, then going shopping. Walking the dogs around the park and arguing whose turn it is to bag up their poop."

Scott tilted his head, smiling. "Really?"

"Really."

"And you think the guy at the bar is that guy?"

Ranger stumbled over his words, then sighed. "He's got as much chance as any, right?"

Scott didn't answer. He stroked Ranger's knee. "I'm gonna get us some more drinks. Don't look at the bar. Distract yourself with your phone or something. Remember, he doesn't exist while I'm in the room."

"Got it."

****

Scott was a genius, Ranger decided, that and a sexual lothario.

He spoke in lower and lower whispers to force Ranger to lean into him. He darted glances at Ranger's eyes and mouth, then told him to repeat the looks on him. It looked sexual and intimate from the outside, but, in reality, they'd been discussing the news. The mundane. Things other people found boring, but Ranger was just happy to be talking to someone.

After two pints, Scott decided the date was over.

"Won't it look bad if we don't stay until closing time?"

"Trust me. We've had two pints, so we're still sober and leaving with smiles. If we got drunk and slobbered all over each other, it wouldn't suggest romance, but trash."

Ranger snorted. "Okay, I'll trust you."

Scott checked his phone. "My taxi is outside. This is how we leave. You follow me out, simple as that. No glance in his direction, no acting surprised that he's here and you didn't notice, no opening the door for me. Understand?"

"I understand."

"The key is not to chase but be chased."

Got it. Ranger frowned. He really didn't.

They both stood up; Scott took the lead and led Ranger out of the bar. He didn't glance at Vince, or Troy, or anyone, and once outside, they headed straight to the taxi without stopping. Scott opened the back door and turned to Ranger.

"What else about me makes you think I should be a model?"

Ranger snorted. "Not this again."

"Trust me."

"Your hair." The wind brushed it in front of Scott's face. He stroked it back, but it was unruly and snagged on his full lips. "It looks so soft. I'm not sure whether it should be stroked gently or twisted with a fist."

Scott smiled, with big dimples and bright-blue eyes. "You're blushing again."

"Yup." Ranger clutched the back of his clammy neck. "I can feel it."

"Kiss me," Scott whispered. "Softly. No tongues. Four presses. Don't nod. Just do it."

Ranger cupped Scott's face. He brushed his hair away from his mouth and kissed him exactly as he said. Slowly. No tongues. Four presses with the last one the longest. He opened his eyes in time to see Scott's flutter open.

"Perfect." He ducked into the taxi with a smile on his face. "Watch me leave, don't look behind you, and walk straight home. Goodnight, Ranger."

"Night, Scott."

Ranger watched him go. The whole time he felt eyes burning in the back of his head, but he didn't turn to face them. He hooked his thumbs in his jean pockets and set off in the direction of home.

CHAPTER THREE

"How?" Ranger ran his hands through his hair as he paced. Life was unfair. It was so unfair. *Jesus Wept!* "How can you be a bigamist?"

He stopped and glared at Mr. Clifton for a response. He mumbled something beneath the gag, but it had soaked through with dribble and Ranger didn't want to touch it.

Ranger had gagged him but left his hands untied. Mr. Clifton was too terrified to move. His eyes were trained on the gun Ranger waved around.

"I mean, I'd get it if you were some sexy as hell guy with a smooth voice, impeccable dress sense, eyes of sapphire, and a body you just want to crawl over, but you're not."

No. Mr. Clifton wore a stained white T-shirt that was miles too big and jeans that emitted a strange smell. His wild eyebrows protruded from his face by an inch, and his eyes were sunk so far into his head it was like peering into tunnels.

"I've been trying to find someone for over a year. Someone to set up home with. Someone to love, and then there are guys like you, jumping from partner to partner, living separate lives around the country. I mean, how did *you* even convince these women you work for the secret service?"

Three women in total. Three women believed they were dating a spy who disappeared abroad for months at a time when in reality he drove 100 miles north to his other family. Once there he played the same trick on that poor unsuspecting woman. Three wives and countless lovers on the side.

"How?" Ranger asked again.

Mr. Clifton wasn't attractive. His tunneling eyes were too close together and darted around his surroundings like a cornered rodent. Ranger leaned closer and spied whiskers growing from Mr. Clifton's nose. Personal grooming was not high on Mr. Clifton's agenda, or not the normal kind at least. While Ranger had been watching him from the window, he hadn't just picked his nose and ate it but slicked his hair back by spitting on his hand. The guy was gross, but he had romantic options. *How unfair was that?*

"The women you've messed about are all beautiful."

Mr. Clifton nodded. Tears rushed down his cheeks.

"Anyway, I've got a list of names and messages to read out, so let's get this show on the road." Ranger cleared his throat. "Rebecca says, 'Rot in hell, you piece of shit.' Ella says, 'Bye-bye, asshole.' Nancy says, 'This is for all the fat jibes and for chasing after my sister.' Oliva says, 'Women across the country will be relieved to hear of your death.'" Ranger took a deep breath. "I should have put on a voice, shouldn't I? Made it more interesting? Given each woman a character. What do you think?"

He looked at Mr. Clifton, but he didn't answer.

"Rude."

Mr. Clifton flopped back into the sofa with his eyes closed.

"I guess you know what they sound like. Try to imagine their voices. That will add to the authenticity." Ranger looked back at the list.

"Where was I... Hope says she's gonna fuck your brother. Again. Ouch. I like Hope, and finally, Harriet says you're scum and she knows you poisoned her—" He blinked as the list slipped from his fingers. Ranger aimed and pulled the trigger.

The pip, splatter, and thud signaled the end of Mr. Clifton.

"Dog. She knows you poisoned her dog," Ranger finished while putting his gun away. "I love dogs. If anyone hurt my boys, I'd burn down the world."

Ranger twitched his nose. If anything, the thick scent of blood pouring into the air was a blessing. Ranger stared at the sorry mess that was Mr. Clifton.

"You were lucky enough to have not one woman but three that married you. Three that wanted to set up home with you. Three women to cook, and clean, and take care of you." Ranger held up his forefinger. "I just want one. One guy and I'd treat him like a goddamn king."

He left the hotel room via the window and took off in a sprint. Yates had sorted the CCTV for the night and found Mr. Clifton's room number. All Ranger had to do was break in through the window, read out the list, and fire between his eyes.

Ranger yanked his phone from his pocket. Rain sprinkled the screen. He wiped it on his jacket before answering.

"Done?" Yates grumbled.

"Yup."

Ranger picked out Dylan's voice in the background. "No, I'm not asking that."

"What?" Ranger asked.

Yates sighed. "Dylan wants to know whether the escort was good-looking."

"Like you wouldn't believe."

"Ranger said he was ugly and must've been using filters."

"Dylan, don't listen to him!"

"Shhh," Yates growled. "Don't give yourself away. Are you almost at your bike?"

Ranger sighed. "I don't ride a bike anymore."

"Oh yeah." Yates chuckled down the line. "You drive a tank."

"It's a people carrier."

"For the dogs?"

"Yes, for the dogs. It's got a great safety rating."

"Whatever. Text me when you're home."

Yates hung up, and Ranger slid his phone into his pant pockets. He jogged along the footpath, took a left by the hairdresser's, and slipped down the alley behind the launderette. The rain got heavier, soaking through his clothes, but he didn't mind. There was no point getting irritated by something as simple as rain. Water dropped down like a waterfall from the blocked gutters, and Ranger stepped beneath them, humming a cheerful tune.

He skidded to a halt at the shadowy figure leaning against the people carrier, puffing on a cigarette. The orange tip glowed as Troy inhaled a deep breath. Rain streaked his face, and he cupped his hand over the end of his cigarette to stop it from going out.

"You've been following me."

Ever since the fake date with Scott, Ranger had felt eyes on his back and a presence lingering close by. Troy had been stalking him, but rather than spin around and confront him, Ranger had allowed him to. He enjoyed being the subject of Troy's fixation.

"Yes." Troy flicked his cigarette away.

"Why?"

Troy shrugged and swung his head in the opposite direction, toward the dead end of the alley. He pushed off from the wall and advanced on Ranger.

"Did you like it when he kissed you, all soft and sweet?"

"It was a nice kiss."

"Nice," Troy spat. "Who wants nice?"

"Me."

Troy narrowed his eyes. "Really?"

"Did you like watching him kiss me all nice and sweet?"

"No. I did not."

Troy forced Ranger to walk backward until Ranger met the wall. Raindrops clung to Troy's lashes. When he blinked, they dropped to his cheeks and ran down his jaw. Ranger followed a drop. He leaned in to catch it with his mouth, but Troy pulled back.

"Don't."

"Why not?"

Then Troy was on him, meeting Ranger's mouth with a grunt. He sucked and bit and bullied Ranger's tongue into submission. His hands slapped the wall on either side of Ranger's head to keep him in place.

Ranger's heart was battering his ribs, jolting his whole chest as they locked their mouths together. He dragged Troy forward by the hips and brought their crotches flush.

A spark of white-hot arousal went through Ranger when their hard cocks rubbed. The kiss was a mess, wet and slippery. It was a mauling with no grace, but Ranger shivered and made sobbing sounds for more, clutching Troy's arse to keep them together.

Troy ended it, pushing off from the wall like it were a vertical push-up.

Even in the low lighting of the alley, Ranger could see Troy's mouth. It shimmered, swollen and wet, looking sexy as hell. The rain ran down it, and Ranger made his move, surging forward to suck his lips before being pinned against the wall by Troy.

Ranger let his head thump back against the bricks. "Go on a date with me."

Troy stroked his swollen mouth. "No." He gestured to the car. "We can go back to yours, fuck and get this over with, but no date."

"No fuck without a date."

"You serious?" Troy tilted his head.

"Deadly."

"Fine." Troy rearranged his jacket and left the alley without glancing back. With no conscious thought, Ranger began to follow him before Scott's advice slapped him in the face.

Don't chase, be chased.

He nodded to himself, jumped into the car, and started the engine.

Troy poked his head back into the alley. "Seriously? For us to fuck, I have to go on a date with you?"

Ranger didn't answer. He gave Troy a warning rev, but it just sounded embarrassing in the people carrier. Troy raised his eyebrows, laughing.

Ranger got his revenge by driving fast through a puddle and soaking him. He grinned like a maniac at Troy jumping up and down in anger as he drove away.

****

Ranger stepped into Blooming Bloomers with a huge smile on his face.

"Oh, Christ," Yates muttered, dropping his head into his hands. "Why are you looking so happy? Actually, I don't want to know."

"Well, I do," Dylan announced, twisting his seat toward Ranger. "How'd it go?"

"You need to study," Yates said.

Ranger raised his eyebrow. "Are you a broken record?"

"You're too much of a distraction."

"Thank you." Ranger checked his reflection in the window, practically glowing. "That's one of the kindest things you've ever said to me."

Yates groaned. "You're impossible."

"So?" Dylan asked, bobbing up and down.

Ranger perched on the table and searched his pocket. He pulled out a folded piece of paper and handed it to Dylan. He took it with a smile. "Your list?"

"My list."

Dating Advice Magazine published an article on the fifty most romantic things to do with your partner. Ranger had shown Dylan, and after some not so gentle coaxing from Ranger, they'd both made a list of six to try.

Dylan opened it out on the table. His eyebrows shot up. "Kissing in the rain."

"Yup. Ticked off."

"With the escort?"

"No. With Troy. He followed me last night."

"He did what!?" Yates roared.

"Relax, he lost me once I parked the car."

"Did you not know he was following you?"

Ranger shrugged. "Maybe I kinda liked that he was."

"You like being stalked?"

"I seem to remember you were hoping to stalk Dylan at the student bar, but he didn't turn up…"

Dylan's brow furrowed. "You said you just happened to be passing through."

"This isn't about me and you. It's about Ranger not being careful."

"Was it a good kiss?" Dylan asked.

"So good." Ranger sucked on his lip thinking about it.

"How come you haven't kissed me in the rain?" Dylan asked.

Yates folded his arms. "We've kissed in the shower; that's practically the same thing."

"It isn't."

Yates peered over Dylan's shoulder. "What else is on this stupid list?"

"Candlelight dinner. A romantic stroll. A movie out. A movie in. Sharing a bath. That's my list anyway."

"Wait," Yates whispered. He touched Dylan's shoulder. "Don't tell me you made a list too?"

Dylan checked the time on his phone. "I really should be going. My lecture starts soon."

He leaned up on his tiptoes to kiss Yates goodbye, then fled as if he was on fire. Yates watched him go before turning to Ranger.

"Oh," Ranger quirked his eyebrow, "where is Donnie again?"

Yates frowned. "Huh?"

"Where's Donnie?"

"Scotland. I told you."

"Then how come he sent me this?"

Ranger handed the postcard to Yates. The Maldives. Without Troy's kiss being on his mind, he might've been annoyed about the postcard landing on his doormat.

"Courtesy of you, an early honeymoon apparently."

"He's winding you up."

"He'd better be." Ranger narrowed his eyes. "Maybe I wanted to go on a holiday to the Maldives."

"Pay for it yourself."

"Rude." He took the postcard back, thought about tearing it up, but couldn't bring himself to rip Donnie and Elliot's names apart. They belonged together, even if they were trying to irritate him.

Yates rocked on his feet. "So…"

"So?"

"What's on Dylan's list?"

"His list of romantic things?" Ranger hugged his stomach as he laughed.

Yates shoved him. "What?"

"All things you'd hate."

"Tell me one thing."

Ranger roamed his gaze across the ceiling, then laughed. "Take a tango class."

Yates's nostrils flared. "Fuck that."

"It's what Dylan wants."

"No way in hell." Yates spun around and walked away. "Oh, and you'd better be more careful around Troy. I'll transfer you the money for Mr. Clifton later."

"Three wives. When you told me, I expected to walk in on some Hollywood hunk."

"Maybe what he lacked in looks he made up for elsewhere."

Ranger scrunched up his face. "I did not want to imagine what his cock looked like."

"Why did you then?"

"Anyway," Ranger said, checking his watch. "I need to go get the dogs. Later, bitch."

"Just call me Yates."

Ranger slipped out of the door. "Never going to happen...bitch."

****

Ranger whistled as he headed down the street. A grin spread across his face as his eyes fixed on the house at the end of the row. The one with the open window and two heads hanging out.

"Hello, boys!"

Ranger knocked on the door and was immediately mobbed by the Dobermans. They bounced around and licked his face as he pushed his way inside. Anna greeted him in the hallway, then bellowed at the dogs to stop jumping. She stood barely taller than five feet, but she could shout with a booming voice that demanded obedience.

"How have they been?"

Anna pointed at Blade. "Perfect. An absolute gentleman."

Blade sat down, chest out, back straight, looking exactly as Anna had described. Ranger couldn't imagine a prouder-looking dog. He beamed at him in the same way he imagined a father would beam at his son.

"But Scope... Well, Scope..."

Ranger turned to Scope, who sat in a slump, with his head hanging low and his droopy eyes fixed on Ranger's knees.

"Not only did he get over the gate into the kitchen, but he opened the fridge and ate my left-over chicken."

Scope belched, then sunk his head even lower in shame.

"How was your date?"

Fake date, but Anna didn't need to know that. She leaned forward, intrigued.

"It was good. A few drinks and a kiss goodbye. Standard date, I guess."

"Yes!"

She punched the air with both fists, putting the dogs on high alert.

"Going on another?"

Ranger nodded. "This Friday."

Scott had insisted.

"Double yes!"

Anna turned away from Ranger and addressed Blade and Scope. "I'll be seeing you for another Friday sleepover."

Scope released another chicken-smelling burp into the air. Anna sighed and went to find their leads. They walked home as normal, but as Ranger watched his dogs fondly, he saw the exact moment Blade detected they were being watched. He bristled and slowed his pace, grumbling at odd intervals.

"It's all right."

Ranger knew who was following. It wasn't the first time Blade had sensed someone acting unusual on their walk. Ranger suspected it was something to do with the footsteps. Troy's clunky boots took each turn they did. Scope didn't seem to mind, but Blade stiffened up and no longer seemed at ease on his walk.

"Relax, bud. I've got him exactly where I want him."

CHAPTER FOUR

Ranger pushed open the doors to The Archer and took a seat at the bar. Vince hurried over to him with wide eyes, beckoning with his chin for Ranger to speak.

"Oh, right. The date went well."

Vince smiled and punched the air just like Anna had. "I thought as much. You couldn't keep your eyes off each other, and you were blushing and smiling. Where did you find him? Out of a catalog?"

Ranger blinked. "Why do you say that?"

"He looks like a model."

"Oh." Ranger laughed. "He's handsome."

He was, no doubt about it, but he wasn't Ranger's kind of handsome. He liked the rough and rugged look. The lip gnawing, tongue fucking kind who kissed in the rain and jumped up and down in a rage when they got soaked by a puddle.

"I could feel myself turning."

"Hey!" Ranger wagged his finger at Vince. "You promised me if you ever got curious, it'd be with me."

Vince slapped his hand to his chest. "And I promise that's still the case. I'll get you a beer."

"Thanks."

The door to the pub opened, and the air shifted. Ranger knew who'd stepped inside without looking over. Troy's gaze hit him with a rush of awareness. He licked his lip, mind lingering on their kiss.

"So, are you seeing him again?" Vince asked.

Ranger caught the drink Vince slid his way. "Tonight, at seven."

Troy whistled, then chuckled darkly as he slipped onto his stool. Two stools away from Ranger's. He spun to face him, though, and lounged against the bar with a cocky smirk twisting his lips.

"What?"

"It's five minutes past seven, right now. Maybe pretty boy got bored."

Ranger looked past Troy to the door. "He'll be here soon."

His text had told Ranger to trust him. He didn't know why but he did.

"Unless he's stood you up."

"We had a good date last week. Why would he?"

"All the others have."

A prickle of pain sparked in Ranger's temple, but relief swept it away when Scott stepped inside the pub. He rushed past Troy and pulled Ranger into a hug. He'd tied his hair back, showing off his perfectly sculpted jaw, and when he smiled, his dimples sunk even deeper than Ranger remembered.

"I'm sorry I'm late."

"It's only five minutes."

"Still," Scott said a quick hello to Vince, then checked his watch while shaking his head. "Movie starts at eight."

"What movie?" Troy asked.

Scott looked at him, and the second his eyes fell on him, Troy stiffened and sucked the air from the room as he pushed his chest out. He looked on the verge of getting to his feet just to slam home his muscle in the face of Scott's beauty.

"*Wilma's Wedding.*"

Ranger's eyes lit up, and he smiled at Scott.

"That sounds like a fucking rom-com." Troy mumbled.

"You don't like rom-com's?" Scott asked.

Troy almost slipped off his stool. "Hell no. Look at me, of course, I don't."

"Well, it's lucky for Ranger that I do." Scott checked his watch. "We probably have time for a quick drink before the taxi gets here."

"I'll get you one," Ranger said.

Scott squeezed his bicep, then moved to the table in the darkened corner. Troy glared at him until he sat down, then he twisted to glare at the bottles behind the bar instead. Ranger didn't speak to him as he waited for Vince to pour a beer, then ambled over to the table.

Scott pressed against him as soon as he sat down and squeezed Ranger's thigh.

"Quick. Tell me something else you like about me."

"Huh?"

"You said you trusted me."

"I do."

"Come on then. Something else that makes me model material."

Ranger sighed as the familiar twinge of a blush grew in his cheeks. "When you smile, you get dimples."

"You like them?"

"Yeah, they're cute."

Scott narrowed his eyes. "Cute?"

"You're cute and beautiful. A winning combination."

"And yet..." Scott placed his hand on Ranger's chest, over his heart. "I don't excite you."

He opened his mouth to apologize, but Scott shushed him.

"You're the first man that's hired me and hasn't asked for sex."

"I told you, I wanted to see if I could make Troy jealous."

"You've certainly done that." Scott smirked. "I can see the steam pouring from him."

"Good."

"I said we were seeing *Wilma's Wedding* to wind him up even more."

Ranger's shoulders sunk. "Oh..."

Uncertainty flittered across Scott's face. "What is it?"

"I thought you were serious."

"Wait. You want to go see it?"

Ranger clutched the back of his neck and shuffled away from Scott. "Well, you know, it would be nice to see it at the cinema... It's not like I can go see it alone. I look odd, and there's no way Yates would come with me. I could ask Dylan, Yates's boyfriend, but that's just weird—"

"I never thought you'd like that kinda thing."

"I do. Jesus, you should see my Netflix list. It's rom-com after rom-com."

Scott narrowed his eyes. "What's your favorite?"

"*Love before Dawn*."

"I love that movie. I'm not going to lie, but a tear crept out when they kissed at the end."

"A tear? I was full-on blubbering."

Scott snorted and whipped out his phone. "I'd love to see *Wilma's Wedding* with you, Ranger."

"I feel like you're gonna say but..."

"No buts." Scott showed Ranger his phone. "I'm booking the tickets, that's all. Where do you want to sit?"

"Bang in the middle."

Scott selected the seats. "All done."

"I'll buy the drink and snacks. Hell, I'll take you for a meal afterward if you want?"

"That'd be nice." Scott squeezed Ranger's thigh. "It's a...a date."

He kissed Ranger on the cheek, so softly it itched. When Ranger glanced over to the bar, Troy was watching, chomping on his bottom lip, reminding Ranger of a few days before, when they'd been soaking wet and grinding in the alley.

"Excuse me." Ranger laughed awkwardly. "Just gonna take a leak."

He hurried into the toilets and splashed cold water on his face. It wasn't the time to get excited thinking about kissing Troy.

"He's sweet, isn't he?"

Ranger straightened at Troy's voice. "He is."

"Too sweet, sickly sweet."

"I think he's the right amount."

"Liar."

When Troy leaned in to meet Ranger's lips, he couldn't hold in his whimper. He felt the rage of it, Troy's teeth on his lips, his tongue pushing Ranger's aside. The force of the kiss winded his mouth if such a thing were possible. Ranger didn't know; he didn't care. He was breathless and dizzy and horny as hell.

Ranger clutched onto Troy's shoulders. And by the time Troy had pushed him into a cubicle, his cock was already painfully hard, bobbing desperately in his pants.

Troy brushed his hand down Ranger's chest before cupping his hardness and rubbing frantically with his thumb. "Bet pretty boy wouldn't blow you in the restroom."

A loud knock on the toilet door froze them in the act. Ranger shoved Troy out of the way just as Vince poked his head inside the toilets.

"Um, taxi's outside. You'd be mad to keep Scott waiting."

"I'm coming."

"If only," Troy drawled, revealing himself from the cubicle. Vince frowned; his gaze dropped to the sizable erection tenting Troy's jeans. Ranger empathized. He was struggling not to stare at it too.

"Right." Vince backed out, turning red. Ranger followed with Troy hot on his heels. Erection be damned, Ranger could feel the heat of it on his arse.

"Have a good one and enjoy the movie," Vince said, not meeting Ranger's eyes or anyone's for that matter.

"No doubt I will."

Troy yanked Ranger back and stepped in front of him. Their chests thudded. His lips twitched with a sneer, but his eyes found Ranger's mouth. They glued to it.

"Excuse me."

"No," Troy mumbled.

"What do you mean no?"

Troy pressed his forehead to Ranger's and tried to force him backward, back toward the toilets, the cubicle where they'd been about to—Ranger shook his head, clearing his dirty thoughts. He wanted to date, not get blown in toilet cubicles. *Although…*

"Troy…" Vince warned.

"Let me pass," Ranger growled.

"Right, I'm getting the hose."

Troy took a step back and whipped around to face the bar. His breathing came out shaky, and Ranger glanced at his locked jaw, his hands curled into fists.

"Ranger," Vince reminded. "Scott's waiting."

"Right."

Ranger left the pub and found Scott outside leaning against a taxi.

"Well?" he asked.

"I think we're getting to him."

"Good." Scott patted the top of the car. "Come on. We've got a movie to catch."

It was on the tip of his tongue to tell Scott about the kiss in the toilets, but in the end, he kept it to himself.

****

"Duck pond first, and then an ice cream."

Scope tugged him in the direction of the ice cream stand despite Ranger's bargain. He sighed and dragged Scope away.

"Can't you be more like your brother?"

Blade shot a sidewards glance at Scope whining, then huffed from his nose. Scope kept flashing sad eyes at Ranger and whining softly.

"I didn't say no ice cream. I said duck pond first."

The hair along Blade's spine stood up. Ranger snorted. "Yeah, bud, I sensed it too."

Ranger rounded the corner and pulled both dogs from view. The clunky boots got louder, then Troy stepped in front of them. Blade growled, and Troy tripped over as he hurried to put distance between them.

"Fuck!"

"He doesn't like you following us." Ranger held his hand out to Troy, but he jumped to his feet without taking it.

"I wasn't. I just happened to be walking the same way as you and your mutts."

"I've never seen you around this way before."

Troy lifted his eyebrow. "I've always been here. You've just not noticed."

"Make yourself useful," Ranger said, tossing Troy a lead. He caught it and stared down at Scope still flashing sad eyes at anyone who made eye contact with him. "What's up with this one?"

"He wants his ice cream, not that he deserves it." Ranger chuckled.

"What did he do?"

"Broke out of his crate, opened a door, jumped a gate and got into his sitter's fridge again, and this time ate a whole ham." Scope lowered his head at his list of bad deeds. "I should've called you Elliot."

Troy's gaze flicked back and forth, studying Ranger. "What?"

"It doesn't matter."

Ranger started walking, and after a sigh, Troy did too. It was a nice day; the sun was up, but the air carried a cool current. Ranger could wear his shades and vest without anyone giving him strange looks. They walked in silence, but Ranger found it wasn't uncomfortable. He didn't feel the need to break it, and neither did Troy.

"We're almost there."

"Where?"

Ranger gestured to the bench in front of them. "The duck pond."

The same 'duck pond' Donnie had once swum across to save Ranger's life. Troy traced his finger along a bullet hole in the bench. "Wasn't there some shoot-out here once?"

"That was over a year ago now."

Ranger slumped as he sat down. For over a year, he'd been trying to find himself a boyfriend. He'd scrolled through every magazine and website for tips, and nothing had worked.

Troy hesitated for a moment, then sat down too. Ranger risked a small smile. All those articles, and it was Dylan's advice about making Troy jealous that looked the most promising.

"So I found your dating profile."

Ranger lit up. "Yeah? What did you think?"

Troy raised his eyebrow. "Part-time stripper?"

"Are you doubting me?"

"Not exactly."

Ranger sprung up from the bench. "I can give you a taster."

"What?"

"Show you some moves."

Troy's gaze lingered on the old couple feeding the ducks. "Not sure that's a good idea."

"Sure is." Ranger swayed his hips as he gripped the bottom of his vest. He hoisted it up, bit by bit, revealing his firm abs. "First, we start with a belly button flash."

"Ranger..."

"Peekaboo."

He flashed it, once, twice, three times for luck. Troy looked as if he was fighting back a smile.

"And then we go a little higher."

"Okay." Troy shook his head. "I get it. Stop."

Ranger ignored him and shut his eyes. He peeled his vest up his body, swaying to an imaginary soundtrack. He got it up to his pecs before reopening his eyes. Blade glared alongside Troy, but Scope at least had the manners to humor him and wagged his tail.

A duck quacked. Ranger shifted to point at it. "See, he's feeling it."

"Congratulations. You've turned on a duck," Troy drawled.

"Did you know ducks have corkscrew-shaped penises?"

"No—what? Why do you know that?"

"Fun fact."

Ranger pinned his T-shirt with his chin and circled his pinkie finger around his nipple. "Time for a game of lick the tit."

"Jesus," Troy breathed. His face glowed red. "Enough already."

"Have I seduced you with my moves yet?"

"No."

The old lady gasped and dropped her loaf of bread.

"At least she's having a good time."

Troy surged off the bench. He yanked Ranger's T-shirt back down while shaking his head. "I think she's having a heart attack."

"Heart-stopping stripper. I can add that to the profile."

Troy laughed. He looked so open when he laughed, and Ranger melted against him.

"Did you like the taster?"

"Not really."

"Your cock says otherwise." Ranger took Troy's hands off his sides and placed them on his arse. "And I was just about to start shaking this for you."

Troy squeezed him, then retreated to the bench. "You're an odd guy."

He spoke the words at the ground as if they weren't meant for Ranger. "I knew you were different, but not this…odd."

"How did you know I was different?"

"I've seen you on dates." Troy snorted. "I've *heard* you on dates."

"And?"

Troy cleared his throat. "The questions you ask…"

"You're not on about the hummus one, are you?"

"If only it was just the hummus… If you were to commit a murder, what would be your weapon of choice…"

"It's interesting."

"Terrifying." Troy shook his head.

"Well, you gonna answer or what?"

Troy looked down at his hands. "My fists… 'If you were an animal, what animal would you be?' I think the guy you asked said something like a butterfly, but you said tiger because you wanted to rip the guy's clothes off. Coming from you, that's terrifying."

Ranger frowned. "How long have you been eavesdropping on my dates?"

"Told you. They're entertaining. You've got the worst luck."

"My luck's changed with Scott."

"Mr. Beautiful, but boring… How was the movie?"

Ranger ignored the sneer in Troy's voice. "It was good."

"You can't be serious."

"Predictable, yeah, of course, Wilma had a childhood crush on her maid of honor, and she was the one that hid the phone in the room to record them going at it to stop the wedding from happening."

"I thought it was Wilma's sister that had planted the phone."

Ranger stopped. "What?"

Troy stopped too. "What?"

"You've seen it?"

"No."

"Then how do you know about the sister?"

Troy shrugged and powered ahead. "Lucky guess."

"Right." Ranger chewed his bottom lip to mask his smile.

"I just happened to be going that way," Troy snapped.

"So you thought you'd follow us and sit for a whole movie?"

"I was hoping you'd get up for another toilet break."

Ranger shook his head. "We're not hooking up in a toilet."

"There's a Portaloo down the road."

Ranger tipped his head back and laughed. When he glanced at Troy, he caught the end of his laugh too.

"I'm in love with your laugh."

Troy eyed him wearily. "What?"

"Your laugh."

"You shouldn't say shit like that."

"But it's true. I love it. It might be my favorite sound in the world."

"There's plenty of better sounds."

Ranger poked him. "Like what?"

Troy's face reddened. "I don't know, like a bird flying into a window or a…a sneeze."

Ranger pressed his lips together not to laugh.

"Don't put me on the spot like that." Troy shuffled and looked away from Ranger. "And don't say you love me."

"I didn't. I said I love your laugh." Ranger scrunched his nose in reply to Troy's glare. "Which I do."

"I'll make a conscious effort to laugh differently then."

Ranger grinned. "Admit there's a part of you that likes me."

Troy raised his eyes skyward. "There's not."

"There is."

"I like marmite but don't want to date it."

Ranger widened his eyes. "You like marmite? What kind of sick fuck are you?"

Troy snorted, then covered his face. "You've got to stop making me laugh."

"Why?"

"I don't want to laugh. It's involuntary. I want to sulk."

"Gotcha," Ranger said. "I've got to make you sulk." He hummed before asking, "Did you see Scott kiss me goodbye again?"

Troy spluttered. "What? No…"

Ranger turned his head away. The end of the night had been weird. Scott had been giving him a look, an odd look, like he thought Ranger might kiss him goodbye. He hadn't, but it was satisfying knowing the thought of it had irritated Troy enough for him to light up a cigarette.

"You smoke too much."

"I smoke when I'm stressed."

"Am I stressing you out, Troy?"

Troy rubbed his temple. "Kinda."

"Go on a date with me."

He groaned. "Not this again."

"One date."

"It'd be awful."

"Why?"

Troy gestured to himself. "I don't do well on dates. Not to mention you'll ask me something stupid like if I was a tree, what tree would I be?"

"One I'd want to climb."

Troy laughed, then groaned. "Ranger."

"It'll be fun, and besides, you're doing okay on this one."

"This isn't a date."

"No," Ranger sighed. "It's a romantic stroll around the park."

He sat down next to Troy. Blade jumped up on the bench to be beside him. He snapped at Scope when he looked as if he would follow.

"Woah." Troy shifted further from Ranger and Blade. "That one's crazy."

Blade watched the ducks on the pond, tatty and loud. Sitting by the water was a lesson in restraint for Blade, one that was finally paying off. It had been weeks since Ranger had needed to jump in after him and wrestle him for a duck.

"He's the top dog, or in their case, top brother. They don't always get on."

"Yeah." Troy chuckled to himself. "I know what that's like."

"You have a brother?"

Troy shifted his jaw. "No. Yes." He sighed. "We don't get on. Ever. I haven't seen him for a few years."

"But you still care about him, right?"

"We've never got on."

Ranger frowned at Troy's non-answer but didn't push. "Sometimes Blade puts Scope in his place. He never hurts him, just reminds Scope that he's top dog and he could if he wanted to, but I've also spied him grooming Scope's coat, licking his face, and when Scope ate a dozen eggs from the sitter's fridge, Blade stayed by his side despite his gas."

"Well, that's definitely love." Troy laughed.

Ranger found himself leaning toward Troy. He looked so nice when he laughed, so carefree, but it didn't last long. His expression tightened, and he shoved along another inch to keep their distance.

"What about you? Any siblings?"

"Not that I can remember." Ranger drummed his fingers against his head. "I had an accident of the shot in the head variety. Can't remember much, but Yates told me I didn't have any siblings, and I never knew my parents, so yeah…"

"That sucks."

"I think I prefer that to having good parents and not being able to remember a single memory."

"My mum had me young. She was great. Can't fault her. She died eight years ago. Things went downhill after that."

"I'm sorry."

"It's not your fault. My relationship with my dad collapsed soon after she died. We've not spoken in years, but I want to. Fuck, I want to. More than anything."

"Reach out to him."

"I'm trying, but it's hard." Troy nodded to himself. "I'm trying."

"Good."

"This conversation is getting too deep for a Sunday morning. What do you say to going back to yours, locking the dogs in the garden, and fucking?"

"I'd say thanks for the offer, but I've got plans today."

"Scott," Troy spat.

"No, actually. Someone else."

Troy drew his shoulders up. "So you're not double-timing Scott, but three-timing him?"

"I'm meeting with a friend."

"What friend?"

Ranger narrowed his eyes.

A twist of unease upset his stomach. "It's none of your business. If you're not willing to date me, I'm not willing to introduce you to my friends."

"I don't want an introduction; I just want a name."

"Tough."

"Fine." Troy handed the lead back to Ranger. He looked as if he was about to say something else but shook his head and trudged back the way he'd come.

Ranger rolled his eyes when Scope whimpered.

"You've known him all of twenty minutes," he said, stroking his head. "Besides, I haven't told you who we're having ice cream with." Scope's ears perked up, and Ranger grinned at him. "Your favorite person in the world, second only to me of course… Dylan."

His tail wagged in a fast blur as he jumped up on the bench. Blade growled him down again, but it didn't lessen Scope's joy.

****

Scope lost his damn mind when he saw Dylan waiting for them at a table. He yipped, and yapped, and bounced up and down. Even Blade couldn't keep him under control. He launched himself at Dylan, licking long stripes over his face.

Dylan fussed over him and scratched the base of his spine when Scope presented it to him.

"I think dogs do that to encourage mating," Ranger said.

"That's gross."

"And yet you're still scratching him there?"

"But…he's a boy dog."

"And?"

Dylan chuckled. "I got you all your favorites. Blade his peach ice cream and Scope his strawberry ice cream, and you a coke."

He passed one of the small tubs of dog-friendly ice cream to Ranger. He opened it up for Blade, who took his time to lick from the pot. Dylan would've needed an umbrella to protect himself from Scope's tongue. Ice cream sprayed everywhere as he gobbled it down.

"Slow down, or you'll choke." Dylan chuckled.

"Choke, it's ice cream. He's more likely to get—"

Scope pulled away sharply with a whine and scratched his ear with his foot.

"Brain freeze," Ranger finished.

"Poor thing."

"Idiot more like." He rested his hand on the table.

Dylan uncurled Ranger's fingers and hissed.

"I don't have a snake in my palm, ya know."

"It still looks sore."

"It's fine." Ranger poked the bag on the table. "What's in here?"

"Something for Yates."

"You've come a long way if you're bringing sex toys to the park."

Dylan's cheeks glowed. "It's not a sex toy."

"What is it then?"

"A present."

"Aka sex toy."

"It's a shirt. I found this silk pattern that was perfect, and one of my friends is doing fashion design, and she made it into a shirt. I've been working in the university shop to pay for it."

"Let's see it."

Dylan carefully got the shirt from the bag, still neatly folded. Black silk and covered in huge yellow lilies. "You know, in honor of Edna."

Ranger kept his face blank.

"It's...it's even got a different pattern on the inside, see?" Dylan showed him. "Tiger print."

Ranger blinked.

"What do you think?"

"Well, it's disgusting."

Dylan's face dropped. "What—"

"Yates will love it, though."

Dylan lowered his face to the table. "Jesus, Ranger."

"Couldn't resist winding you up. When Yates sees that shirt, he'll get so excited he'll probably explode all over the shop."

"There was something else," Dylan said, putting the shirt in its rightful place. *Where no one could see it.*

"What is it?"

"So um...Yates is acting weird."

Ranger unscrewed the lid of his coke. "How?"

Dylan leaned over the table. He bit his lip, fighting with himself. Ranger waited to see if he'd reveal the problem, but when he didn't, he took a mouthful of coke.

"He's been sending me these tango videos."

Ranger spat his coke out on the table. He laughed, wiping his mouth.

"You okay?" Dylan asked. He leaned over the table and thumped weakly on Ranger's back.

"Yeah, went down the wrong tube. Tango videos, you say?"

Learning the tango was a hundred percent *not* on Dylan's list.

Dylan nodded. "It's weird. I mean, he doesn't seem like the type that wants to dance, does he?"

"No. No, he does not."

"Maybe he's having a mid-life crisis."

"Bit of advice, my freckled friend, don't say that to him."

Dylan looked away. "What if I embarrass him? Jesus, I'm just going to embarrass him, and he'll dump my arse."

"Hey." Ranger flicked Dylan's hand. "Stop that."

"But do you really see me all in black with flared pants and an open shirt, prancing around a room?"

"More so than Yates, he's going to look hilarious."

"If it's what Yates wants, I'll do it and try my hardest not to trip over my feet and face plant the floor."

Ranger patted his shoulder. "That's the spirit. Actually, I've got something which might help you out."

He tugged his wallet from his jeans and leafed through the coupons. "Free Tango lesson, Thursday the 17th at Darling Dance studio. You could give it to Yates next time you see him, see his face light up."

Dylan took the coupon. "You just happened to have this, huh?"

Ranger held open his wallet, flashing his coupons. "I come prepared."

"What's the news with you?"

"Well..." Ranger leaned back and tugged his list from his pocket. "You got a pen?"

Dylan raised his eyebrow as he swung his rucksack onto the table. "Sure."

He leaned over and watched as Ranger ticked off 'a romantic stroll.'

"With the escort?"

"No." Ranger snorted. "With Troy, ten minutes ago. Scope liked him."

"Scope likes everyone. It's that one you've got to convince."

Blade stopped eating his yogurt and turned to Dylan.

Ranger swore his eyes narrowed a fraction.

"He's doing it again."

"Doing what?"

"Trying to stop my heart with a look. I can't believe they're brothers."

Ranger shrugged. "I won't ever know for sure, but they look similar."

"All Dobermans look similar. They look evil."

"They're misunderstood," Ranger said, petting Blade.

Ranger's neck prickled, and he looked down at Blade and saw his hair at his scruff standing up. Their stalker was somewhere close by, watching as usual. Ranger smiled, enjoying the burn of the eyes on his back.

CHAPTER FIVE

Ranger couldn't recall the last time he'd been bowling. It must've been before his accident, maybe when he was a kid. He watched Scott bowl and tried to force up a memory, but there was nothing, only a sense of sadness before it pitched into anger, and he winced.

He clutched his head until it passed.

Scott whooped and leaped into the air. "Strike."

Ranger peeled his eyes open. "Nice one."

"You okay?"

He let go of his head and sat up straight. "I'm good. Remind me again why we're here?"

"Bowling's fun."

Even Ranger had admitted it had been fun, but after an hour, he wondered what it was supposed to achieve. They couldn't make Troy jealous if he wasn't around.

"You're up." Scott tugged him up by the arm and shoved him toward the bowling balls. "Show me the weapons."

"Huh?"

"Your guns."

Ranger tilted his head. "Real guns?"

"Your arms, you idiot."

"Oh." Ranger took his turn while Scott acted as a personal cheerleader. He wasn't even aware of how many pins he knocked down, but by Scott's pitying 'aww,' he suspected not many.

"So when are we going to The Archer?"

It was Friday, and there was a high chance Troy would be there. It seemed the logical place to be.

Scott waved his question away. "Later. I'm having fun."

He bounded over to the bowling balls and chose his favorite bright orange one. Ranger didn't retreat; he stood close to him.

"You're charging me by the hour, right?"

"Right."

Scott's easy dismissal brought out Ranger's headache. He frowned, shadowing Scott as he went to take his turn. It wasn't that he didn't like Scott's company. It was just he was paying for a service he didn't want.

He cringed. Even in his head, it sounded bad. Scott shot him a smile that was *all* dimples.

"What's wrong?"

"I think we should head over to The Archer."

"Don't be a dick, Ranger."

He took a step back. "How am I being a dick?"

"You're ruining a perfectly nice date."

"But I don't want one with you."

Scott winced and hugged the ball to his chest. Ranger wanted to suck his words back into his mouth, but at the same time, he didn't. It was the truth.

"Look, after this game, we'll go to The Archer."

"You said that before."

"I paid for ninety minutes, so we might as well use them."

A sharp pain exploded behind Ranger's eyes. He huffed as he shifted from foot to foot. "No. I paid."

He'd paid for the drinks, the food, and the bowling. He wouldn't have minded paying if it was a real date that he wanted to be on, but Scott had hijacked the night. Every time he expressed his annoyance, Scott revved up for a row. Ranger couldn't afford a row. He couldn't afford to get angry.

Scott spun away and launched the bowling ball down the alley. It thudded, bounced, and ended up in the gutter.

"Goddamn..." Scott clutched his shoulder. Pain etched across his handsome face, and Ranger's headache fizzled to a manageable throb.

"You okay?"

"Pulled it, that's all."

Ranger herded him back to the seats, and Scott slumped. He sighed. "You're not a dick. I shouldn't have called you that."

No, you shouldn't have. Ranger shook the thought away and sat next to him. "It's okay."

"It's not okay. It's just...I don't get this often." He gestured to the bowling alley.

"You don't get dates?"

"I get picked to escort for my looks. I rarely get to know someone out of the bedroom. You don't look at me like I'm a piece of meat, and I thought you were having fun with me."

"I am." Ranger scrunched his eyes shut. "I was."

"I'm sorry."

Ranger took over rubbing Scott's sore shoulder. He groaned, leaning into the touch like a dog starved of affection.

"That feel good?"

"So good." Scott slipped onto the floor and nestled his way between Ranger's legs. Ranger stiffened for a moment before carrying on. There was nothing in it. He was massaging Scott's pain away, that was all.

Scott stretched his neck to the left, giving Ranger more access. "Where did you learn to do this?"

"I took a course at the regional college. I do scalp massages too."

"Show me."

Ranger slid his fingers into Scott's hair and began on his scalp. Scott moaned and drew his knees up to rest his head against. When he stopped, Scott elbowed his calf. "A little longer, please. It feels nice."

Ranger obliged. "I do foot massages too."

"You're a man of many talents."

"I may look intimidating, but I do nice things."

"Do you cook?"

Ranger hummed. "I took courses on that too, and one on how to make cocktails, and coffee. One on massages, homemaking, and first aid."

"First aid?"

"So I can save your life if the need arises."

Scott chuckled and tipped his head back to look at Ranger.

"Why all the courses?"

"I wanted to be ready."

Scott spun around to face him, leaning up on his knees. His eyes dropped to Ranger's mouth. "Ready for what?"

"My boyfriend."

"You really want one, don't you?"

"I'll treat him like a king, make sure he's happy."

Scott's bright smile faded, and he shifted his gaze away. "And you think that guy is Troy?"

"I don't know. I find him attractive—"

"But you find me attractive too, right?"

Sure, he was attractive. Angelic almost. No doubt he should be a model, but for hair and skin products, not for piercings, and tattoos, and bare-knuckle boxing. His heart quickened as he imagined Troy on the cover, shirtless ,with his nipple piercings shining, and sweat gleaming on his muscles.

"Right?" Scott said again, squeezing Ranger's thighs. His eyes sparkled under the lights, two baby-blue diamonds screaming their beauty. Ranger didn't want to be the one to shatter them.

"Of course you're attractive."

He was, subjectively he was stunning, but he didn't rush heat through Ranger's veins like the thought of Troy did. Wasn't beauty in the eye of the beholder anyway?

Scott slumped against his thigh. "You kept me hanging there."

"Sorry."

"I'm gonna call us a taxi."

Ranger bounced his feet on the floor. "Great. I know us *dating* is starting to get to him. He'll give in eventually and let me take him out."

Scott didn't say anything. He got up, fished his phone out of his pocket, and went to make a call. He came back ten minutes later with a coy smile on his face and held his hand out to Ranger.

"Taxi coming?"

"It'll be here in thirty."

"Thirty?"

Scott slotted his fingers through Ranger's and dragged him out of the bowling alley. It was dark outside, and the air had a bitter chill. Scott kept tugging Ranger, and he didn't protest, even when he was pulled between two buildings and out of sight of the street. It was gloomy; the dull lamp on the wall flickered on the verge of going out.

"What are we—"

Scott's mouth covered Ranger's before he could finish. He jolted back in surprise and knocked his head against the wall. Scott's tongue didn't demand entry but coaxed and teased. If it had been Troy on him like that, he would've melted to a puddle on the floor, but Scott's soft lips and smooth upper lip weren't doing it for him. He moved his mouth away and laughed softly.

"Hey, what's going on?"

"I'm feeling a bit frisky, that's all."

"Frisky?"

"I want to treat you like a king." Scott pouted. "My king."

He fluttered his eyelashes at Ranger and kissed down his T-shirt as he got to his knees. Ranger tangled his fingers through Scott's hair in an attempt to stop him, but he only moaned and dove his face into Ranger's crotch.

He cringed, wondering what the right etiquette was for that moment. Thanks, but I'm not interested? No doubt it would damage Scott's pride being turned down. He leaned back on his heels and gazed up at Ranger.

He was in shadow, except his eyes that caught a distant light and shone. Calm ocean blue not badass bitter brown.

"I won't charge you for this," Scott said, scraping his hair back. He rolled a hairband off his wrist and secured his hair in place. Far too neat and ordered for Ranger's preference.

"You said you were charging by the hour."

Scott laughed and pinged Ranger's belt buckle open. "This last hour will be free. I don't want to be paid to do this."

Ranger swallowed. "And what's exactly is 'this'?"

"I'm gonna blow you. Then you're gonna take me home and fuck me."

"Right…Well."

Scott's nimble fingers undid his jean buttons and yanked them down. "Well, the thing is…"

"You're not hard," Scott whispered. He dropped back on his heels. "I…I thought you'd find it hot, the whole public sex anyone could see scenario. Other guys do."

His expression pitched with sadness. Ranger found himself laughing off his lack of arousal to make Scott feel better. "It's cold, that's all."

"I'll warm you up."

Scott pulled down Ranger's boxers and snuggled his face deep into Ranger's crotch. He began kissing his flaccid cock. The sensation left Ranger grimacing. Feather-light kisses that were absolutely not helping the situation. Ranger winced, wondering how to end the awkward encounter without humiliating Scott. He was beautiful, but not Ranger's kind of beautiful. Ranger's "beautiful" was prickly and angry with a near-permanent frown and piercing eyes.

He had biceps that bulged, and hard hands, and fucking nipple piercings, and wouldn't tease, he'd take, just like he took Ranger's mouth in a kiss the week before.

He groaned as a current of arousal went through his body. It fed to his flagging cock, and it managed a small rise, but Scott didn't use it to his advantage. He didn't fuck his mouth over it or use both hands to jerk him to get him going any further. Scott licked with too much caution. Too much theater. It was a show, not an experience, and Ranger's cock withered with disappointment. He could keep thinking of Troy to get hard and endure an unsatisfying blowjob, but thinking of guy A while being sucked off by guy B was a dickish thing to do.

Ranger wasn't a dick; he was nice, or he was at least trying to be.

"Stop."

Scott leaned back. "What's the problem?"

"Ranger's not the problem in this scenario. It's you."

An orange cigarette end glowed in the mouth of the alley. Troy's boots clunked as he stepped closer, all menacing swagger. His glare targeted Scott.

"Me?" Scott said.

"You," Troy repeated. "If it were me on my knees in front of Ranger, his cock would've burst his jeans open and a big dollop of precum would've spat on the ground."

"Fuck," Ranger murmured, shuffling his back on the wall. Troy took another slow drag on his cigarette. It glowed red like the devil, but Ranger couldn't look away. He wanted him closer; he wanted him there.

"Now get up," Troy snapped, pointing at Scott with the cigarette.

Scott staggered to his feet. Ranger could see him staring from the corner of his eye, but he couldn't look away from Troy. An aura surrounded him, something dark and electric.

"Here's what's gonna happen. You're gonna leave the alley and get a taxi home, and I'm gonna blow Ranger so hot and fast I doubt he'll last a minute."

Ranger made a sound that was unfitting of the powerhouse he was. A frail whimper. That was the challenge Troy had set him, last a minute. He already doubted himself.

"Off."

Ranger yanked his boxers down further to join his jeans around his knees. Shoes, he had to remove his shoes first—

"I wasn't talking to you. I was talking to him." Troy shoved Scott away. "Ranger no longer needs your services."

"Wait." Ranger gaped. "You know Scott's an escort?"

"Course I do, but escort or not, he's not sucking on your cock."

Ranger was hard, so unbelievably hard. Even the cool chill of the alley didn't deter his wagging cock. He grabbed it and swirled his thumb around the head. The wet against his thumb made him moan.

"No touching," Troy growled.

Ranger let himself go, but he felt the build-up of precum at his tip before it dripped. Troy had made him drip.

"You can stand around and watch if you want, pretty boy, pick up some pointers on how to please a guy like Ranger."

Ranger closed his eyes to regain some composure. When he opened them again, Scott had gone, and smoke wafted up from between his legs.

Troy blew a hot breath over the head of his cock. The precum clinging on simmered, and Ranger couldn't resist thrusting his hips forward.

"Someone's needy." Troy laughed.

He held his cigarette between the V of his forefinger and middle finger as he clutched Ranger's hips. He took Ranger deep into his mouth, and his knees shook, but all too soon Troy withdrew and snarled in disgust.

"Urgh, you taste like pretty boy's mouth." Troy flashed a fierce frown at Ranger. "That won't do."

He shoved his cigarette between his lips and used both hands on Ranger's cock. His sweeping palms used Ranger's drooling cock to smear wetness up and down his length.

Ranger whimpered, unable to help it. Troy used Ranger's excitement to lube his cock, never stroking with enough focus to get off, but soaking his skin in his own arousal. Ranger thrashed, rolling his skull against the wall.

"Troy, you're killing me."

"When I suck you off, I only want to taste you."

His cock twitched, drooling more precum over Troy's palms. Ranger whined pitifully at his desperate display. It was embarrassing, but he couldn't deny his toes were curling. Troy took a hand away to hold his cigarette and blew hot smoke over Ranger's cock. It tingled, and he hissed in a breath through his teeth.

"And a little of me."

Troy started rubbing him with the power Ranger knew he possessed.

The alley filled with the sound of slick slides and rough breaths. Ranger touched the top of Troy's head, not silky soft strands, but short and prickly. He moaned, rocking his pelvis in time with Troy's hands.

"I'm gonna come."

Troy snorted. "I've not even put my mouth on you yet."

The fist around his cock didn't relent. It beat at him until Ranger's back arched, and his stomach contracted.

"I can't *not*," he gasped.

Troy took Ranger into his mouth and, with one deep suck, pulled him straight to the back of his throat.

Ranger was coming before he had time to process the change in sensation or the spongy wall his cock had been slammed against. Pleasure rippled through him as he unloaded in pulses. Troy stayed put, mouth around him, swallowing everything until Ranger began to come down to earth, heaving and shuddering and seeing fucking stars.

Troy pulled Ranger's cock out slowly, keeping his lips tight, cleaning off the cum and saliva that covered his skin. His lips popped, and he pinned Ranger to the wall with a sharp look.

"You didn't even last a second with my mouth on you."

He grinned up at Ranger, not a beautiful bright grin, but a mocking dirty one.

"You played dirty."

"It's the best way to play." Troy got to his feet and dusted his knees, not looking at Ranger.

"How did you know we were here?"

"I've been following you." Troy turned back to him. "Does that freak you out?"

"No. It's nice to be chased for once rather than doing the chasing."

Troy nodded. "I think I gave pretty boy a scare."

Guilt descended on Ranger. He flashed a look at the entrance of the alley, but Scott was long gone.

"How long have you known he was an escort?"

"I managed to find him after your first date, lots of scrolling, but there he was. The pretty boy you were trying to make me jealous with."

"It worked."

Troy narrowed his eyes. "Marginally, but the guy just pissed me off more than anything."

"Because you were jealous."

"No. Because he's been taking advantage of you."

Ranger gestured to himself. Double the weight of Scott. Muscular, strong, there was no way Scott could've taken advantage.

"I don't think so—"

"On your second *date*, you paid him back for the movie ticket, then paid for the snacks, afterward he decided he wanted to eat out at Prime Italia, which costs a goddamn fortune, and he didn't even eat all the courses. And after that, he wanted to try the new cocktail bar on Fleet Street."

"How did you—"

"I've been following you, remember?" Troy narrowed his eyes away from Ranger. "And then today you're bowling, you didn't seem like you wanted to be here, but he kept throwing his weight around and threatening to have a tantrum."

"I didn't want to get annoyed."

"You bought him food and drink, even let him spend money in the arcade. You were spoiling him."

Ranger frowned. "He's an escort. I'm paying for his time."

"That time should've been on what you wanted to do, not what he wanted to do. I met my limit when I saw you stroking his hair."

"Scalp massage."

"Whatever. It was the way he looked at you afterward. Like he *wanted* you. Like he wanted you more than a client, and I wasn't just gonna stand around and let him have you."

"So you interrupted his blow job and took over?"

"Yeah." Troy's lips lifted with a cruel smile. "And you loved it, and now…"

He flicked the butt of his cigarette onto the floor and stamped out the glow.

"Now?" Ranger asked.

Troy stalked over and pulled up Ranger's boxers and jeans. Ranger took over to fasten the buttons and secure his belt, eyeing Troy's mouth with an overwhelming need to taste him.

Troy nodded, satisfied, then pulled Ranger away from the wall, and grabbed him by the back of the neck. He marched him from the alley toward an awaiting taxi.

"You're gonna take me home and let me fuck you."

Ranger's stomach flipped, and he missed his footing. Troy either didn't care or notice and continued to drag him up the road.

CHAPTER SIX

The thing was, Ranger had never bottomed for anyone. *Never.* Even without remembering his life before he got shot, he was certain that beastly part of him never lifted its arse in the air and asked for a pounding.

But Troy wanted to fuck him, and Ranger wanted Troy, so it looked like it was happening. Getting in the taxi and the journey home all passed in a blur. Ranger's nerves jumped from paralyzing uncertainty to knee-trembling excitement. He was gonna have sex with Troy, not in the way he'd imagined in his head, but still...

Troy flung cash at the driver before dragging Ranger out of the taxi. His hand clasped around the back of Ranger's neck, taking him toward the front door.

"Keys!"

Ranger jumped at the bark of his voice. He slipped his keys from his jeans and handed them over to Troy.

His heart hammered with anticipation as Troy led him through the house via the hold on his neck.

"Wait..." He tripped. "How did you know where I lived?"

He'd not told the driver the address, Troy had.

"Later." He growled.

It was unexplainably arousing being handled with such possessiveness. Troy hadn't only chased him, but he'd captured him too, and like he was a hostage, he was being pushed from room to room.

"Bedroom?" he asked.

Even the gruffness of his voice made Ranger shiver. "First one on the left."

Troy pushed him inside and let go. When Ranger turned to face him, he was already simultaneously taking his T-shirt off and slipping out of his shoes. His bronzed skin pulled taut over his muscles, and the two studs flashed at Ranger, tempting him closer.

"Wait for it," Troy murmured.

"Wait for what?"

Troy undid his jeans and shuffled out of them. His boxers were compromised by his huge cock, the waistband stretched with a teasing gap, but Ranger didn't have to wait long before Troy was yanking them down. His erect cock bobbed free, long, and thick, a frustrated shade of purple at the tip.

That wasn't the reason Ranger's heart skipped a beat. Oh no. It was the metal glinting at him. Troy had a piercing, a Prince Albert piercing, and it wasn't a thin hoop; it was huge, the size of a bull's nose ring.

Before he could move, or possibly faint, Troy pointed at him. "Off."

Ranger couldn't process anything; his mind was frazzled. Instead of pulling his T-shirt off, he grabbed on to it and ripped it in two.

Troy swallowed hard. "Man, that was hot."

Ranger's jeans were too thick and tough to rip. He growled as he struggled to remove them. Troy didn't help matters. He took hold of the piercing and used it to shake his cock. Precum sprinkled the carpet. He let it go, and it wagged up and down before settling under the weight of the piercing.

Once he was down to his boxers, Ranger dropped to his knees and opened his mouth to receive Troy's cock.

He could have wept as the metal slid against his tongue and shot an awed glanced at Troy. The piercing moved as he sucked. He could slide his tongue through it, around it. When he pulled back, he gripped Troy's base and stared at his cock. The weight of the hoop tugged at his slit, opening it enough for Ranger to flutter the very tip of his tongue against.

Troy cursed and smashed his fist into the wall.

"Quiet," Ranger told him. "Don't interrupt."

"Interrupt?"

"I'm having a moment right now. A moment with your cock." Ranger hooked his finger through the hoop and lifted Troy's cock higher. He tipped up onto his tiptoes and made a sound of discomfort, but Ranger ignored him.

"You're the most beautiful thing I've ever seen." He showered Troy's tip with kisses, then captured the head in his mouth. He hummed around the piercing, and Troy jolted up the wall.

"Fuck, Ranger."

He pulled back. "I said, 'Don't interrupt. We're getting to know each other.'"

"Stop speaking to my cock."

Ranger sighed, rubbing Troy from root to tip. "Ignore him," he told the piercing. "He's trying to ruin our fun, but I won't let him. I'm gonna fucking worship you. I'll clean you every day with my tongue, and I promise to play with you every time you're out."

Troy's cock twitched at Ranger's cooing. He licked away the pearly drop that formed.

"Fuck, but most of all I want to see what it looks like when you come."

Troy panted, rolling his hips. "It's different. It—

"Shush." Ranger narrowed his eyes. "I wasn't talking to you."

He crept his hand up Troy's body and yanked on one of his nipples. He moaned and thrust his hips into Ranger's face. Precum smeared against him, and he chased the ring with his tongue to lick at it. A hint of the salty taste wasn't enough. Ranger took the head of Troy's cock into his mouth and started sucking. Both of his hands found their way up to Troy's chest, and he played with all three piercings at once until Troy was shuddering and moaning.

"Stop!"

Ranger dropped back on his heels and looked at Troy with wide eyes. "Did I hurt you?"

"No." Troy chuckled. "I was about to cum."

Ranger licked his lips. "That's a good thing."

"It is, definitely, but I want to come inside you. The first orgasm is always the most intense, and I want it while I'm fucking your brains out." He looked down at Ranger like he was hungry. Like he was starved. It sent a thrill racing through Ranger's body. He couldn't deny Troy. He found he didn't want to deny him.

"All fours. On the bed."

Ranger did as he was told and waited. Troy came up behind him and yanked his boxers down. The sudden vulnerability made Ranger clench and rock forward on his knees.

"Fuck..." Troy groaned.

"What is it? Is something wrong?"

Troy grabbed him by the arse and began kneading his cheeks. "You're big and beautiful."

Ranger had never dwelled on the size of his arse before. Jeans always fit him snuggly; he guessed that meant he had a large arse. It hadn't mattered either way until Troy was groping him, moaning at the supple flesh, and muttering dirty words at Ranger's hole.

"Stop speaking to my arse," Ranger said over his shoulder.

He flinched at the feel of teeth on his cheek. "Fuck you."

"That's better."

"I was still speaking to your arse. I'm making it promises like you promised my cock."

Wetness dripped down Ranger's crack. He stiffened as Troy's finger rubbed against him.

"You're a glorious little hole," Troy panted. "Surrounded by such spongy cheeks. God." He pinched one. "There like memory foam. I bet they mark easy. I can't wait to see my handprint on them."

Troy stuck his head between Ranger's legs and sucked on his balls. He cried out, shuffling away, but Troy pulled him back by his hips.

"Stay on all fours while I suck your balls."

Ranger tried his best to keep still, but Troy's mouth moved everywhere. It drenched him with licks and kisses until he couldn't stand it.

"I can't wait to slap my body against this." He was back to groping, sighing with pleasure at the feel of Ranger's arse. "You've got enough padding for me to fuck you as hard and fast as I want."

Ranger shivered and dragged his sweaty forehead against the mattress. It sounded hot and *not* hot at the same time. He mumbled against the sheet, "I've never bottomed."

Troy licked a stripe directly over Ranger's hole. "Huh?"

"I've never bottomed."

Ranger's arse suddenly went very cold without Troy's breathing to warm it. He glanced over his shoulder and found Troy sitting on his heels, frowning at him. His eyes searched Ranger's as his lust came to a screeching halt.

"But you jumped straight on the bed and let me see your hole."

"Yeah."

He did do that, and he was hard, and panting, and sweating everywhere, but he'd be lying if he said he wasn't slightly unsure and a little confused.

"You weren't just doing that because I wanted you to, right?"

Ranger scrunched his face as he thought. Was he on all fours just because Troy wanted him to be? Or did he want Troy to fuck his virgin hole?

"You've got to want it too," Troy said firmly. He shuffled back on his knees, getting further away from Ranger.

It might have only been an inch or two, but the gulf between them suddenly felt a mile. He missed Troy's groping hands, and his wet mouth, and the feel of his fingers swiping over his hole.

"Fuck," he whimpered.

Troy stiffened. "What is it?"

The realization poured heat through him, but he still shivered.

"I want you to fuck me." He shifted back on his knees, moving his arse closer to Troy and his beautiful cock. "Yup, I want you to fuck me."

"You're not just saying that because you feel like you have to?"

"No." Ranger swallowed. "I want it, and it's kind of freaking me out how much I do."

"You sure?"

"Troy…" Ranger whined.

"Making sure." Troy snorted, reaching for Ranger's arse. "Where's your lube?"

"Don't want any."

Troy rolled his eyes. "We need lube, for me as much as you." He tugged at his piercing. "You want this beauty to slide into you nice and easy, right?"

"Fuck yes." Ranger swung his arm in the direction of his bedside cabinet. "Top drawer."

Troy rushed to retrieve it, but before he coated Ranger's hole in lube, he got to work on it with his tongue and lips first. He licked and sucked until Ranger lost all ability to think.

"I'm guessing no one made out with your arsehole before?"

Ranger panted. Each lick shunted him closer to the edge. "I don't think so."

"What do you mean you don't think so?"

"Can we have this discussion later?"

Troy hummed and applied pressure with his fingers until Ranger's body accepted them with a sudden give. They were wet and slippery and glided past his ring of muscle.

"Oh my…" he gasped in a shrill voice. He dropped his head to the bed but kept his eyes and mouth wide open as Troy slid his fingers in and out.

Troy chuckled behind him. "Oh my? You suddenly turned posh Ranger?"

"Oh my…"

He couldn't get the last word out. Troy stroked against something that made him spasm. A bundle of live wires that fed into his cock. They took him to the brink of coming and let him linger. It was bliss, fizzling bliss. He breathed slower just to cope, but his heart was pounding. Each pulse point around his body beat like a drum. He looked between his legs at his hard cock—even that jolted with each contraction.

"Do you mean to say 'oh my God'?" Troy chuckled.

Troy stroked the sacred ball of pleasure again. Ranger gasped and fisted the bedsheet.

"Oh, my fuck…" he yelled.

"I won't be able to pound you tonight, not with it being your first time."

First time. Even hearing those words got Ranger excited. His body had gone through a whole range of first times he no longer remembered, but this was the *first* time. His first time. He was certain of it.

Pain erupted in his temples, and he winced.

Some distant part of him yelled at him, told him he didn't do this, he didn't submit and let someone fuck him. It was pathetic. It was an insult that anyone could ever think they could top him, let alone get him in this position.

It raged and roared, putting Ranger in a panic. The old him told him to fight against the humiliation. This *first time* had never happened because it wasn't supposed to. He wasn't a bottom or a switch. He was a terrifying alpha male.

He suspected Troy must've sensed some uncertainty. "Don't worry. I'll go easy on you."

The odd prickling in his head started, the red fog spreading and thickening. The him of the past would've killed Troy for touching him this way. No doubt about it. It was an indignity, an insult, a humiliation.

"Don't..." he gasped.

"Don't what?" Troy asked, his voice pitched with worry.

Ranger clawed at the bedsheets, blocking out the voice in his head.

"Don't keep me waiting."

It was now or never.

Troy put his cock to Ranger's entrance. He applied pressure. The pain threatened to push him into flight or fight mode, and he knew which one it would be. He stared at his hands on the bed, scrunched into the mattress. They trembled with their locked grip. He didn't know whether he was trying to hold on or curl them into fists to launch an attack.

"Relax," Troy told him. "You've gone all rigid."

Ranger's body denied Troy entry, and so did his mind. He didn't do this. He didn't get fucked. He was the fucker. The muscles in his face twitched and pulled his expression into a snarl. He didn't want that expression and buried it into the mattress. He needed to tell Troy to stop before he launched at him, but he didn't want to give in to the old Ranger's philosophy. Submitting didn't make you weak, or pathetic, or a whore.

"Troy," he whined.

Troy shushed him and pressed deeper. Ranger's arsehole ached like it was bruised, like Troy's cock was causing him blunt trauma. His body didn't let him in. He was too tight, too conflicted. He had to stop the situation before he lost all control and battered Troy to death. Ranger closed his eyes against the red fog and willed it to disperse.

Troy's gruff voice didn't make sense in his ears.

"What?" Ranger asked.

Fingers clawed at Ranger's hips. "I said, I can handle you."

Could he?

He could.

Ranger didn't know how. Most people who angered him died under the spell of the red fog, but not Troy. Troy had punched him back, hard enough to crack his ribs and clear his mind so he could function again. Troy had a fighter's hands and a body in a similar shape to Ranger's. He was tough, and strong, and brimming with self-confidence.

I can handle you.

Ranger gasped as his hole opened. He expected a rush of scorching pain, blood to pour from his crack, but nothing happened. His body stretched to accommodate Troy as he eased himself deeper. The fog vanished, and the panic at losing control went with it. The whole thing hit him as underwhelming. He'd expected agony or pleasure, but instead, it was neither. Just a searing stretch of a sensation.

"That was the hard part," Troy said, adjusting his knees on the bed. "Now, the fun bit."

He rocked his hips, working the lube in and out in small movements. Ranger's eyes fluttered. Okay, there was the pleasure, building pleasure.

"Fuck, you're tight."

The movements got faster and deeper. Ranger's hole hurt, but the deeper sensations inside masked it. There was pleasure, and pressure, and a drag of something hard each time Troy drew back.

Ranger groaned when he realized what it was. "That's your cock ring."

The tension he held in his body left him, and he gave in completely to the sensation of being fucked.

"Sure is," Troy moaned. "Your arse is tugging on it perfectly. I'm not gonna last." He dove back in with a groan. "I just need to push it in the right position, and you'll go crazy at the feel of it."

Ranger wasn't sure what he meant until it rubbed against the ball of firing pleasure receptors. The sensation was as pleasurable as Troy's fingers, but knowing it was the mouth-watering piercing Ranger had admired making him feel that good brought his cock to full mast and left him delirious with the need to dirty the sheets.

"Jerk yourself at the same time," Troy said.

Ranger propped himself up on one arm and reached for his cock with the other. He started tugging himself, thinking of the piercing inside him, adding charge to his prostate each time they touched. He moaned, imagining sparks inside his body. They burned hotter and hotter each time they throbbed.

"You're so fucking tight," Troy said again, picking up speed. "You feel so good. Your arse is magic, and your hole is a vice. Goddammit, Ranger, I'm losing my mind back here."

Ranger had already lost his. He chased his orgasm while Troy plundered his arse.

He needed to warn him he was about to come, but no words came out, only a groan, which Troy answered with a groan of his own. Cum splashed the bed as it swept inside his channel. It was an erotic thought to lose cum and gain it at the same exact moment.

They twitched and shivered together, both going weak-kneed before collapsing side by side on the bed.

"Fuck me," Troy panted, flinging his arm over his face.

Ranger chuckled, daring to slide closer to him. Troy didn't protest; he lifted his arm and peeked a look at him. Then dragged him closer. Ranger smiled so hard his face almost split in two.

"I mean it," Troy panted. "Next time. You're gonna fuck me."

Ranger stiffened, then rolled on top of Troy and pinned him to the bed.

Troy narrowed his eyes. "What the…"

"You owe me a date."

CHAPTER SEVEN

Ranger woke to a startled cry. He flipped off the bed and crashed his knees into the floor as he grabbed his gun wedged against the mattress. No one launched at him. Gunshots didn't pierce the air or his skull. He took a breath as he scanned the bedroom. The door was open, and Troy's clothes and boots were gone.

"Troy?"

Ranger hurried out of the bedroom, gun at the ready. Troy stood at the bottom of the stairs, pointing a trembling finger in the direction of the kitchen.

"Who the hell is that?"

"Oh." Ranger chuckled lightly and lowered his gun. "You give me two seconds to put pants on, and I'll introduce you."

He was standing in the nude, heaving for breath, flashing a gun, but that didn't get Troy's attention. His focus stuck to the scene in the kitchen.

"I don't want to be introduced to a corpse."

"Two seconds," Ranger repeated, darting into the bedroom. The front door clunked and rattled; Troy was doing his best to undo as many of the bolts as he could before Ranger came back. Ranger snorted. He'd locked the doors and windows after Troy had fallen asleep. The locks protected him from the outside as much as they protected the outside from him.

His home was a fortress, and he liked it that way, but it had a tendency to freak out anyone who tried to escape in the morning.

Ranger bounded down the stairs in time to see Troy aim a fist at the window.

"Woah," he said, skidding to a halt beside him. "There's no need for that. The glass won't break, but you will."

"Let me out of here, Ranger."

He yawned and stretched out his arms. "After breakfast, I'm starving."

Troy's furious gaze followed Ranger into the kitchen, but he still teased the idea of smashing the window to escape. In the end, he sighed, and his heavy boots plodded after Ranger.

"Troy, meet Gavin. Gavin, this is Troy."

"What the fuck is it?" Troy asked. His nostrils pulsed, and his top lip curled over his teeth.

Ranger kissed Gavin on the cheek. "Morning, honey."

"What the hell?" Troy said. He ran out of breath and gasped. "I mean…I've obviously died and ended up in hell."

"I kissed him to make you jealous. Did it work?"

"No, just made me feel a bit sick."

Ranger looked at Gavin sitting in his chair, blank of all emotion. Blue eyes, blond hair. Ranger had drawn all over his arms to make his skin look tattooed. Even so, he had no curiosity toward testing him out. When he'd unwrapped him, he'd feared Yates had lost his mind and gifted him a corpse for his birthday, but no, just Gavin the Gaybot as Dylan had nicknamed him.

"Are you gonna explain?"

"He's one of those high-tech sex dolls. Electric. He's low on charge. My best mate Yates got me one for my birthday. He's a replacement for a boyfriend in case I can't find one."

"Why have you kept it?"

Ranger sighed at Gavin. "Are you gonna tell him, or shall I?"

Troy bowed over, squeezing his temples. "What the actual fuck is happening?"

"I was messing with you again. Truth is, I did put him in the wheely bin outside after Yates gave me him, but I felt guilty and had to bring him in, and now he kinda lives with me."

"I thought…I thought he was one of your targets."

Ranger studied Troy intently. He shifted his gaze away, unable to look Ranger in the eye.

"Targets? Wait. You know what I do for a job?"

Troy nodded, still not looking at him.

"How?" Ranger asked.

"I did a little research on you."

"I see." Before Ranger could ask more, Troy was back to pointing at Gavin.

"So, a high-tech sex doll?" Troy said. "Does it move and talk and stuff?"

"He only moves a little, his arms and legs shift back and forth an inch, but I can program him to say things."

"Like what?"

"Good morning, Ranger. Have you had a good day? You're a nice person. You'll find love. Don't give up. Goodnight, Ranger."

"That's sad, sweet, and creepy all at once."

Troy gestured to the plate on the table. The cutlery, the wine glass. Gavin had a placemat with his name on it, despite not being able to eat...and not being alive.

"What's with this?"

"Sometimes I practice dates with him."

"Does it...does it have a hole?"

Ranger drew back and smacked his lips in distaste. "Now, who's the weirdo?"

"I just meant if it's a sex doll, it's gotta have a hole, right? Otherwise what's the point?"

"Troy, would you like to try out Gavin?"

"No! Urgh, this is too messed up for a Saturday morning."

"I don't know where else to put him, so he sits at the table." Ranger yanked open the fridge. The fridge magnet pinged off, dropping Donnie's postcard to the floor.

"Damn."

"Looks nice," Troy mumbled.

The Maldives looked more than nice, but Donnie and Elliot weren't really there. They were just trying to wind him up. Ranger slipped the postcard beneath the cutlery drawer. "If you're lucky, I might take you one day."

"Yeah, okay." Troy rolled his eyes.

"I'm serious. But first, you've got to let me feed you."

Troy was getting the works. Even though Gavin's presence had left him sickly pale, Ranger suspected he had a big appetite. He hoped so. He'd waited so goddamn long to cook someone's breakfast.

"How tall is it?"

"He," Ranger corrected. "Just under six feet."

"What's his body like?"

"He's got washboard abs and big arms."

"What's his cock like?"

Ranger cracked an egg into a glass, then glanced over his shoulder. "I think I'm starting to get jealous of Gavin."

Troy shrugged. "I was curious, that's all."

He took the seat next to Gavin and patted his pockets to locate his pack of cigarettes. A sigh of bliss left him as he slotted a stick between his lips, but Ranger rushed over and batted it away.

"Damn it, Ranger!"

"I want you to appreciate the taste."

Troy slouched. "Come off it. You can't cook."

"Sure I can. Sit and keep Gavin company until I'm done."

"Fuck keep Gavin company," Troy mumbled. "It's a robot."

"It has feelings."

"Of course it doesn't."

Ranger smiled as he mixed up the batter. "Bet he's giving you the evil eye right now."

Troy didn't reply for a few minutes, then he cursed and hissed in Ranger's direction, "Isn't there a switch or something to close its eyes?"

"*His* eyes," Ranger said. "Gently lower his eyelids, and they'll stay down."

"Fine, here goes."

They snapped back open. Troy screamed. It rang in Ranger's ears. He stifled his laugh with his hand, but it was no use. Troy heard and cursed at him. His chair screeched against the floor as he put as much distance as he could between him and Gavin. He came over to Ranger and sat up on the counter.

"I knew you were an odd guy, but that's too odd."

Ranger frowned at him. "How am I odd?"

"All those dates. So eager, and excited, and brimming with desperation."

"So what, I want a boyfriend. Why is that so bad? My two closest mates are in relationships, and I'll admit it, I'm jealous. I want what they have."

"And what do they have?"

"Yates has got Dylan, and he adores him. He's the only guy I've seen Yates all soft and gentle around. He takes care of him, watches out for him. I want that."

"Yuck."

"Then there's Donnie. Too confident for his own good, gets his ego smashed to pieces by some kid. He keeps Donnie on his toes, keeps him entertained. I want that. He adds excitement to Donnie's life."

"Some kid?"

"Not a kid, Elliot must be in his mid-twenties." Ranger thought about it, and Troy looked as confused as he felt. So what, he didn't know the age of his best mate's boyfriend.

"The point is I want the excitement. I want to take care of someone, but most of all I want what the four of them all have, but I don't."

"Which is?"

"Love. I want to be loved."

Troy slipped down from the counter. "Well, keep trying, and I'm sure one day it might happen."

"I want to be loved, and I want you to star in my love story."

"People…" Troy ran his hand over his head. "People don't talk like that."

"I'm not 'people.' I'm Ranger. So I'm wondering whether this is going to be a friends-to-lovers situation. I hope it's not enemies-to-lovers."

"I'm tapping out of this conversation." He went to leave, but Ranger rushed over and caught his arm. "Where are you going?"

"Home."

"Stay for breakfast, please."

Troy scrunched up his face. "Ranger, this isn't a good idea."

"I'm only asking for breakfast. I'll even put Gavin out of the way."

"I dunno."

"I'm doing pancakes, with bacon and maple syrup, squirty cream, and ice cream with roasted hazelnuts on top."

Troy licked his lips. His stomach gurgled.

"But if you're more savory, I can do pancakes with avocado, and bacon, with pine nuts sprinkled on top and a balsamic dressing."

"Jesus. They both sound good, but the sweet pancakes have me salivating."

Ranger flexed his eyebrows. "So, you'll stay?"

"Just for breakfast, and only if you put the sexbot out of view."

"I've got just the place."

He heaved Gavin up from his chair and dragged him to the guest bathroom, chuckling under his breath at the thought of scaring the shit out of Troy yet again.

****

Troy slumped back in his seat with his hands rested on his belly. He'd eaten everything. *Everything.* Ranger could do nothing to control his pleased smile.

"Okay, I take it back. You can cook."

"Thanks," Ranger said, clearing away the plates. He filled up the sink under Troy's watchful eye and began washing the plates and cutlery.

"If I was a nice person, I'd offer to do that," Troy mumbled. "But as I said, I'm not a nice person. I'm an arsehole."

Ranger rolled his eyes. "I'm happy to do it."

"You're happy to wash plates?"

"Yeah."

"And what if I told you to iron my clothes and wash my boots too?"

Ranger shrugged. "If you couldn't do it yourself for some reason—"

"What if I just didn't want to? Would you be happy to do it for me?"

A scratch of pain went through Ranger's head. He didn't answer Troy's questions and carried on washing the plates and pans. Troy's boots clunked as he got up. Ranger still feared he would dart for the door, but instead he came over and grabbed a dishcloth off the side. Ranger cleaned and Troy dried. Neither of them spoke as they went about their individual tasks.

Ranger finished first and turned to Troy. "What is it you do as a job?"

The plate Troy was drying slipped from his grasp, but Ranger was quick; he caught it. He raised his eyebrows at Troy, still expecting an answer.

"Boring, office work."

Ranger frowned. "You work in an office?"

"Yeah, so what?"

Ranger drained the sink. "You're lying, but why not just say you don't want to tell me? I wouldn't force you to talk about anything you don't want to."

Troy finished the last plate and set it down on the side.

"How about a different question?" Ranger said, smiling. "Are you working today?"

"No. Not unless my…boss calls me."

"Do you like your job?"

"I'm not…where I want to be."

"And where do you want to be?"

Troy didn't answer. Ranger fidgeted in the resulting silence.

"Would you like me to kill your boss for you?"

"He'd be more likely to kill you." Troy flung the dishcloth at Ranger and broke the moment. "Right, I'm gonna take a leak, then I'm gone. Where's the bathroom?"

"The door under the stairs."

Troy jogged from the room. Ranger didn't have to wait long for him to find Gavin. Troy screamed, one of the high-pitched and ear-ringing variety. Ranger doubled over with laughter.

"Too easy!"

Troy cursed at Ranger before slamming the bathroom door shut.

Ranger ventured into the hallway and found Gavin lying on the floor, his blue eyes beaming guilt into Ranger's chest at being cast off. He sat him up against the wall and refused Gavin's eye contact.

The toilet flushed, Ranger heard the taps going full blast, then Troy stepped out. He jumped when he saw Ranger waiting by the door and beat his hand to his chest.

"You trying to kill me?"

"There would be no trying. If I wanted to, I would."

Troy grimaced, stepping over Gavin's legs. "You're rather confident, but don't you remember my punch in The Archer floored you?"

It did. When the fog cleared, Ranger found himself staring up at the ceiling. His ribs had screamed in pain.

"I can handle you," Troy repeated from the night before. Ranger shivered thinking about it. Troy's eyes darkened, and Ranger imagined he was thinking about it too.

"So I guess we should swap numbers."

Ranger lit up. "To arrange a date?"

Troy smirked. "No, for sex. How about enemies with benefits?"

"Enemies?"

"We aren't friends."

"We're not anti-friends, though."

"I'm not going to date you, Ranger. This is just sex, understand?"

Ranger grinned. "I understand. My phone's upstairs."

He rushed upstairs to find it, and while he was in his room, he grabbed the handcuffs from his bedside cabinet. They were going on a date whether Troy wanted to or not.

"What the hell are you doing up there?"

"I'm getting dressed."

Ranger tugged on a fresh T-shirt, changed sweatpants and pulled on some socks, then doused himself with aftershave in record time. He dove into his ensuite to brush his teeth with his left hand while preening his hair into position with his right.

"Ranger!"

"Almost done." He snatched his sunglasses from the dresser and hooked them over his T-shirt. "I'm ready."

Troy stood with his arms crossed and his foot tapping on the floor. "What the—"

"Here," Ranger said, thrusting his phone in Troy's face. He took it with a huff and tapped in his details. When he handed the phone back, Ranger took it with one hand while snapping a cuff around his wrist with the other. Troy gaped, but before he had a chance to react, Ranger had tightened the cuff and fixed them together.

"What the fuck?"

Ranger smiled at him. "You owe me a date."

Troy yanked the cuff. "Unlock it right now, Ranger!"

"The key is upstairs."

Troy rushed at the stairs, but Ranger had anticipated his reaction and pulled him the other way. Troy swung around and collided with the wall. He growled, launching at Ranger.

They fought, bicep against bicep, Troy's right arm against Ranger's equally equipped left. Troy's boots slipped on the floor. Ranger took advantage and pulled him to his chest. They collided with a thump.

"Goddammit, Ranger!"

"Go on a date with me."

"No." Troy swung his left arm back, ready to punch. When it came at Ranger's face, he caught Troy's fist in his right hand and held it.

"We can spend all day rolling around the floor fighting, but I'll win," Ranger said, still smiling.

"No way."

"I will because I watched you eat, drink, and smoke; you favor your right hand. You carry most of your punching power in that arm, and it's secured to me. You can't get a good swing. Your left arm is weaker—"

"I'm not weak," Troy growled.

"Weaker," Ranger repeated with a snort. "You still have a lot of power in your left arm, but not as much as mine. I'm ambidextrous. I have the same strength in both hands and arms. I can take on your restrained right hand and control your weaker left hand. You won't win against me."

Ranger crushed Troy's fist in his hand to make his point, then released him.

"Bastard," Troy hissed, shoving Ranger in the chest.

"One date. That's all I'm asking. As soon as we're done, we can come back here, and I'll undo the cuffs."

"We can't spend a whole day chained to each other."

"If I undo them, you'll run."

"I promise I won't."

Ranger bopped Troy on the nose with his finger. "Liar. Now come on, tickets are for ten."

"Tickets?"

"Movie tickets."

Troy scrunched his face up. "Please say it's not a rom-com."

CHAPTER EIGHT

Ranger wasn't cruel enough to make Troy sit through a rom-com. He'd picked a film based on what he thought Troy would like. *The World Title.* An underdog story of a boxer defying the odds. Troy relaxed a fraction when Ranger showed him the ticket and stopped yelling out for someone to help him.

He snatched the tickets from Ranger's hand. "I want popcorn and drinks."

"Coming up," Ranger said, tugging Troy along by the wrist. The handcuffs got a few curious glances, but no one wanted to intervene.

"Social experiment," he said to the cashier. "We're spending the day chained to each other to see if we're compatible."

Troy shoved his way forward. "Which we're not."

The woman at the counter adjusted her cap and smiled. "I dunno, I think you kind of suit."

"Don't say that," Troy growled, stepping behind Ranger. "Dear God, don't say that."

"Thank you," Ranger said, taking their snacks.

"You better have been thanking her for the food, not her comment."

"I thanked her for both."

"I could yank your arm right now, and you'd spill popcorn all over the floor."

Ranger cast him a quick look. "What's the point of that? You won't be able to eat it."

Troy huffed and allowed himself to be led into the theater.

"I could shout and be a pain in the arse and get us kicked out."

"You could do that, but I think a part of you wants to see the movie."

Troy muttered something Ranger couldn't hear, but he didn't deny it. He led Troy around the corner but came to a stop when he saw their seats occupied by a group of teenagers. The closest one had his feet up on the chair in front, munching chewing gum like a goat.

Ranger blinked as he took all of them in. One guy and girl locked together by their lips. One girl throwing popcorn around, and another laughing hysterically. Then there was the gum chomper whose lip smacking made Ranger's pulse increase.

"They're our seats, right?" Troy said.

Ranger swallowed. "Right."

He couldn't move; his feet had fixed themselves to the floor. Troy dragged him forward but didn't speak when they drew the attention of teenagers. He looked at Ranger and raised his eyebrow.

"Sorry, guys." Ranger laughed awkwardly. "But I think you'll find we booked these seats."

"So?" The gum-chomping guy pulled his feet off the chair in front and swiveled toward Ranger. Despite the gum he chewed, Ranger could smell the alcohol on his breath. He heard bottles clunk under laughing girl's feet.

"So, I want to sit in the seats I booked."

"We aren't moving."

Ranger opened his mouth to speak, but popcorn sprayed in his face. The girl staggered as she stood up, another handful of popcorn at the ready. "Fuck off."

"Oh fuck," Ranger whispered.

The pain in his head started as a tingle, but it got tighter, sharper.

Troy looked at him. "Huh?"

Ranger hissed, touching his temple. He had to push the anger away. Easier said than done when chewing gum was spat at his chest. It dropped down, landing on the top of his shoes. The flare of outrage inside his skull was almost too much. If he lost it, it would be a blood bath. There would be real cuffs on him as he was led away in a police car.

He stared at gum as the guy's laugh cackled in his head. His restraint slipped. He had to leave. Fight or flight had kicked in, but with him, it came on steroids, flight or kill everyone in the vicinity.

Ranger backed up a step, but Troy stopped him from going any further. He narrowed his eyes at Ranger, tilting his head, trying to understand him, but how could he explain it? Anger and him didn't mix; people ended up dead.

"What are you doing?" Troy asked.

Ranger tipped his head back, gesturing behind him. He tried for a smile, but it was too much effort. "I'm gonna get an usher to move them."

The group burst into hysterics, mimicking Ranger's voice, mocking him. His sight warped and twisted before filling with a pink hue. Troy watched him with wide eyes. His eyebrows nipped together as he tried to understand Ranger's reaction.

Ranger couldn't speak, his mouth was too dry, but he pleaded with his eyes for Troy to leave with him, forcing a twitching smile and tilting his head toward the exit.

Please, please, please.

Troy stepped closer, Ranger was so grateful he could've kissed him. His eyes were full of fury, and his frown so fierce it put a deep crease between his eyebrows.

He crouched down and picked the piece of gum off Ranger's shoe.

"We'll watch something else."

"No," Troy said. His voice shook with a threat. He held the piece of gum between the thumb and forefinger of his cuffed hand and yanked Ranger back toward the teenagers.

The gum chopping guy stood up, full of misplaced confidence as he matched himself against Troy. "Go get the ushers—"

Troy punched him in the gut with his left hand so hard spittle flew from his mouth. He bowed forward, gaping and drooling with pain. Troy sat him upright and shoved the piece of gum in his gawping mouth. He fell back onto his seat, but Troy didn't stop. He covered the guy's mouth and used his knee to keep him pinned in place.

"Swallow it, you piece of shit."

He did. Troy moved his knee, grabbed him by the T-shirt, and hauled him from the seat. He landed on his hands and knees in the aisle and crawled down the steps, sobbing.

"The rest of you, fuck off."

The group rushed past and helped their injured friend off the floor. Troy pulled Ranger by the wrist and made him sit in their seats. Once the group had gone, Troy swung his head toward Ranger.

"Why didn't you—"

"Don't." Ranger swallowed. "Just don't, let's…let's enjoy the film."

He reached for the blister pack in his pocket and popped out two strong painkillers. They never worked, but he took them anyway. His headache robbed him of an appetite. It pulsed and flared, and he knew from experience it would last a few hours before it mellowed to a comfortable level.

He handed the popcorn and drink to Troy and let his arm go limp so he could eat. Ranger felt Troy's eyes on him throughout the film.
He didn't turn to face him. He couldn't even muster the willpower to force a smile. Instead, he stared at the screen, not taking anything of the movie in, and massaged his throbbing head.

****

"So, what did you think?"

They left the screen without Troy shoving on their cuffed hands and asking for help. That meant progress in Ranger's eyes.

"It was alright," Troy said with a shrug. "How's the head?"

The inferno had softened to a bearable level, but he still needed to wear his shades. Bright lights seemed to make it worse. "It's alright—"

"Hey…Ranger!"

Vince rushed toward him, all smiles, until he saw who Ranger stood beside. He stared at the handcuffs joining Ranger and Troy together. "Um…"

"We're on a date."

"We're not on a date. I'm a hostage." Troy stood up on his tiptoes and yelled across the foyer. "But no one gives a shit!"

"Role play," Ranger whispered.

Vince chuckled, scratching his head. "So, um. I wanted to talk to you."

"Yeah?"

"Don't mind me!" Troy snapped, looking away.

Ranger watched as Vince grew redder and shiftier. "What did you want to talk about?"

Vince averted his gaze. "Us, I mean—we know each other from The Archer, but it might be fun to do something outside of it, you know, get to know each other a little better."

"Fuck this!" Troy announced, dragging Ranger away.

Ranger looked at Vince. "I'll text you."

"You won't," Troy growled. He pushed open the doors to the cinema, yanking Ranger through with him.

"Why not?"

"I turn my back for five seconds, and Vince is trying to get his cock in your mouth."

"He wasn't—"

"He was."

Ranger turned back and waved at Vince through the door. "You really think so?"

"Cut it out."

"You get quite possessive, don't you?"

"Vince was trying to hit on you *while* we're on a date."

Ranger tried to fight off his smile. "Thought this wasn't a date? Thought you were my hostage?"

"Whatever."

"You hungry?"

"No."

"I booked us a table at *Kings Kitchen*. The burgers there are amazing."

Troy's stomach gurgled, so Ranger poked it. "Your gut likes the sound of it, at least."

Ranger led the way, noting with a burst of happiness Troy was no longer resisting him but walking by his side. They made their way down the street, and Ranger couldn't resist trying his luck and touching Troy's hand. He snatched it away, the cuff went clunk, and Troy glared at him the rest of the way.

"It was an accident." Ranger chuckled as they got to the door.

"It wasn't. You tried to hold my hand."

"I was aiming for your pinkie finger. Thought we could join them."

"Urgh," Troy pulled Ranger inside and toward the waiter waiting at a tall table. He looked up and smiled, but it didn't reach his eyes.

"I booked a table under Ranger, twelve-thirty."

The waiter tapped away on his electronic device. His face scrunched, and he shook his head.

"Something wrong?" Ranger asked.

"I just seated the last group for twelve-thirty."

Ranger slipped his phone from his pocket and checked the time. He showed it to the waiter, and they both stared at it as the clock changed to exactly twelve-thirty.

"But I'm on time."

"Hmm, yes, I can see that." He smiled at Ranger again. This time it reached his eyes, and he wriggled his nose.

"I booked last night on your website."

Troy elbowed him in the ribs. "Bit presumptuous of you."

The waiter nodded with fake sympathy. "I can see your booking here on the system, but a group of four came in just before you."

"So what, you gave away my table?"

"If you read the terms and conditions, you'll see there's no guarantee."

"But I turned up on time. I paid your deposit."

"Which will be transferred back to you in up to five working days."

He smiled at Ranger, then turned to Troy. "Is there anything else I can help you with today?"

"You could get us a burger from the back," Troy muttered.

"Sorry, we don't do takeout."

Ranger pointed past him to an empty table. "Why can't we have that one?"

"That's a table for six."

"It's empty."

"The party for that particular table will be arriving momentarily."

"So they're late?"

"Only by a few minutes or so."

Ranger took off his shades and pressed his thumb and forefinger into his eyes. He saw stars as he tried to get a grasp on the situation. "I turn up on time for a table I've booked, and you've given it to someone else, yet that table is late, and you're holding it for them."

"I can see why you might feel this is unfair, but I'll make it easy for you to understand. That is a table of six for six paying customers. They will spend far more than you two."

"Dunno about that," Troy said.

His voice was muffled in Ranger's head. Everything was muffled, and soft, and fuzzy around the edges. He brought his fist down hard on the table. It split with a snap. Someone gasped. He stared at the broken table and traced the sharp edge with his finger.

It cut him, but he didn't feel it. Blood dripped down his finger, but he didn't feel it rushing against his skin. He didn't register the warmth. He wiped his bloody finger on his sweatpants.

"I've called security," the waiter blurted. When Ranger looked up, the waiter was standing on the other side of the room, clutching onto the doorframe that led to the restaurant. Lots of faces had turned toward them.

"I'm sorry," Ranger said. He hissed in pain, but it wasn't his finger, but his head. "I didn't mean—"

"I suggest you leave. We've got all we need on the security camera there."

Ranger spun around and found it targeting him from above the door. Ranger could've bested the security guy in a fight with ease, but that wasn't the point. He didn't want to be escorted out or told he was banned from *Kings Kitchen*.

"It was a misunderstanding about the tables."

The waiter shook his head. "I apologized profusely, but he didn't accept. He got aggressive and threatened me."

"But I didn't…or I didn't mean to. I don't know."

Fuck, his head hurt. He grabbed it with both hands.

"Come on," Troy murmured.

For a moment, Ranger had forgotten they were cuffed together. Troy pulled him outside and marched him up the street, away from the restaurant.

"I didn't mean to get angry—"

"Are you kidding me right now, Ranger? The guy deserved to go through the fucking wall. Why…" He huffed, shaking his head.

"Why what?"

"Why are you letting people walk all over you?"

"I don't wanna be that person that terrifies the shit out of everyone when they're angry."

"So your solution is to never get angry."

"Yeah."

"That's just stupid."

Ranger stopped. The cuffs clunked as Troy was forced to stop too. Ranger could see the challenge in Troy's eyes, could tell he'd keep on pushing and pushing, and he didn't want to deal with it. He reached for his shades to help with his throbbing head, but they weren't there.

"You dropped them," Troy said.

"I'll go back—"

"You kinda trod on them too."

"What?"

He hadn't registered the crunch under his feet at all. He groaned, knocking his fist into his forehead. "I need them."

The cars screeched past them. He winced at the shrill ring of a bicycle bell and groaned at the honk of a horn. The pounding in his head had company in his gut. It swelled and sloshed, churning up his breakfast. "I'm gonna be sick."

"What?"

"My head." He tapped it, but even that touch was raw agony.

"This way," Troy said, tugging Ranger's arm. Troy took him away from the street and pushed him up against the wall.

"Not even a blow job will fix this."

Troy snorted. "Close your eyes."

"What?"

"Do as I said, or I'll jab my fingers into them."

Ranger sighed and closed them. He frowned at the pitter-patter of rain and clap of thunder. "What the—"

"Shush," Troy growled. "It's from my phone. It'll help you block out everything else. I listen to it to block out my neighbors when I wanna jerk off."

"It's…it's still too bright."

He could see painful pink through his eyelids.

Ranger's wrist lifted, but he kept it limp, trusting Troy. Warm hands came up and covered his eyes. He took a deep breath in the dark and imagined rain and thunder. Ranger didn't know how long he stood against the wall, but Troy didn't complain or remove his hands from over Ranger's eyes. He waited until Ranger shuffled and let out a soft sigh.

"Better?" Troy asked.

"I can handle it now."

Troy peeled his hands away just as Ranger opened his eyes. "You sure?"

He blinked. "Yeah. I no longer feel like I'm gonna be sick."

Or kill anyone.

"That's good to know, although being sick in that restaurant would've been ideal."

Ranger snorted. He fished his hand in his sweatpants pocket and revealed the key.

"Hey? You said that was at your place."

"I lied," Ranger said, undoing their cuffs. He shoved them in his pocket and sighed at the ground.

Troy rubbed his wrist as he watched Ranger.

"So um…" Ranger struggled to look Troy in the eye. "I'm gonna go."

"Go?"

"Yeah."

Ranger started walking, but Troy pursued. "What I said is the truth. Bottling up your anger is a stupid idea."

"I don't want to deal with this right now."

"So what are you gonna do?"

Ranger looked at him. "I'm gonna go get my dogs and cuddle up with them on the sofa as I watch some rom-com where the characters fall head over heels in love and everything is painless and wonderful."

"That sounds awful…"

The disgust was evident in his voice, and Ranger smirked. "Bye—"

"But I guess I'm in."

"What?"

"You heard me."

Troy strolled beside him, lit cigarette between his lips, glaring at everyone who dared block their path. Ranger's smile for him wasn't fake, and the butterflies in his stomach were very fucking real.

****

Blade's excitement at seeing Ranger was quickly overshadowed by Troy's presence. His tail dropped between his legs, and he huffed at Ranger. Scope bounded over and allowed Troy to stroke his head, tail whipping back and forth like a puppy. Never in a million years did Ranger think dogs could express shame toward each other; that was before Blade and Scope. Blade was one step away from shaking his head at the indignant display of his brother licking Troy's hands and whimpering with excitement.

They walked them home, side by side, not talking, but in what Ranger felt was a comfortable silence. Even the cars rushing by and the chatter escaping doorways seemed muffled with Troy by his side. He hoped Troy shared the feeling of peace, but when he glanced at him, he noticed a look of contemplation tightened his features. Troy scanned the ground as if something bothered him.

"We're here," Ranger said. Troy looked up at the house and waited for Ranger to unlock the door. He let the dogs go in first, who immediately made themselves at home on the sofas.

"You don't have to come in," Ranger said.

Troy strolled forward, brushing Ranger aside. "Well, I am. Someone has to provide damning criticism of your movie, and it'll have to be me."

He stepped into the living room, tapping away on his phone. Ranger didn't ask who he was messaging but sat down with a sigh. Scope collapsed onto him, and Blade stepped off the sofa to lie on his feet.

"Shit," Ranger hissed, looking up at Troy.

"What?"

"You must be starving."

Troy wagged his phone at Ranger. "I sorted it. I'm assuming you like pizza?"

Ranger nodded.

"It'll be here in thirty."

Scope whined and set his big black eyes on Ranger. He felt himself reacting immediately. "Okay, okay, I'll get you and your brother your dinner."

He went to stand, but Troy pushed him down by the shoulder. Blade growled, getting to his feet in one fluid motion while Scope dove over the back of the sofa to hide.

"I'll do it," Troy said, backing away from Blade. "Where's the food?"

"Cupboard next to the fridge. There's dry food and wet food. You share a tin between their bowls, wet food first, then three handfuls of dry food each—"

"Yeah, yeah, yeah," Troy said, trudging off.

"Hey," Ranger yelled. "I'm not done. After the dry food, there are individual pots of homemade gravy in the fridge. You need to heat the pot for exactly thirty seconds and pour it on top. Otherwise, they won't eat it."

"They'll eat it," Troy shouted from the kitchen. Ranger listened as Troy opened every drawer and cupboard on his quest to find dog food.

"Do you want me to help?"

"Stay right where you are."

Blade and Scope trotted off to see what Troy was doing, leaving Ranger to relax fully into the sofa. His whole body felt tired, overworked. No gym session even came close to making him feel so utterly overwhelmed as restraining his emotions did.

Troy dropped down on the sofa next to him. "Done."

"Did you follow my instructions?"

"I put food in their bowls, yes."

Ranger chuckled and grabbed the remote on the arm of the sofa. Netflix came up on the screen, and Troy groaned as he knocked his fist to his head.

"Really?"

"Yes, really." He picked one on the list and sunk into Troy's side. Troy stiffened, but halfway through the movie, he softened and even flung his arm over the back of the sofa so Ranger could press into him more.

They ate pizza, they rearranged to fit the dogs around them, and Ranger gazed at Troy as if he were the sun and stars all rolled into one. He leaned back and pulled out his list.

"What's that?"

"Nothing."

He leaned forward, opened the list on the coffee table, and grabbed a pen off the side.

"Seriously?"

"It was in a dating mag. You're supposed to pick six things on the list that you want to do with your love interest."

"Love interest?"

"Yup."

Ranger put a line through see a movie out and see a movie in.

"And what do you get when you complete the list?"

"Hopefully a boyfriend." Ranger turned to Troy and grinned.

"Stop looking at me like that."

"Why?"

"I don't deserve that look."

Ranger opened his mouth to argue, but before he got the chance, Troy pushed his head onto his lap. The angle bent Ranger's back into an uncomfortable position, but when fingers began working his scalp, he found he didn't care.

"Does it always hurt?"

Ranger nodded against him. "Yeah."

"Have you been to the doctor?"

"Oh yeah, I've got my very own pharmacy upstairs. They only tackle the tip of the iceberg."

"Where does it hurt the most?"

Ranger tapped his temple, and Troy immediately started rolling his thumb against it. He moaned and mashed his face into Troy's thigh, drooling on his leg.

"Feel good?"

"Yeah, you're about halfway down the iceberg down."

Troy scratched his nails against Ranger's scalp. He moaned, repositioning himself on the sofa. The fingers in his hair worked their magic, and in no time he struggled to keep his eyes open.

"I miss looking at this…"

"What?"

Troy followed the shape of the snake with his forefinger. "That mean arse tattoo of yours. It used to glare at me across The Archer."

"How long have you been watching me?"

Troy swallowed, then flicked Ranger's head. "Hey, this head massage comes at a price."

Ranger tried to stop his eyes from spinning back, but it felt too good. "Which is?"

"I want you to wake me up with an orgasm."

Troy was staying the night. He was *staying* the night.

Ranger pressed his cheek into Troy's thigh. "That's not a price. It's a fucking reward."

Troy tipped his head back and let out a sharp bark of laughter that sent Scope scurrying from the sofa. Ranger's heart verged on bursting with happiness.

The savage voice left behind by the old him, sniggered in his head, *too good to be true...*

CHAPTER NINE

The birds hadn't even begun tweeting, and only the faintest hint of the sun bled through the blinds, but Ranger was on the move or shifting at least. He shuffled a few inches down the bed, checked Troy was still snoring softly next to him, then shuffled down a few more.

He bit his lip to stop any giddy chuckles from escaping.

When he got to his prize, he sighed and slipped the sheet over Troy's crotch. There it was, that piercing that had sent sparks through his body. Ranger flashed a look to the top of the bed. Troy's face tightened as he was exposed to the cooler air of the bedroom, but he didn't wake. His forehead relaxed, and he continued breathing evenly.

Ranger bit his lip as he stared at Troy's cock. The only cock he'd ever had inside him, and what a specimen it was. Even soft it was big, and the head a perfect helmet shape. The hoop came out of Troy's slit and hooked beneath the head of his cock. Working the top of it with his tongue was easy, but Ranger wanted to toy with the underside, the most sensitive part. He set about wooing Troy's cock with his tongue, his lips, and the occasional word or two.

"You're beautiful."

Ranger tongued at the ball on the hoop before closing his teeth on it and giving a little tug. Troy flexed his hips and groaned softly. He rubbed the sleep from his eyes before peering down the bed.

"It's a bit early, isn't it?"

"Shush." Ranger narrowed his eyes. "Don't interrupt us."

Troy groaned and spread his legs wider. Ranger nestled between them and began working Troy's cock with his hand. In no time he was hard and releasing blissed sighs against the side of the pillow. Ranger whined at the slide of the ring against his tongue. He couldn't resist drawing the hard metal into his mouth and biting it.

"Easy," Troy gasped. He gripped onto the bed and stiffened his legs, too afraid to move with Ranger performing risky bites. Ranger went back to sucking on the head and stroked his hands up Troy's body to get to his nipples.

Troy sunk into the mattress with a groan. "I'm gonna come so fast if you play with them all together."

Ranger lifted his head but kept twisting his nipple bars. "Is that your weakness?"

Troy bucked his hips. "Yes."

Ranger smiled as he crawled up the bed. He latched on to Troy's nipple piercing and started sucking.

"Fuck."

Troy fisted the sheets and shook his head against the pillow. "Your mouth feels really good."

Ranger let Troy's pink nipple go with a pop.

"And what about my hand?" He slid it up and down Troy's shaft, picking up speed. The piercing dragged against this palm.

Troy hummed. "That feels good too."

Ranger lowered his mouth back to Troy's nipple while watching his face. "And what about both?"

He sucked, and he jerked, and Troy cursed and pleaded. His hips moved to meet Troy's hand, and he gritted his teeth as he growled, "I'm gonna cum."

"Then cum."

Troy's growl morphed into a gasp. His body tightened, shuddered, then relaxed. Ranger abandoned his nipple for a close-up view of the action. He hooked his finger through the ring and held Troy's cock up. His eyes popped wide when Troy's head began contracting. His shaft spasmed too, and he let loose a long moan. His cum didn't shoot out; it rushed over the side of his cock, oozing down his shaft. Ranger kept hold of the ring until the cum stopped flowing.

"You've got a dribbler."

He released it and looked up at Troy with awed eyes.

Troy flung his arm across his face and laughed. "I guess you can call it that. It doesn't squirt out anymore."

"It's hot." Ranger wetted his lips. "It's seriously hot."

Ranger admired Troy's cock, and the cum that had left him in a thick stream, like lava from a fucking volcano. Ranger groaned as he ducked down to taste it. A quick taste turned to a feast.

"You have no idea how much I'm into your cock."

Troy's chuckle vibrated down his body. "I think I do."

He stroked his hand through Ranger's hair. "How's the head?"

"It's leaking down my thigh."

"I meant your actual head."

"Oh. My actual head, the one on my shoulders." Ranger laughed. "It's okay now."

Troy hummed and beckoned him closer, "Now...how's your other head?"

"Close to bursting."

"Want me to relieve the pressure?"

"Fuck yes."

Ranger nodded so hard it gave him whiplash. Troy grabbed him by the hips and pulled Ranger up his body. He narrowly avoided kneeing Troy in the face as he straddled him high up on his chest.

"These need to come down," Troy said, running his hands down Ranger's sides and taking his boxer shorts with them. He licked his lips as he took Ranger in and opened his mouth wide. Ranger took that as a solid invitation and leaned his body closer, not breathing as he concentrated on getting his cock to Troy's lips.

He mouthed at his cock before plunging it deeper. Troy mumbled something Ranger didn't understand but then began to knead Ranger's arse with a vengeance. There was no doubt in Ranger's mind; Troy was into his arse. He pressed his fingers into it, scratched it, stroked it, all while swirling his tongue against the underside of Ranger's cock.

The first slap came as a surprise, jolting Ranger forward, near enough choking Troy beneath him.

"Shit, 'm sorr—"

Troy smacked his arse again, pushing Ranger deeper into his mouth. He yelped, then shuddered at the dual sensations, slickness against his cock, and raw heat on his arse.

Troy's hand made his whole body judder. He stroked Ranger softly between strikes, but the heat of the slap continued to tingle.

"My arse is gonna be so red after this," Ranger breathed at the headboard.

Troy moaned and slapped him harder. He hissed at the strike, then hissed again at the slosh of Troy's tongue, rubbing at the sensitive seam.

"Fuck, Troy." He curled his fingers into the headrest. "Just suck it."

For all the licking and slapping, Ranger couldn't help wishing for Troy to suck him too. A mumble that was definitely a chuckle vibrated against Troy's cock.

He slapped Ranger so hard he fell forward, impaling Troy, but rather than shove him away and struggle away from the giant crushing him, he started sucking. How? Ranger didn't know, didn't care.

Troy's mouth was brutal, unrelenting, and the sensation of fingers pinching his stinging arse heightened it all. He gaped at Troy, his cheeks sucked in, all of Ranger's cock stuffed inside his mouth.

They locked eyes, and Ranger's surrender happened hard and fast directly down Troy's throat. He didn't choke or splutter; he'd been expecting the onslaught, and once Ranger had slipped out and collapsed, he rolled onto him.

"Now, while your arse is still stinging, I'm gonna fuck you again."

Troy's devilish smile vanished at the sound of a phone. His phone. Ranger didn't recognize the ringtone. Some tune from the nineties.

"Leave it." Ranger panted.

Troy glanced at the caller before shaking his head. "I can't."

"But we were about to—"

"Another time."

He swung his legs out of the bed and found his jeans. Ranger couldn't see Troy's expression when he looked at his phone, but his shoulders stiffened. "I've got to take this."

Troy stalked into the bathroom and closed the door. The lock clicked. Ranger sat up against the headboard. He resisted the urge to run over to the door and press his ear against it. Trust was important in relationships; all the magazines said so. If Troy didn't want Ranger to hear the conversation, he just had to accept it.

The door flew open. Ranger smiled at Troy, but there was no smile back. He pocketed his relic of a phone.

Troy went about gathering his clothes without looking away from his task.

"Something wrong?"

He faced away from Ranger as he got dressed. His muscles were locked tight, and when he turned his head, Ranger saw that his jaw was clenching and releasing.

"Troy?"

Troy hung his head and put his hands on his hips, still not looking at Ranger. "Nothing's wrong. I've got to go, that's all."

"It's not even six in the morning."

"So what?" Troy gripped the back of his neck and turned to Ranger. "That's how it is, and I'm not gonna stand here and argue with you about it."

Ranger swallowed. "Well, thanks for yesterday. It was the best date I've been on."

Troy frowned. "The date was a disaster."

"But you fixed it."

"Fixed it?"

"Yeah." Ranger tapped his head. It was aching, as always, but softer than before.

"Look…" Troy stared off into the corner. "Send your dogs to the sitter on Friday."

Ranger's eyes lit up. "Why?"

"We're meeting up."

"A date?"

"No. Not a date. Two guys meeting up."

"It's definitely a date."

Troy groaned and flung open the bedroom door. "Friday. I'll text you."

Scope launched at him and sent him crashing into the bed. Troy slipped down, and Scope was on him, licking his face and kissing Troy's neck with his nose. Ranger could relate. He wanted to do that, but he doubted Troy would tolerate that from him.

Troy struggled to his feet. "Fucking mutt."

He brushed by the ecstatic Doberman. Scope whined and sought solace in a hug from Ranger. He listened as Troy stomped downstairs, cursing when the bolted and chained door blocked his escape.

"Let me out!"

Ranger pushed Scope off his chest and found his sweatpants on the floor.

"Let me out, or this time I really will smash the window."

"Okay, okay."

He rushed down the steps to see Troy already puffing away on a cigarette, rubbing his forehead. He was wound up so tight he looked a step away from snapping. Ranger undid all the locks, and Troy rushed out without a backward glance or a kiss goodbye.

Even a wave would've been nice. Ranger's hand hanging limply by his side was lifted by Blade's head. They both watched as Troy broke into a run and disappeared down the street.

"That was my best date." Ranger patted Blade on the head. "My best date and he's running away from me like that."

Blade breathed heavily from his nostrils and turned back to go into the house. Ranger followed him into the kitchen where he sat down next to his bowl. His untouched bowl from the night before. Troy had put the dry food in first. Blade glanced at his bowl with such disdain a laugh crept out of Ranger.

"I'm sorry, buddy," he said, picking up his bowl. Troy had turned his kitchen upside down in the quest for dog food. He frowned at a left-open drawer before glancing at the fridge. Huh…something was missing, but he couldn't work out what. Blade pushed his bowl across the floor with his nose.

"Why can't you be more like your brother, huh? He's not fussy about food."

Ranger turned to Scope, who was trying to gnaw his own leg off for fun. He froze in the act and slowly let his leg drop from his mouth.

"Maybe not." Ranger scraped Blade's bowl into the bin, then filled up the sink to wash it. "What do you say we visit Yates and Dylan today?"

Scope shot to his feet, wagging his tail. Ranger raised his eyebrow at Blade, who shifted his gaze away and let out one long sigh through his nose. He'd never admit it to Yates and Dylan, but his dogs reminded him of them so much.

****

Now, Yates had specifically told Ranger to stay away from the bakery opposite Bloomers, but Ranger was in a good mood, and his tastebuds demanded something sugary, and colorful, and what Yates didn't know couldn't hurt him.

He tied Blade and Scope up outside and stepped into Stud Muffins.

Two brothers were inside, Newt behind the counter and Mickey at a table, reading. Ranger thought back to his bible, his holy grail, Dating Advice Magazine, and the how to make a good impression section.

Always greet with a compliment.

"Well, aren't you as sweet-looking as the cakes?"

Newt smiled at him with a twinkle in his eye. "Sure am."

Ranger hadn't been lying. Newt had a round face, pink cheeks, and eyes that weren't blue and weren't green either. They were closer to turquoise. A hairnet tamed his copper-red hair, keeping it from his face. He was striking across the street and more so up close. When he smiled, he looked younger, not that Ranger had an accurate guess on his age, but cherub came to mind. Sweet cherub.

One down.

Mickey lowered his magazine to reveal his scowl. Shaved head, and notches missing from his eyebrows. He was the savory to Newt's sweet.

Stone was stoic, Newt was cute, but all Ranger had learned about Mickey was he had an inability to dress himself and never wore a T-shirt. His flawless chest was on display, not as nice as Troy's, but still impressive. Ranger zeroed in on what he was reading, Muscles and Men, not a porno like it should've been but some health and fitness magazine.

Find common ground.

"You should try reading Thump and Mind. It's got some good articles in it about keeping focused on your fitness goals and staying motivated."

Mickey glared, Ranger glared back.

A car grumbled past. A crow cawed in the distance. The shadows in the bakery moved with the passage of time.

"I might just do that," Mickey said, removing his prolonged eye contact. "Thanks."

Ranger inwardly beamed. *It was all going so well.* He turned back to a still smiling Newt.

Inquire about the family.

"How're your parents?"

Newt glanced at Mickey for help.

"They're both dead," Mickey said, turning the page.

"Oh…right…so how's business?" Ranger asked.

Mickey shuffled, Newt stiffened.

"Which business?" Newt asked.

Mickey flung his magazine across the bakery. "Subtly at its finest. The bakery is doing fine, thanks for asking. Now it's my turn to ask a question."

"Okay, shoot?"

Be open and engaged.

"What the hell is up with your dog?"

Mickey pointed to the window. Scope had both paws on the window, and his face pressed to the glass so he could see inside. As soon as Ranger looked at him, he yelped and dropped back to the pavement.

"When I find out, I'll let you know."

"Did you want something?" Mickey asked. "Other than stick your nose in our business and bring up our dead parents."

Steer away from uncomfortable topics.

Ranger ran his finger across the display case before stopping on a twirly pink cupcake. "Ah, that one looks perfect."

Newt grinned. "That happens to be my favorite."

"Bullshit," Mickey coughed under his breath.

Newt craned his neck forward, and his pendant swung free from his neck, flashing blue at Ranger.

"That's a pretty necklace."

Newt straightened up and grabbed it. "Thanks."

"What is it?"

"Neptune."

"Neptune? Like the planet?"

Newt nodded. "It's my favorite."

Show an interest.

"Why?"

"It rains diamonds."

Even if it screams bullshit.

"Oh really?"

Mickey groaned and looked pointedly at Ranger. "I'm gonna save yourself an hour of your life. Don't ask why, because he will tell you in the most boring, droning detail you can imagine."

"Fuck you," Newt spat.

"I'm being honest."

Ranger looked back at Newt. "Well, my favorite is Pluto."

Newt's sunshine smile dimmed. "Pluto isn't a planet."

"Isn't it?"

"No, in 2006 the international Astronomical union reclassified what counts as a planet."

Mickey groaned at the ceiling. "Here we go."

"What is it then?" Ranger asked.

Newt crossed his arms. "Pluto is a dwarf planet."

Ranger shrugged. "There's still planet in the title, so it's a planet."

"It's not a planet."

"It is."

Newt's cheeks reddened. He attempted to glare, but all Ranger could think was cherub, angry cherub, and that made him laugh.

Don't antagonize.

"It's not!"

Too late.

Mickey jumped to his feet. "Are you calling my brother a liar?"

"I don't think so." Ranger looked down at Mickey, flaring his nostrils and shaking his fist. "Am I?"

Mickey widened his eyes and pointed a shaky finger at him. "What the hell are you asking me for?"

"I don't know; I think I've confused myself."

"No shit, you've confused me too."

Mickey trudged around the counter, picked a cupcake, and boxed it. A different smile pulled at Newt's lips, not sweet or angry, but evil cherub.

"Just take your cake and leave." Mickey handed it over, and Ranger smoothed his thumb against the logo on the box.

"How much—"

"It's on the house." Mickey pointed to the door. "Pluto is not a planet, and you'd better remember that. Spread the word."

Newt lifted his chin. "There's actually a space exhibit coming to the museum if you want to learn—"

"Newt, zip it," Mickey said. "And you, get to it."

Ranger got the hint and left. He stopped by the window to wipe off Scope's paw prints until Mickey shooed him away.

"Come on, boys." He untied them from a lamp post. "You've got to look both ways before you cross."

Blade did because he was Blade, but Scope bounced into the road without a care in the world.

The bell to Bloomers rang out.

Ranger held the door open for Blade and Scope. They stepped inside, one tail wagging and one not. The table Dylan studied at was empty. Ranger watched Scope's tail as he realized. It dropped between his legs, and he turned to give Ranger a disappointed look.

"I'm sorry, bud."

Yates came in from the office and pointed at the dogs. "You can't bring them in here."

Always greet with a compliment.

"Your shirt looks nice—nah, I can't do it. It's hideous as always."

Yates looked down at himself. If anything, the shirt was tamer than usual, white with pink flowers and green leaves down the sleeves, but even so, it still had a nauseating effect.

"Dogs and you, out."

"What's wrong with my boys? They're on leads."

"They're intimidating. They'll put off the customers."

Ranger looked at each dog. Yes, Blade was intimidating at first sight. He stood stiffly, head up and alert, and liked nothing more than staring someone down. He was a powerful dog, a proud one.

Then there was Scope.

Scope, who was reaching around to lick his own arsehole.

Ranger remedied the problem by turning the sign on the door to closed, much to Yates's annoyance.

"Did you know Pluto isn't a planet?"

"Who gives a fuck about Pluto—wait…that better not be from over the road?" He wagged a finger at the cupcake box.

"Sure is, and you know what? I think there must be something in the water around here."

"What do you mean?"

"You moody about your flowers, and the cherub is tetchy about his planets." He opened the box and showed off his pink cupcake. "Looks good, doesn't it?"

"I told you to stay away from the brothers."

"But it was just too tempting." He took a bite and hummed his pleasure. Blade glared, Scope whined, and Yates looked seconds away from tackling him to the floor.

"So good—" He took another bite, only to pause and reach into his mouth for the hard thing lodged in his teeth.

"What is it?" Yates asked.

Ranger studied the object in his fingers. "A nail."

"It probably fell out of the ceiling or a display cabinet or something."

"It's a fingernail. A whole fingernail." He dropped the cupcake. It splattered on the floor and was promptly eaten by Scope. "Fucking hell, Yates? Are they Sweeney Todding it across the road?"

"Of course not."

"Those little shits!" He spun around to face the window, and sure enough, both brothers were watching. "I'm going over there—"

"Absolutely not! Leave it, and don't go back for seconds."

"But—"

"No, buts, I'm not having you blowing their brains out all over the buns and pissing off Stone."

"What is it about Stone that has you cagey?"

Yates huffed. "I'm not cagey. I leave him to his business, and he leaves me to mine. It works. Besides, who do you think ran to help me when the shop got petrol bombed? Stone did. I owe him, and that means the least *you* can do is steer clear of him and his brothers."

"Fine."

"Where's the nail now?"

"Scope ate it." He patted him on the head. "I wonder if it'll come out whole, scratch its way out of there," he cooed at Scope. "You kinky bastard."

Yates turned his face to the ceiling. "I think I've hit my Ranger limit for today."

"Where's Dylan?"

"He's got an appointment with a counselor, a relationship counselor. He'll be back soon."

Ranger gritted his teeth. "Are things between you that bad?"

Yates narrowed his eyes and put venom in his glare. "For him and his sister."

"Ah, I see."

"He's got a lot of work to do to repair their relationship, and he knows it, but he's trying his hardest," Yates said. He stopped trying to kill Ranger with his stare.

"What happened to the fiancé anyway?"

Yates didn't answer.

"He's still alive, right?"

"He's alive."

Ranger lifted his eyebrows at Yates's bluntness and didn't press any more. There were other ways to hurt a guy than to kill him, and Yates had people everywhere.

"And just so you know, me and Dylan are doing fine."

Ranger hummed. "A counselor is kind of like a therapist, right?"

"I guess they are similar."

"There's loads of romance movies where the patient falls in love with their therapist. Just saying…"

Yates's top lip twitched. "Do you want to go through the window?"

Ranger looked at the pane of glass. "Not really, besides, these two won't let you. All I've got to do is say the *word*."

Yates rolled his shoulders, glancing at the dogs.

"Checkmate, bitch."

"If it's a job you're after, there isn't one yet."

"I wanted a catch-up." Ranger brimmed with the need to tell Yates all about Troy and their date. He opened his mouth, ready to unleash a detailed description of events, but Yates's buzzing phone interrupted him.

Yates answered. "Is it done?"

Ranger didn't hear the response, but Yates nodded and mumbled, "Good. I'll see you soon."

He hung up and dropped his phone back to the counter.

"Donnie," he said. "Finished the Scotland job."

"Right."

Yates sighed. "Dylan keeps on at me to invite them over. He wants to meet them properly. I told him it's a little complicated considering the situation."

"They need to keep a low profile."

"Exactly."

Ranger frowned. "Invite them over, like a double date?"

"I wouldn't call it that, but—"

"Can I come?"

"If it ever actually happens, then of course. You've boasted about your kitchen skills for ages. You could cook something."

Ranger licked his lips. His heart took off in a giddy beat. "Can I bring Troy?"

Yates blinked. "Troy?"

"Yeah."

"The guy you were trying to make jealous with an escort?"

Ranger's smile spread from ear to ear. "It worked. We went on a date yesterday."

"And how was it?"

"Awful, but the end was good. The last few hours of that night were probably the happiest of my life."

Lying on Troy's lap with a full stomach and the dogs curling around them. It had been picture-perfect. Ranger's eyes welled up just thinking about it.

"And he's asked me out on Friday." Ranger kept his focus on Yates's mouth, waiting for it to grin, or for him to say something positive, but his lips didn't stray from their firm line.

"What?" Ranger asked.

"I dunno. There's something about him."

"You've only seen him once."

Yates turned his head. "I know, but…"

"But nothing." Ranger rubbed his head, inwardly cursing Yates for making it hurt again. It had been close to clear all morning, with barely a hint of pain, but it started to grow fierce and fast in his head.

"I thought I recognized him."

"When you saw him, his nose was strapped and his face was swollen. You didn't get a good look at him." Ranger took the dog leads in one hand and drummed his fingers against his temple with his other.

"And yet my gut told me there was something not right about him."

"Bullshit!" Ranger's breaths came out in pants. "Why can't you be happy for me, huh?"

"Happy that you're dating the guy that broke your ribs?"

"I like him."

"What's his surname?"

Ranger stepped back. "What's that got to do with anything?"

"Let me run a check on him."

"No."

"Why not? It'll make me feel easier about him."

"I'm not fucking this up to make you feel easy."

Yates's nostrils flared. "How old is he? What does he do for a job? Where was he born? Where does he live?"

"Stop it."

Blade's growl thundered out, but it didn't stop Yates. He glared at Ranger, their eyes locked. Yates heaved in anger as much as Ranger did.

"My point is you know nothing about this guy."

"I know," Ranger said. "I know I don't. But I want to know about him, and I don't want it to be you who tells me, but him. I want him to trust me enough to tell me."

"I could save you a lot of time. Then you'll know whether he's worth pursuing or not."

Ranger couldn't look away from Yates, and Yates couldn't look away from Ranger.

"Back off," Ranger growled.

"I can't."

Yates's face twisted with a snarl, and Ranger knew his expression matched. He couldn't feel his hand around the dog leads or smell the flowers close by. The situation was bad.

"I know he is worth it. I know we could be great together. We will be great together."

Yates laughed. "You've been on one date, *one* date."

"When you know, you know."

Ranger knew he had to leave. He couldn't lose his temper, especially not in front of the dogs. Scope would cower under a display table in fear, but Blade, he'd react, he'd go for Yates too. He opened the door to the shop and took a step back.

"My gut says there's something untrustworthy about him."

Ranger shook his head. "And my gut says he's trustworthy."

He thought about that morning, Troy ducking into the bathroom to take a call. That wasn't unusual, it was considered polite. But it was the lock clunk that'd followed Ranger dwelled on. Troy had shut him out completely. He'd secured away a piece of him. So what, he reasoned. They were only just getting to know each other. Date two was on the horizon.

"If Dylan was here, he would've been happy for me. He would be rooting for us."

"Dylan?" Yates snorted. "That's who you want rooting for you and Troy? The kid who put all his attachment on the only father figure in his life until it became the toxic mess he's still trying to dig his way out of."

Ranger took a step back and collided with someone. He didn't turn around but looked down at Scope, who was facing that direction and wagging his tail with untamable joy.

Fuck.

"He is digging his way out, though."

"If his sister was a lesser person, she would've left him to drown. Fuck, I thought about it."

Ranger winced, stepped aside, and revealed Dylan behind him.

Dylan, with an expression that could only be described as crushed. Yates took a shrill intake of breath. The anger cleared from his face. He unknotted his arms and let them drop limp at his sides.

"Dylan—"

"I know I deserve that, but…"

He turned, and his feet pounded the path as he fled. Scope whined as he lowered his head to the floor and ceased wagging his tail.

"Goddammit!" Yates rushed out from behind the counter and squeezed past a growling Blade.

He stopped beside Ranger, breathing hard. Ranger stiffened, expecting Yates to throw a punch, or grit out a stream of insults. Instead, he met Ranger's eyes.

"You wear your heart right there on your sleeve with nothing to protect it, and I worry about it. I worry about you."

Ranger gaped, thinking of something, *anything* to say back.

Yates took off, limping down the street.

CHAPTER TEN

Ranger approached Troy, who was leaning against a wall. He tipped his head back, closed his eyes, and breathed a cloud of smoke up into the atmosphere. A sports bag hung off his shoulder, and he tapped one of his sneakers to the floor as he waited.

"Hey..."

Troy flicked his cigarette away. "Hey."

Ranger tore his gaze from Troy and looked at the huge sign above his head. The paint had flaked, the wood had rotted, and letters were missing.

OXIN CLU

The longer Troy stood beneath it, the more worried Ranger became in case it dropped and decapitated him.

"You wore sweatpants and a vest like I asked." Troy glanced at Ranger's shoes. "And sneakers, good."

He'd gone for soft cotton sweatpants and a tight white vest. His arms bulged, and he'd received plenty of appreciative looks as he strolled down the street. Troy was wearing a similar outfit. White sweatpants with red trim and a tight red vest. Ranger greeted both nipple piercings with a look, then smiled at Troy.

"I read in a magazine red is the best color to wear on a date."

"This isn't a date."

"So boxing?" Ranger said. He shrugged to himself. Sparring with Troy could be fun; they'd no doubt both work up a sweat. "I guess it's a good choice."

"Good choice?"

"Our first date was a night in with pizza. It makes sense that our second date is something active."

"I told you, it's not a date."

Ranger shifted his gaze along the wall to the door of the gym. The smashed window had been boarded up, and a graffiti tag had been sprayed repeatedly over the door. No sound came from within the building, only the busy street behind them. The place was in a prime location but was a complete eyesore.

"Come on," Troy said, pushing off from the wall. He trudged over to the door, then searched his pocket for the key.

"Is...is this your place?"

Troy glanced over his shoulder. "Yes."

Dust assaulted Ranger's senses as soon as he stepped inside, and he sneezed. He ran a finger over the front desk, gathering a thick clump of dirt. His nose twitched with the scent of damp and ash.

"Woah…what happened?"

"What do you mean what happened?"

"Well, don't be offended, but it's a goddamn mess."

Troy licked his lips. "There was a fire."

"No shit."

"Everyone knows about it."

Ranger tapped his head. "If I did know, I don't remember."

Troy strolled through what Ranger assumed was the reception area into the main gym. Dust sparkled and twirled in the air; cobwebs dominated the ceiling. Ranger tripped and looked down. A door off its hinges lay on the floor. He searched the room and found where it had come from. When he peeked inside, he spotted lockers and a bench for people to get changed.

Troy didn't speak as his feet crunched over the debris. He jumped up onto the boxing ring in the middle. A skylight shone down on him, and he held his hand out to pull Ranger inside.

"So you own a boxing gym?"

"I own bricks and ash. That's all."

"It's cool though, right? When are you gonna fix it up?"

Troy didn't answer. The zip filled the silence. He opened the bag wide enough for Ranger to look inside.

"So we're gonna take turns?" Ranger asked.

"We're gonna fight."

Ranger stepped back. "Practice fight."

"No, a real fight. I'm gonna go at you hard, Ranger. I suggest you don't go at me like it's a *practice*. It could cost you some teeth."

He threw a glove in Ranger's direction, then another. They skidded against the dusty surface and stopped at Ranger's feet.

"This doesn't seem very romantic."

He put them on anyway and knocked them together.

Troy chuckled. "It's not. This isn't a date, this is boxing."

"I don't want to hurt you."

"You won't."

"I will if I punch you in the face."

"Come on, Ranger." Troy slipped his gloves on. "Fight me."

"Wait, let's take a minute."

"Ground rules. Not the head and not below the belt. Chest hits only."

"Troy, I don't want to—"

The rest of Ranger's words dissolved with a gasp and a stream of spittle. Troy caught him in the ribs, and he went down to his knees, coughing and spluttering. He propped himself up with his gloves as he tried to drag the air in the room into his lungs.

Troy circled him. His face tense and his eyes piercing. He looked down on Ranger like he were vermin, a cockroach in his decrepit gym.

"You know, you're pathetic," he spat.

Ranger got to his feet and managed to block Troy's next punch. He backed away, intent on leaving. If it was fight or flight, he was choosing to go. He spun around to climb out of the ring, but Troy wrapped his arms around his chest and hauled him back.

"All those dates, trying so hard. It was embarrassing to watch, but I couldn't not. I had to keep coming to the bar. It was too entertaining not to."

Ranger used both gloves to deflect Troy's next strike. The force of it bent his wrists and shook the muscles all over his body. It spread through him like a shock wave, leaving him gasping.

"I honestly thought you couldn't get any more pathetic. Then I saw you with those kids in the cinema. Kids. They humiliated you, and the waiter afterward did too. You stood there, blubbering and apologizing. I was so embarrassed I almost left you there on your own."

Troy curled a punch into Ranger's side. The pain radiated through him, ending with a deep ache in his ribs. They were familiar with that punch. The same hook that had broken his ribs the last time they came to blows.

"You really think I'd be interested in you?" Troy laughed. He laughed like he'd done that night at The Archer, full of mocking. He'd waved cash in Ranger's face. He had forgotten afterward, but the laugh made him remember. Cash because he'd won the bet the whole pub was participating in. How long until gullible Ranger realized his date had escaped out of the window. Ranger had heard them all, the whole pub rumbling with laughter until he lost control of his anger and went for Troy.

"I wouldn't be seen dead with you."

Ranger lifted his gloves in front of his face. The red gloves Troy had given him. His vision filled with hazy pink, a cloud of fog he had no hope of wading through. It would only disperse once he was done, once Troy was a bloodied mess on the matt.

He should fight the anger, he knew he should, but it was so tiring always pushing the headache aside, always containing rage that wanted to be let out.

Troy's punch hit Ranger's gloves into his face. He backed off, whipping his chin with the gloves. His nose dripped blood, but he couldn't feel it, or smell it, or taste it on his lips. He was numb to everything but the inferno of anger, so he did all he could do.

He let Troy have it.

****

The scent of sweat filled Ranger's nose, fresh sweat, well-worked sweat mixed with an aftershave he recognized and one he didn't. It ran through his hair, tickling his scalp. His racing heart slowed in his chest and brought him more awareness. His sweatpants and vest were glued to his body, and he was no longer vertical but was laying down as he slowed down his breaths. The surface beneath him tremored slightly, but he ignored it and instead opened his eyes. His spinning sight snapped back into position. The huge window above him showed him the gray sky, and rain patted against the pane. The surface beneath him kept vibrating, and Ranger finally turned his head to find the source.

Troy lay on the floor beside him. Sweat dripped down his face, and he was laughing. Not in malice or mocking, but a laugh that made his eyes sparkle and his cheeks redden. It was the first time Ranger had seen him looking happy, actually happy, and the look was directed at Ranger.

"You have a nice smile," Ranger said.

Troy's laughter came to an end, but he still grinned at Ranger. "For thirty-five minutes you've been trying to punch it off my face."

The last hour came back to Ranger in a rush. The second date. They'd been in the boxing ring, and Troy had demanded they fight each other.

Ranger gaped and rolled onto his side to face Troy. "I'm sorry, I didn't—"

"Don't you dare apologize. You did exactly as I asked. You did exactly what I wanted you to."

"Why?"

Troy rolled on his side and looked at Ranger. "How's the head? And just so we're sure, I'm talking about the one on your shoulders."

Ranger blinked. "It's…it's empty."

"Well yeah." Troy chuckled.

"No, I meant, it's not there."

"What isn't?"

"Pain. There's always a pain, but right now…"

There was no pressure at all.

"There's not?"

Ranger's eyes began to sting. "No."

Troy cupped his face. At some point, he'd removed his gloves, but Ranger was still wearing his and used one to pin Troy's hand against him.

"That anger, or rage, or whatever you want to call it, doesn't give you headaches. Stopping it from coming out does."

"I don't like losing control. What if I'd have killed you?"

"I would've brought it on myself for being an arsehole."

"That doesn't make me feel any better."

"I know you don't like losing control, and if you'd been in a ring with anyone else, you would've killed them, but I can handle you."

"You can handle me."

Troy hummed, then flopped onto his back. He rubbed his stomach. "Only just. You're incredible, Ranger. I had to duck and weave like crazy not to be hit in the head, and when one of your punches landed, it flung me across the ring like we were in a movie or something."

He smiled up at the ceiling, seemingly reliving it. Ranger's unease about the fight started to fade, but then he spotted the red smears high up on Troy's vest.

"You're bleeding."

"My fault, not yours. I didn't take my nipple studs out." He tugged his vest over his sweaty abs and showed Ranger his nipples. "See, they're still there."

"Good." Ranger slumped. "I wouldn't think you're hot without them."

Troy reached for Ranger's gloves and took them both off. He threw them aside and watched as Ranger stretched and curled his fingers.

"You would've been a great boxer."

"Maybe I still could be with the right trainer."

Troy shot him a glance. "Maybe."

"Is that what you wanted to do with this place, train people up?"

"We're not doing this, Ranger."

"Doing what?"

"Having a heart to heart."

Ranger pouted at the ceiling. "I'm only trying to get to know you."

"You know the most important thing…"

"Which is?"

"I've got a hot cock."

Ranger laughed. His stomach muscles roared in protest. "Yes, that's true, but I want to know more. How old are you? Where are you from? Where do you live?" Ranger took a deep breath. "What's your job?"

"They're the type of questions you ask on a date, and I told you this isn't a date."

"What was it then?"

"I…well…" Troy stewed over his words. "I guess I wanted to help you."

"And you did, on both of our dates, you helped me. I can't help but wonder what magical thing you're gonna do on the third one."

Troy shook his head against the floor, but his lips lifted in a slight smile. "You're persistent."

"Yates calls me annoying."

"That too."

"So come on. If you can go anywhere and do anything on a third date, what would you choose?"

"Ranger…"

"I don't mean with me, but hypothetically."

Troy sighed. "Rome."

"Rome?"

"I'd visit the Colosseum, go beneath where the gladiators once walked. Touch the rocks that their sweat and blood once stained… Yeah." Troy patted his sweatpants pockets and found his squished cigarette box. He peeked inside, huffed, then threw the box out of the ring.

"That's the third date sorted then."

"Look, I know you're worried because your mates have found someone, and you think you'll never find Mr. Right—"

"I'm not worried anymore. I've found him."

Troy groaned and pinched the top of his nose. "Mr. Right isn't me. I'm Mr. Fucking Wrong. I don't do relationships. I certainly don't do love. I've got this far without either."

"I'd rather be in love and live a short life than never be in love and live a long one."

"Why are they the only two choices?"

Ranger shrugged. "They just are."

"You're a hopeless romantic."

"A hopeful romantic, actually."

Troy scrunched his face up, then rolled away and presented Ranger with his back. "I'm hopelessly horny, so put that cock you're shifting around in your sweatpants to good use." Troy yanked down his pants. "There's lube in my sports bag."

"What?"

Troy sighed. "Get your cock out, and shove it in me."

"We're in the middle of a conversation."

"It was feeling too close to a heart to heart, so fuck me already. This is a one-time deal kind of thing."

Ranger spun away so fast he got head rush and ended up crashing back to the floor. He found the bag, and the lube inside, and crawled back to Troy.

"You better have enough energy left to fuck me good, Ranger."

"I've still got plenty of energy," Ranger said, tugging down his sweatpants.

"No foreplay." Troy shifted his arse back. "Just fucking fuck me, got it?"

"Yes, I've got it."

Ranger tugged his vest up and held it in his teeth. He tugged up Troy's too so their hot skin could press together. Troy squirmed and complained as Ranger got him ready. He only stopped bitching when Ranger began pushing inside of him. Troy sighed with bliss and gave up on his fidgeting. Ranger groaned as he bottomed out.

"Yes, like that."

Ranger shook his head. "No."

"No?"

He pulled out and tugged Troy onto his back. Troy widened his eyes and opened his mouth like he might protest, but Ranger nudged his cock at his hole.

"Like this," he said, sinking back inside.

The missionary position was intimate. It was special. Not merely fucking, but fucking with passion. Troy moaned as he flexed his hips.

"And we can talk like this too."

"Talk? I don't wanna talk!"

Ranger ran his hand through Troy's sweaty hair and held on as they touched and teased each other with their tongues. Ranger didn't know why it was so important, but he needed his bare chest on Troy's. He needed to kiss him while feeling their slick chests brush and the firm stomachs stamp each other with sweat. He needed to tug Troy's hair, and nip his lips, and steal glances at Troy's beautiful cock sliding against his stomach as Ranger fucked him.

But wait, he needed to find things out about Troy too.

Ranger stopped. "So, where're you from?"

"Damn it, Ranger!"

"Answer me, and I'll continue."

"Basildon."

Ranger rewarded him with a slide of his cock. Troy tilted his hips for Ranger to go deeper.

"How old are you?"

"Thirty-four."

He pulled out and pushed back inside just to feel Troy's hole spasm in shock.

"And where do you live?"

Ranger knew he hit the right spot when Troy's eyes rolled back. "Um, a few streets from here."

"And did you buy the gym because you wanted to train people up?"

"That was the dream once."

"It can still come true."

"I don't think—"

"It can," Ranger said, pushing in deep. Troy groaned while clawing at Ranger's back. "Goddamn."

"I'd join, I'd join in a heartbeat. I'd be your fucking poster boy."

"You'd be such a good poster boy. So fucking hot and sexy." Troy shivered. "Enough already, fuck me hard like you said you would."

"If you promise to come home with me afterward."

"Ranger, I'm not sure that's a good idea."

"The takeaway on the sofa, the movie, the dogs around us. I know you liked it."

Troy squeezed his eyes shut. "I did."

"Then come home with me, and we'll do it all over again. We can do it as many times as you want."

"I wish—"

"Don't wish. Do."

Troy conceded with a low moan. "Okay, fine. Now fuck me already."

Ranger did as he promised. He fucked Troy with every ounce of energy he had left until his thrusts lost their rhythm, and his hips jerked. He looked into Troy's eyes as he clenched Ranger to orgasm.

"Fucking hell," he moaned, knocking their foreheads together.

Ranger's cock spasmed in Troy's arse, shooting his load. Troy kept clenching and releasing, clenching and releasing, milking Ranger's release until he had nothing left to give. He collapsed in a heavy heap on Troy's chest, sticky and sated.

"I didn't finish," Troy mumbled.

Ranger laughed breathlessly. "Give me a minute."

"No. I don't think I will." Troy flipped Ranger over and pinned him to the floor. "I think I want to fuck myself to orgasm using that tight hole of yours."

"I like the sound of that."

Troy chuckled. "There was me thinking you'd need some convincing."

"I'm already convinced," Ranger whispered.

He was *the one*.

CHAPTER ELEVEN

"This was the worst decision of my entire life."

Ranger rolled his eyes and ignored Troy's meltdown.

"Literally the worst decision."

Ranger splashed him. "That's a bit dramatic, it's only a bath."

"With candles and bath salt and...two dogs watching us."

The dogs hadn't been part of the plan, but they'd insisted on coming into the bathroom, and Ranger couldn't say no to them. Blade glared. Scope panted. It got even weirder when Scope sat down to lick himself.

"It's relaxing," Ranger argued.

"Is it?"

"Yes. Can't you feel the aches and pains in your muscles melting away?"

"Those aches and pains you speak of are getting worse. Guys as big as us are not meant to share a bath. Have you even thought about how we're gonna get out?"

Their bent knees were wedged together, and their muscular bodies had created a suction effect against the side of the bath. Ranger couldn't move, but he wasn't going to admit it.

"They're gonna find us like this in a few days when the dogs have eaten us."

"You," Ranger corrected. "They won't hurt their dad, and when Blade and Scope eat enough of you, I'll be able to escape."

Troy flung his arms up. "Well, isn't this fucking romantic? You're talking about your dogs eating me."

Blade's stomach rumbled, and Scope licked his lips.

"You can at least wait until the water turns cold, you blood-thirsty mutts."

Ranger laughed, and to his surprise, Troy shook his head and laughed too.

"This is ridiculous. Why put this on your list?"

"I thought it would be nice. In the movies, it looks nice."

"But we're not in the movies, Ranger. This is real life. I could ruin this bath right here and now by releasing a—"

"Don't you dare," Ranger splashed him again.

"I'm just saying I could."

"But you won't. It's on my list, and I want to enjoy it despite the taps digging into my back and the smell of lavender making me nauseous."

"Why lavender?"

"Home Keepers magazine says it's number one for creating a relaxing environment."

Troy squeezed his temples, muttering under his breath. "Did I just hear you correctly? Did you say Home Keepers magazine?"

"There's loads of good shit in there. For instance, did you know you can get rid of bloodstains with toothpaste?"

"You." Troy pointed at Blade. "Get over here and bite my head off. I don't think I can take it anymore."

"If you keep ruining this, I'll drown you."

"In what? An inch of water?"

Ranger broke out into a fit of laughter. It wasn't long until Troy joined in too. The whole situation was ridiculous.

Blade stood up, huffed dramatically, then left. Scope bounded after his brother, leaving Ranger and Troy alone.

"Can you make them dance?" Troy asked.

Ranger dragged his eyes away from the door the dogs had just left through. "What? Blade and Scope?"

"No, you idiot." Troy splashed him. "Your pecs."

Troy demonstrated, jerking his chest and flashing his nipple piercings. Ranger had to lean to see him around their knees.

"I can do that too."

He shifted away from the taps and made his pecs dance just like Troy had asked.

"That's hot."

"Don't you dare jerk off in this bath."

Troy grunted and put his arms on the sides. "What are we supposed to do then?"

Ranger frowned. "I'm not entirely sure. I think we talk about deep stuff."

"Screw this," Troy muttered. He tried to get up, but Ranger put pressure on his knees and trapped him in the bath.

He slumped. "Deep stuff, huh? Like how I was deep in your arse earlier?"

"I was deep in yours first."

Troy hummed, groping himself again. "That was good."

"Hey!" Ranger snapped, flicking water in his face. "No touching yourself. We're discussing deep stuff, remember?"

"Like what?"

"Hopes and dreams. The future."

Troy tipped his head back. "The future…"

"Yeah, come on."

"I'm not sure about this."

"You said you wanted to run your own boxing club."

Ranger watched Troy's throat as he swallowed. "Yeah. I did."

"That's a dream right there. And you said you wanted to get back in touch with your dad."

Troy squeezed his eyes shut. "Fix things with my dad and fix up the boxing club."

"Both sound achievable."

"Maybe. They are but…"

Ranger splashed him. "Hey, no buts. They are achievable. Leave it at that."

"I guess I don't need to ask you about your hopes and dreams. They're pretty transparent."

"What are they then?"

"You hope to find a boyfriend, and you dream of a happily ever after."

For once Troy didn't say it with a sneer.

Ranger nodded. "Spot on."

"That's enough deep stuff for one night." Troy yawned. "I'm beat."

"I guess we should attempt to get out of the bath."

"You go first. I want a good view of your arse while you're sprawled over the floor."

****

Ranger woke to the sound of his phone buzzing on the bedside table. He swiped for it, but Troy's arms snaked around him and tugged him away from the interruption. Ranger couldn't control the smile tugging up his cheeks.

After thirty minutes of trying to escape the bath, they'd climbed free and spent another night chilling on the sofa with a movie and the dogs slotting between them. Troy had taken it upon himself to provide the inner monologue of characters, leaving Ranger's stomach an achy mess from laughing.

"It's too early."

Ranger fought against Troy's hold, but he clung on and tangled their legs together. When they'd fallen asleep, it had been him trying to curl his body around Troy's, but at some point during the night, they'd rolled over, and Troy had glued himself to Ranger's back.

"It could be important."

Troy kissed the back of his neck. "What's more important than this?"

Ranger sunk back with the biggest grin possible on his face. Troy was right. *Nothing* was more important than *this*. He closed his eyes and enjoyed Troy's arms around his middle and his scent filling his lungs.

"I love that you're a cuddler."

Troy tutted. "We don't speak that word."

"Love or cuddle?"

"Both words." Troy yawned, drawing Ranger away from the phone another inch. It rattled on the table, breaking the calm between them.

"It'll stop eventually," Troy mumbled.

The caller persisted, and Ranger sighed, reaching out for it.

"It's Yates," he said, switching the phone to silent. "He probably wants to form a search party and go looking for Dylan."

Troy's arms stiffened, and his leg slipped free of Ranger's. "Search party?"

"They had a tiff, and Dylan can be quite sensitive."

"How sensitive?"

"If he sneezed, he'd probably burst into tears afterward, that kind of sensitive."

"Odd. I thought Yates was a tough guy?"

"Opposites attract. You have piercings, I don't. I have tattoos, you don't. See? Opposites attract."

"You're listing differences, not opposites. We've got a lot more similarities anyway."

"Like what?"

"We both like pizza."

"So does everyone."

"We both switch."

Ranger hummed. His arse ached from where Troy had taken him for the second time.

"I've only done that with you."

"I've unlocked a whole new world for you to explore."

"When's your birthday?"

"Um…End of June."

"Mine's the beginning of July. We're both Cancers."

Troy groaned. "Please don't tell me you believe any of that shit."

"I do actually, and cancers can be compatible, really compatible. They can be soulmates."

"What about your friend's star signs?"

"Yates is a Scorpio and Dylan is a Pisces. They're said to be compatible too."

"Yet they've had a tiff?"

"They'll work it out, and if Yates needs a helping hand, I've got plenty of dating advice so he can make it up to him."

"Remind me, how many of your dates did a runner?"

"We weren't compatible. I was waiting for Mr. Right."

Troy slid his hand over Ranger's mouth. "Don't say it."

He couldn't physically say it but said it with his eyes, and he knew Troy had understood when his eyebrows snapped together, and he shook his head.

"Ranger…"

"What?" he mumbled beneath his hand. "I didn't say anything."

Troy lowered his hand.

"If things were different…"

"What things?"

"Just…things."

Ranger hummed. "Give me one thing."

"Okay fine, if I wanted to be in a relationship, maybe then I'd date you, but I don't. I've got other shit going on. It's not…it's not important to me."

"Yates said that once and you should see him now, like a lovesick dog."

A whine leaked under the door. "I wasn't talking about you!"

Scope's footsteps faded away down the landing.

"Answer me this, do you enjoy spending time with me?"

"If I say no, you're not gonna jerk me off, are you?"

Ranger laughed, pushing their foreheads together. "Answer me honestly."

Troy sighed. "Then yes, I've enjoyed spending time with you, but—"

110

"No buts. There doesn't need to be. Leave it there and leave me happy. That's all I want. I'm not after the world, only a slither of happiness."

"Happiness comes and goes."

"I know, but don't take it away from me just yet. Let me be happy for now."

Troy opened his mouth to reply but sighed instead of speaking. He smiled softly and searched Ranger's eyes as he whispered, "Okay."

"How are you feeling?"

"Achy, bruised, a bit sore."

"Same." Ranger snorted.

"I've got today off if you want to do something and keep that happiness going a little longer?"

Ranger blinked. "Wait, are you serious?"

"I'm serious."

"I don't think we have enough time to fly over to Rome for our third date."

Troy rolled his eyes. "No, but we could do something a little closer to home."

"Like what?"

"Who knows, maybe a dog walk, a picnic, and stroll along the river? Or we could take out a rowing boat and I could serenade you."

Ranger shoved Troy's chest. "Now you're teasing me."

"Maybe…"

"But maybe not?"

"You should hear my singing voice."

Ranger laughed. "I'm sure it's beautiful, second only to the sound just before you come."

"What sound?"

"When you clench your teeth and suck in air. Makes me get goosebumps."

Troy huffed as he rolled onto his back and spread his legs. "I think I need to hear it again."

"I'm up for that."

"I seem to remember you bragged about having strength in both hands. Prove it."

Ranger laughed as he rolled onto his back and took a cock in each hand. Troy flung off the sheet and folded his pillow for a good view. He sighed as Ranger jerked them with the same speed and sweeping motion he performed on himself. He took extra care of the cock ring.

Ranger twisted his toes into the mattress as he squirted his load and watched on expectably as Troy's cock gave in and dribbled out his cum as his eyes flipped back. They both sighed.

"That's one hell of a good morning," Troy mumbled.

Ranger wiped his hands on the bed before grabbing his neglected phone to find out the time. "It's only…"

His voice trailed off when he saw the missed calls from Yates. Twenty calls. He'd been calling nonstop.

"So what time is it?" Troy asked.

"Eight."

Troy plucked the phone from his fingers. "Come on, we need to shower."

"I really should call—"

"Let's shower."

He yanked at Ranger's hand until he gave in and got up, then led him into the bathroom. Ranger showered and brushed his teeth in record time. Troy kept reaching for him and seeking Ranger's mouth with his own, but he ducked away and swatted him. He needed his phone. He needed to see why Yates was calling.

"I'm starving," Troy mumbled, rubbing his belly. "Let's take the dogs and walk somewhere for breakfast."

Ranger's heart melted a little before turning to stone. Yates was calling again. He glanced at the phone, then at Troy beckoning Ranger to him.

"Leave it," Troy said. "This is a once in a lifetime offer, remember?"

"It's a date?"

"Yes, I'm asking you out on a date, now come on."

Something was wrong. Ranger could feel it every time another missed call notification popped up on his phone. Yates was frantic.

"Hey." Troy snapped his fingers. "Breakfast, put that away."

He tapped his foot on the floor as he waited for Ranger. Troy's eyes darted away; his fingers hooked into his pockets on their quest to find cigarettes.

Ranger's heart said to go with Troy, but his head told him to call Yates back. It wasn't about which he trusted more, it was about *want*. And right then, Ranger wanted to ignore whatever was happening at the other end of the phone and go with Troy.

"I know a little place," Troy said.

He opened the door, and in no time Blade and Scope came bounding down the corridor and leaped into the room. Scope's tail whipped against Ranger's legs as he got dressed. He yelped happily, spinning in circles, the polar opposite to Blade, who made a grumbling noise and ran his nose over the sheets on the bed. The scent of the bed irritated him enough that he sneezed as he jumped off.

"Wet food, dry food, gravy, in that order, right?" Troy said.

Ranger gripped the back of his neck. "Right."

"Come on then, boys."

They followed Troy out of the room. Ranger lingered behind with his phone still in his hand. Yates had stopped calling. Maybe he'd sorted the problem out on his own. Maybe the hooks digging into Ranger's insides were a false alarm.

"Hey Ranger, get your arse down here."

Ranger got to the top of the stairs before his conscience caught up with him. He leaned back against the wall and looked down at the door that led to the kitchen as he answered Yates's call.

"He's taken Dylan!"

The air left Ranger's chest in a rush. "The sister's fiancé?"

"No. Marco Russo."

"Wait, what?"

"He knows Elliot is alive. I don't know how he knows, but he's taken Dylan and given me an ultimatum. Give up Elliot, or they'll kill Dylan."

"Have you called Donnie—"

"He's here. He's at Bloomers. I need you, Ranger. Dylan needs you."

Troy came out of the kitchen and stood at the bottom of the stairs. The tip of his cigarette glowed red, and he beat his foot on the floor.

"I'll be right over."

Ranger hung up and hurried down the steps.

"Problem?" Troy asked.

"I need you to go."

Troy snorted. "Most of the time you're pleading with me to stay."

Ranger ducked into the kitchen. Blade and Scope were licking their bowls to a mirror shine.

"Thanks for feeding them." Ranger grabbed their leads from the side and clipped on their collars. "I've got to go."

"You should've left the call."

"What?"

Troy shrugged. "We could've had the morning together."

Ranger ushered Troy toward the door. "As I said, something came up, and I've got to go."

"Something more important than your happiness?"

"Yes, my friend's happiness."

He undid all the locks and bolts and opened the door wide for Troy to leave.

"Ranger?"

He patted his pockets, checking for his wallet, his keys, and his phone. "Yeah?"

Troy took his face in both hands and pressed their lips together. Ranger almost got lost in the kiss, but the fear in Yates's voice sobered him up, and he took a step back.

"What was that for?"

Troy smiled, but it didn't reach his eyes. "Goodbye, Ranger."

He took off down the street, and Ranger resisted the urge to follow. He opened up the people carrier and loaded Blade and Scope inside. When he looked up to see if he could spot Troy, he'd already gone.

CHAPTER TWELVE

Roses crunched under Ranger's feet as he took his first few steps inside the shop. He winced at the sound of the bell. Soil and trampled flowers lay strewn all over the floor. The display tables had been flipped too, all except Dylan's table and chair at the front. Yates hurried out of the office, followed by Donnie and Elliot.

"They made a mess of the place too?" Ranger asked.

"I did this," Yates growled, pointing a stern finger at the door. Ranger locked it and flashed a brief smile at Elliot and Donnie.

"So what happened?"

"What happened?" Yates heaved. He whirled on Donnie and shoved him in the chest. "This idiot hasn't been keeping a low profile, and now Dylan's paying the price!"

Donnie shoved back. "Who was it that asked us to come back for a visit in the first place?"

"I fucking regret that now."

"Hey," Elliot tried to muscle in between them, but Donnie pulled him away and hid him behind his back. Ranger swaggered over and placed himself between the two warring men. By the look of their rustled clothes, it hadn't been the first time they'd shoved each other.

"Where did they take Dylan from?" Ranger asked.

"He was staying over at his sister's. She told me his friends turned up, and he left with them. I didn't want to panic her and acted like it was completely normal, but then I got the call from Brock."

"Brock?"

"He's one of my dad's heavies," Elliot said.

Yates closed his eyes as he pulled at his hair. "They said they'd taken Dylan and would only give him back once I handed over Elliot."

"How long did they give you?"

Twenty-four hours."

"What about your army bitches?"

Yates glared. "That's not enough time for them. Besides, I've got nothing to work on. I don't know where Marco would've taken him." He looked at Elliot, who shrugged.

"What exactly did Brock say?" Ranger asked.

"He said they knew Donnie was abroad with Elliot, and I have twenty-four hours to get you back!"

"We're not invisible."

"No, but I expected you to be careful, and you haven't been if they know Elliot's alive. You must've fucked up."

Ranger pushed them apart and kept a hand on each of their chests. "That's not important right now. We've got to work out how to get Dylan back."

"It's simple, we hand over Elliot."

Donnie pressed his chest against Ranger's palm. "Not gonna happen."

"I want Dylan back; I don't care if I have to sacrifice your boyfriend to get him."

"Hey," Ranger snapped. "We won't be sacrificing anyone. Jesus. We know we're in trouble when I'm forced to be the rational one." He slid his hand up Yates's chest and grabbed his shoulder. "We will find Dylan, but we're not giving up Elliot."

"If something happens to him—"

"The only thing that's gonna happen is him being rescued, understand?"

Ranger turned to Donnie, who nodded. "I won't let him trade Elliot, but I will die for Dylan if that's the way this goes."

Yates slumped and took a step back. Donnie stopped posturing but threw a protective arm over Elliot's shoulder.

"So what's the plan?" Ranger asked.

"I haven't got one yet," Yates admitted. "They said they'd call with a rendezvous to swap Elliot for Dylan."

"My father would never let you walk away," Elliot mumbled. "You know that, right? He'd kill me, you, and Dylan."

Yates gritted his teeth. "Let's not put kill and Dylan in the same sentence for the foreseeable future, okay?"

"Sorry."

"How much do we know about Russo's gang?" Donnie asked.

"Only what I found out about them when they hired us to kill Elliot. Four main members." Yates turned on his heels and trudged into the back. Ranger followed behind him with Elliot and Donnie at the rear.

"Eric Sanchez, Adam Rice, Matt Gear, Sam Phillips."

Ranger didn't recognize any of the men on screen.

"And their associates."

Ranger's jaw dropped at the last picture. His heart took an extra hard thump, but his brain remained calm like he'd been expecting to see

Troy on the screen. Like he knew. His gut had been telling him something was off, but he'd ignored it all because he wanted a piece of happiness.

"What's the last one's name?"

Yates looked at him. "I don't know."

"Cayden," Elliot said. "The last picture is Cayden."

"How do you know that?" Donnie asked.

"So, erm…He used to be my father's right-hand man."

"No." Ranger smacked his fist against the wall. "He's not called Cayden."

"He is."

No. It was Troy, minus the stud in his eyebrow. His dark-brown eyes, his shaved head, and his tight T-shirt that hinted at the nipple piercings beneath it. Ranger backed into the wall and slipped down to a crouch.

"What is it?" Yates asked.

"That's Troy…"

Yates spun back around to face the screen. "Troy? As in the guy you've been seeing?"

Donnie flashed a grin, but it vanished as soon as it came. "Wait, you've been seeing one of Russo's men?"

"I didn't know that. I met him in a pub. He said his name was Troy."

Yates's jaw ticked. "Did you tell him anything about Elliot?"

Ranger smacked the back of his head against the wall. "Yes. I spoke about you and Donnie both having someone." He groaned. "I mentioned Elliot…my kitchen."

"What about your kitchen?"

"He searched it. He must've found that postcard you sent me. That's why they think you're in the Maldives."

Yates scrubbed his hands over his face. "Motherfucker."

"I'm sorry, I didn't know. I…"

But he'd always suspected there was something odd about him, something guarded.

"You were so fucking desperate for someone to love, Jesus, Ranger. You told a stranger about Elliot and Dylan."

"I'm sorry. I don't know what else you want me to say?"

Yates clutched his head. "I don't want you to say anything. I want you to do. I want you to help me get Dylan back."

"First of all, we need to work out where they're keeping him," Donnie said.

"And do you know who's likely to know?" Yates stared straight at Ranger. "Troy or Cayden or whatever the fuck he's called. He'll know. We get him, and we can find out where Dylan is. Where does he live?"

Ranger shook his head. "He only ever came to mine."

"Damn it, Ranger."

"But he has a gym. Vine Close."

"The one that burned down," Yates mumbled.

Ranger stared at him blankly, and Yates sighed.

"It burned down years ago. Two people died."

"I didn't know that, or I didn't remember. The point is he said he lived not too far from there."

"And you have his number?"

"He uses an ancient phone." Ranger squeezed his temples. "You won't be able to track it."

"I will if he picks up your call."

"What's your plan?" Donnie asked.

Yates took a deep breath. "We're getting over to Vine Close. Ranger, when we're there, you're gonna call him, keep him talking for as long as you can. Donnie, I'm gonna send you in when I find him."

"I'm going too," Elliot said.

"He won't go down easy," Ranger said. "Even when I'm out of control, he can handle me."

Yates and Donnie shared a look.

"What?" Ranger asked.

"Nothing," Yates mumbled.

"And what are we gonna do once we have him?"

Yates's gaze skirted over to the desk and the pair of sheers lying on top. "We're gonna make him talk."

****

Yates was going to cut his boyfriend into pieces. Well, they'd never actually got to the boyfriend stage, but still, Yates was planning on hacking chunks off him. The same thought went round and round Ranger's head. The voice in the back of his head chuckled darkly, pleased at the idea, but his heart ached. Troy was an arsehole, no doubt about it, he'd always warned Ranger he wasn't a nice guy, but a part of him was.

A part of Troy was a good person. Ranger had seen it.

It was so hard to get to, but it was in there.

Ranger parked outside the gym, and Donnie turned the collar of his jacket up as he slipped from the car. Elliot grabbed his hand to stop him from leaving. "Donnie…"

"I know," Donnie winked. "You're the love of my life too."

"No, not that." Elliot nipped his lip. "Be careful, not cocky. Cayden is dangerous."

Ranger winced. There was that name again. Cayden, not Troy.

Donnie kissed him softly on the lips. "Be right back, baby."

"Enough," Yates snapped. "Your loved-up display is making me want to shoot you both."

Donnie slammed the car door shut and jogged across the street. Elliot started bouncing his leg on the floor the second he was gone from their view.

"Always remember he's a professional." Ranger smiled. He tried to install some confidence in Elliot, but from his replying blank stare, Ranger knew it hadn't worked.

"A *professional* I ran rings around."

"Point taken."

"Ranger." Yates met his eyes in the mirror. "Call him."

"What if he doesn't pick up?"

"I'll find him eventually; this will just make it happen a lot sooner." He gestured to the laptop on his thighs. "I'm ready when you are."

Ranger took a deep, calming breath, then another. One more for luck.

"Which means make the call right fucking now before I lose it."

"Okay." He pressed his thumb down over Troy's name and held the phone to his ear.

Troy picked up after the third ring, and Ranger's breath snagged in his throat. His lips moved, but he couldn't think what to say. Elliot flapped his hands, encouraging Ranger to speak.

"Hi," he said finally.

Troy snorted. "You're not gonna scream and shout and threaten to kill me?"

"Why would I do that?"

"Because you know Dylan's been kidnapped because of me, but if you think about it, it's not actually my fault."

"You told Marco—"

"Yeah, I told him Elliot was still alive, but he shouldn't be alive, should he? He paid Yates to kill Elliot, and instead of doing the job, he faked it and took the money."

Ranger glanced at Yates in the mirror. His face tightened. There was truth in Troy's words. They'd deceived Marco, a man notorious for getting what he wanted. There were bound to be consequences at some point.

"You tricked me," Ranger whispered. "You pretended you were interested in me—"

"I told you it was a bad idea we date. I made that clear from the start, but you kept on and I…"

Elliot waved his hands again, encouraging Ranger to say more, keep the conversation going.

"You what?"

"It doesn't matter."

"I know you care about me."

"I used you to find out whether Elliot was alive."

"You still helped me outside the restaurant. You still met me yesterday. You still came home with me when I asked."

Troy was quiet for a long time, then sighed. "What can I say? You've got a comfier bed than mine, and a stocked fridge, and a tight, warm arse."

"You didn't want me to answer the call from Yates. You wanted that lie to keep going just a little bit longer."

"And now the truth is out. Yates has twenty-four hours to bring Elliot back and hand him over."

"Donnie won't give Elliot up."

"Then shouldn't you be helping Yates find them instead of calling me?"

"Dylan's a good guy."

"He sounded pathetic the way you described him."

Yates ground his teeth together, breathing heavily through his nostrils. His eyes were fixed to his laptop as he tapped away, trying to locate Troy.

"He's not. He's vulnerable. He's sweet. He encouraged me to ask you out."

"So he's stupid too."

"You shouldn't have involved him."

"Like you told me, Yates adores him. Dylan was the easiest way to get to Yates, and Yates is the only one who can find Donnie and Elliot."

"Where is Dylan? He's not part of this."

Troy barked a laugh. "That's your game, is it? You're trying to guilt-trip me into revealing where they've got Dylan. Give it up, Ranger. It's never going to happen."

Ranger watched as Yates turned the laptop toward Elliot. He tapped out a message for Donnie.

"Was it all a lie?"

"You and me should have never happened."

"But it did, and I wanna know… Was it all a lie?"

"Goodbye, Ranger."

He hung up. Ranger twisted to Yates in the back. "Should I call him again?"

"No need. I know where he is." He passed the laptop over to Ranger and climbed into the front. "And so does Donnie. We better get moving in case he needs a hand."

"He'll definitely need one," Ranger muttered.

He pointed out of the windscreen. "Oatlands Avenue. Head that way, and I'll direct you."

****

The second they pulled up beside the house, Yates flung himself out of the people carrier and rushed through the open door. Ranger blocked the doorway with his bulk, trapping Troy inside, and keeping Elliot outside.

"What the hell, Ranger?"

Elliot shoved him in the back, but Ranger didn't move.

"Donnie would kill me if you got hurt."

Something smashed and crashed, and angry voices hissed and cursed. Troy sprinted from a doorway but skidded to a stop in front of Ranger, wide-eyed and panting.

"They'll kill me."

Ranger nodded. "Quite likely."

"And you're okay with that?"

"Yes."

Yates came up behind Troy and smashed him over the head with dumbbell weight. He dropped to his knees before collapsing on his side. Ranger pinned him with his foot just in case.

"Where's Donnie?"

"Panting for breath on the living room floor. This bastard floored him with a punch." He kicked Troy's shoulder. "Let's get him ready."

"For what?" Ranger knew, he knew, and he still asked.

Yates gripped his shoulder. "Once upon a time you used to do the dirty hits, full of torture and pain. I need that Ranger again."

He swallowed. "But he's not here anymore."

Yates huffed. "Then I guess I'll have to step up."

He took hold of Troy's arm and dragged him back the way he'd come. Ranger stepped into Troy's home and took a proper look at the place. The wallpaper was peeling, there were watermarks in the ceiling, and mold was growing in the corners of the hallway.

He stepped through an archway into the kitchen. Dirty plates and cups were stacked in the sink. The rubbish bin overflowed with takeout cartoons, and a full ashtray sat in the middle of the table. He thought of Troy's jibe about Ranger's bed being comfier and his fridge fuller. The fridge confirmed it had been true. Troy's fridge was empty except for a half carton of milk and a block of moldy cheese.

Donnie stepped into the room, hugging an arm around his ribs. "Goddamn."

Ranger snorted. "He's a fighter."

"No shit. When he punched me, I didn't think I'd ever be able to breathe again."

"He broke my ribs when he hit me."

"I think he's broken mine." Donnie took a deep breath and managed to straighten. "How you feeling?"

"Me? I'm not the one who just got punched."

"No, but I'm imagining you're hurting right now."

"Oh, you know me, good-*new* Ranger always picks himself up and tries again."

Donnie pulled a pained expression. "You liked this guy, though."

"What do people say? Plenty more fish in the sea. Hopefully, next time I won't hook a shark."

"You've always liked the sharks."

"I don't fancy getting bitten anymore."

Donnie scratched the back of his head. "If you want to…you know, sit this out."

"No. I want to be here. I want to find out where Dylan is. I owe Yates, and I owe you too."

Yates huffed and cursed as he hauled an unconscious Troy into the kitchen. He pointed at one of the chairs, and Donnie slid it to him. "This room's better."

Yates pulled Troy up and dumped him onto the chair. At some point, Yates had removed Troy's shirt, and his two nipple studs caught Ranger's eye.

"What's wrong with the living room?" Ranger asked.

"It's carpeted. It'll be easier to clean when we're done."

Donnie watched Ranger carefully, then looked away. He took the duct tape from Yates and secured Troy to the chair. His hands were bound together at his back, exposing his chest. Plenty of space for Yates to work on. He pinched at one of Troy's nipples, leaving Ranger wincing.

"Leave them alone."

"Huh?"

Ranger rubbed his brow; his headache was returning. "Don't touch them, okay? Punch, hit, cut, but leave the piercings."

"Fine," Yates huffed. He forced a rag between Troy's lips and tied it at the back of his head. "We just need this arsehole to wake, and then we can get started."

Ranger's stomach dropped.

"I'm tempted to call Stone."

"Stone? The bakery guy?" Ranger placed his hands on his hips and shook his head. "Surely you're not hungry at a time like this."

Yates growled. "I'm not hungry. I'm angry."

"I don't see how a cupcake can help."

"Forget it." Yates flicked Troy's face. "I'll handle it."

Troy's eyes fluttered before flying open. He shouted around the gag and fought to be free, but Donnie had duct-taped him to the chair legs from his ankles to his knees.

"You're gonna tell me where Dylan is. The quicker you tell me, the more likely you'll get out of here alive."

Troy laughed, a deep rumbling laugh. He raised his chin as if challenging Yates to get started. He kept laughing and laughing until Yates yanked open one of the kitchen drawers and found a knife. He dove at Troy, knife aimed at his heart, but Donnie stepped in and stopped him.

"Drop it."

"I'll cut that fucker open."

"He can't tell us where Dylan is if he's dead."

Elliot pushed off from the doorway, and Troy's eyes snapped to him. He stopped chuckling and glared at Elliot as he strolled in front of him. Troy's nostrils pulsed harder and harder, and he mumbled something under the rag.

Elliot hooked it with his finger and pulled it down. Troy licked his lips but didn't say anything. Yates stopped struggling, Donnie frowned, and Ranger tilted his head, wondering why Troy's eyes twitched with a new level of anger.

Elliot smirked. "Lost for words, big brother?"

CHAPTER THIRTEEN

"Don't ever call me that again."

Elliot delivered a cocky grin. "But it's true, brother."

"Wait just one minute," Donnie said. He let go of Yates, who'd frozen in shock and stepped up to Elliot. "I think there's something you've not told us."

"It all happened so quickly; I didn't get a chance to tell you." Elliot pointed at Troy. "Cayden here is my brother."

Ranger folded his arms tightly. Cayden, *fucking Cayden,* not Troy.

"You never said you had a brother," Donnie said. "You told me you didn't have any family."

Elliot shrugged. "We try to pretend the other one doesn't exist. We're half brothers. We've got the same bastard father."

Ranger gaped. "You're Marco Russo's son?" He blinked. "And Elliot's half brother?"

Troy lowered his gaze and heaved harsher and harsher breaths toward the floor.

"Our dad married young," Elliot said. "He was too young and too immature. He slept with any woman who took his fancy."

"Like your whore of a mother."

Elliot twitched his nose. "Maybe he wouldn't have felt the need to sleep with prostitutes if your mother hadn't been such a bore in the bedroom."

"My mother was a good woman."

"So was mine! Our father harassed her and chased her until the day she died. We never felt safe, always moving around, always fearing for our lives."

"Are you trying to get sympathy from me?"

"No, it's clear you don't have any."

"Not for your mother, no."

"What did she ever do to you?"

"Nothing. But she was no saint."

Elliot took a step back. "She was a goddess compared to yours."

"Goddess's can be spiteful. Why else would she send photographs of you to my mother? Why would she torment her like that? And expose details about her and our father's various rendezvous? Because she was jealous bitch." Troy shrugged. "Who knows, maybe she liked being chased. Maybe she liked the danger and the adrenaline of always having someone after her."

The color drained from Elliot's face.

"Enough," Donnie said, steering Elliot away by the hip. Ranger heard him whisper in Elliot's ear. "Don't let him get to you."

"I was eight when the first photograph of you arrived at our house. It broke my mother's heart. Every year she sent them, addressed to my mother, not our dad, and he vowed to hunt both of you down and wipe you from this earth."

"He failed," Elliot growled. "I'm still here."

"Not for much longer."

"Wait," Ranger shook his head. "I don't understand."

"There's no surprise there."

"You said you haven't spoken to your dad for a long time." Ranger glanced around the shabby room. "He's loaded. Why would he let you live in a place like this?"

"I fucked up."

"How?"

Troy shifted his gaze to Elliot. "I didn't kill him when I had the chance."

"You caught Elliot?" Yates asked. He squeezed the bridge of his nose. "How the hell did you catch him?"

"It wasn't hard."

"I was careless back then," Elliot murmured.

"Six years ago, I made the biggest mistake of my life and let you go. You called me your brother, sobbed and pleaded for your life, and I fell for it." He looked back to Ranger. "Compassion is a weakness. I showed it to Elliot, and I lost my father's respect. He didn't kill me, but he cast me out and burned my boxing club to the ground. Even when word got to me that Elliot was dead, he didn't forgive me. I chose to protect the child of a whore over avenging my tortured mother."

"Stop calling her a whore!"

Donnie shushed Elliot and moved him out of Troy's view.

"How did you know Elliot wasn't dead?" Yates asked,

"There were always rumors. The three of you were involved in the hit. Donnie vanished, Yates is far too unapproachable to get close to, but Ranger... Every Friday you go to The Archer. I thought Elliot might show, or Donnie might turn up, and you'd let something slip when you were drunk, but no, I had to bear witness to your awful dates instead."

Ranger looked away. "You didn't have to keep coming back."

"I told you before they were entertaining. I thought maybe Elliot was really gone, and the rumors were just rumors, but then you mentioned him like you were talking about the weather, talking about nothing serious. And there it was, my chance to get my dad's respect back. Using Dylan as bait to find Elliot, and here he is…"

"Yeah, I'm here," Elliot rushed forward despite Donnie trying to keep him back. "But our dad isn't. None of his men are. No one's coming to rescue you. The only reason he wants me dead so bad is for his pride."

"Yes, our father is a very proud man. Let's not forget Yates took his money for a hit that didn't take place. That's just bad business practice and suicidal to disrespect him like that." He twisted to find Yates. "You must've known that decision would come back on you one day. It's just a shame Dylan has to pay the price."

"Don't," Yates growled the word through his teeth.

"Believe me when I say they'll kill Dylan if you don't hand over Elliot. Ranger told me he's a sensitive guy. I'm sure my dad's men will have fun with him before they kill him, and that's on you."

Yates launched his fist into Troy's face. Blood flung from his mouth and splattered against Ranger's vest. He stared at it as pressure increased in his head. It pulsed between his ears, growing and shrinking against the side of his skull.

Donnie had been right. He needed to sit this out.

He left the room, wincing at the wet, slapping sound of Yates punching Troy again. Ranger peeked a look in the living room at the red punching bag hanging from the ceiling.

Being out of the kitchen wasn't enough; he needed to get out of the house.

****

Donnie greeted Ranger at the front door with a pained smile. He lowered the grocery bag, heart in his throat. "Did Yates…"

"He's alive," Donnie blurted. "He's still alive. He spent the last ten minutes goading Yates into killing him. Me and Elliot had to intervene. We pulled Yates out of there for a break and a rethink."

Ranger hugged the grocery bag to his chest. "Let me try to get through to him."

Donnie dove his hand inside the bag and pulled out a carrot. "By cooking for him?"

"I've got an idea."

"Have you got some truth serum in here, huh?"

"Not quite."

"Come on then, what's your idea?"

Ranger smiled and followed Donnie into the house. "First, I'm gonna clean him up."

"Then?"

"I'm going to cook for him."

Donnie sighed tiredly. "Ranger…"

"Then he's gonna tell us where Dylan is."

"Food isn't that convincing."

"It's got some surprising uses."

"You gonna shove an onion up his arse?"

Ranger shook his head. "Not quite. Unless he asks me nicely."

Yates appeared with red-rimmed eyes. "If I go at him, I'm gonna end up killing him. Torture was your specialty, not mine."

"There's no need," Ranger smiled. "I've got this."

"You've got this?"

"Yup. I make a mean carrot dish."

He winked.

****

Donnie held the door open for Ranger, and he stepped into the kitchen. He winced as he looked at Troy panting for breath. Yates had decided on body hits instead of punching Troy in the face. His breaths rattled as they came out.

Troy lifted his head. "I've been wondering where you were. I thought you'd want a front-row seat after I humiliated you."

"It's funny," Ranger said, putting the bag on the side. "I don't feel humiliated."

"You feel angry?"

"I don't feel that either. I feel…sad."

"I told you us dating was a bad idea, but you didn't listen. This wasn't your love story. This was…enemies to lovers to enemies again."

"You've never been my enemy."

Ranger started unloading the groceries onto the side. Carrots, onions, celery, coriander, chicken stock, and a crusty loaf of bread. "I don't think you're up to eating much, so I thought soup. A good soup is hard to beat, especially when you're feeling tired."

"What?"

"It's the food to have when you're ill."

"I'm not ill, Ranger. I'm being beaten to death. Besides, it'll only come up again when your friend returns and kicks me in the gut."

"Probably, but you can enjoy it on the way down."

Ranger looked at the table of implements Yates had set up. Knives, and sheers, and secateurs. None of them were splattered in blood—yet. He moved them onto the kitchen counter and pushed the table toward Troy.

Ranger met Troy's eyes as he placed a small candle in the middle of the table. It wasn't until he lit it that realization dawned on Troy, and he chuckled in disbelief.

"You're kidding, right?"

"Candlelit dinner. It's romantic."

"I'm tied to a chair, bloodied and bruised—"

"And whose fault is that? You only have to tell us where Dylan is, and we'll let you go."

Ranger turned back to the bag on the counter and pulled out a bottle of white wine. "It's the second cheapest. I read you're supposed to pick the second cheapest. I don't know why." He placed the bottle on the table and searched the cupboards for wine glasses. There were none, and he had to settle for two mugs instead.

"I'm not having dinner with you."

"You can't really escape it." Ranger searched the cupboards. One of the doors dropped from its hinges, but Ranger caught it in time and lowered it to the ground. "Your home is a dump."

"Fuck you."

"I take it you don't have a food processor?"

Troy looked away, muttering something Ranger didn't catch.

"The soup will be lumpier than it's supposed to be. Sorry."

"Sorry?" Troy leaned back as far as he could in the chair. "I can't do this. This is worse than being punched and kicked. Bring the other guy in. The angry one."

"Yates is taking a break. You're stuck with me."

"The other one then." Troy grimaced. "The one always touching up Elliot."

"Shut up and wait patiently while I cook."

Troy chuckled. "That's no way to speak to your date."

"Good job you're not my date then."

Ranger cracked his knuckles and got to work making soup. As soon as the pan started to boil, he dropped it to a simmer and added the vegetables. It chased away the scent of blood and sweat in the air. Ranger took a deep breath, less on edge. He turned to Troy, who'd been staring at him the whole time.

"It just needs to simmer for twenty minutes."

Troy clacked his tongue. "Right…well. It smells good."

"Thank you." Ranger smiled and sat down opposite Troy. The candle flickered on the table. "This recipe was in Home Cooks magazine."

Troy's lips twitched. "Of course, it was."

"They claim it's the best carrot and coriander recipe in the world."

"You've spent far too much time reading magazines and watching Netflix."

"I know." Ranger smirked. "You've spent far too much time trying to win favor with your father, who doesn't give a shit about you."

"He did once, and I want him to again. Is that so bad?"

"When you're willing to sacrifice your brother—"

"He's not my brother."

"Yes, he is. And let's not forget about Dylan. He's innocent in all of this. Why is getting your dad's favor back so important?"

"I've got nothing else, no one else. I made one mistake."

"Letting Elliot go when you had the chance to kill him wasn't a mistake."

"Of course it was, his mother—"

"Tormented yours, I heard, but was that Elliot's fault? Was it his mother's fault for being jealous, or yours for not realizing what was going on behind her back? No. It was your father's. I don't care how big and powerful you think he is. He's a piece of shit that someone needs to wash the fuck away."

Troy snorted. "You won't kill him."

"It's not for me to kill him, but I will save Dylan. I will make sure Elliot isn't hurt. I'll put my life on it."

"For your friends' boyfriends?"

"For their happiness, yeah. It's worth a hundred times more than mine or my life." He opened the bottle of wine and poured some into both mugs. "This is probably the only candlelit dinner I'm gonna have."

"I told you before, you're gonna be fine. You'll meet someone right in the end—"

"Maybe I would've one day, but in all honesty, I doubt I'll still be here this time tomorrow, so this"—he gestured to the pan steaming on the stove, the wine in his mug—"this is as good as it's gonna get for me."

Troy shifted his gaze away. "Ranger—"

"Don't ruin it. Please."

Troy swallowed hard. "Walk away from all this. It was Yates who lied. It's Elliot my father wants dead. They're not after you, go." He flashed a look at the door. "Get out of here. Walk away."

"I'd never leave my friends like that. I love them too fucking much." He downed his mug of wine and smacked his lips together. "You know what? That's not bad. Want to try some?"

Troy poked his tongue out. "Sure, why not?"

"It'll sting." Ranger leaned over the table and helped tip the wine into Troy's mouth. "Not bad."

Ranger shuffled back to get to his pocket. He pulled out a folded square of paper.

"The list." Troy sighed.

"Different list. These are questions to ask on a date."

"What?"

"Just go with it, Troy. It's the least you can do." He ran his eye down it with a grimace. "A lot of them are about family, siblings, parents, and childhood. Do you mind if we skip those subjects? I don't want to lower the mood."

"Please do."

"Okay then." Ranger scanned the list for a good starting point.

"Where do you see yourself in five years' time?"

Troy laughed. It came out different, wetter somehow, but it was an actual laugh, not his mocking chuckle. Ranger smiled at him. "What?"

"Where am I gonna be in five years' time? I'm guessing I'll be worm food in the ground courtesy of your friend in the other room."

"He won't put you in the ground. He'll put you in a lake."

"Fish food then." Troy chuckled. "That's good to know."

Ranger ticked off the question. "What's the scariest thing you've ever done?"

"Scariest thing?" Troy tilted his head. "When I mocked you into fighting me. That was pretty damn terrifying. If you had training and knew what you were doing, I'd be dead, but I was quick on my feet, managed to dodge and weave, but yeah, the scariest thing I've ever done, but also one of the most exciting, and dare I say it…but satisfying too."

"Satisfying?"

"You told me the headache stopped."

"It did. You made it better."

Troy shuffled, then jutted his chin out toward Ranger. "What about you? The scariest thing?"

"It's always scary when I lose control, but outside of that, nothing scares me."

"Come on, you must've done some scary shit. You're an assassin."

Ranger shrugged. "It doesn't worry me. I don't feel fear. If you ask Yates, he'd probably say the scariest and stupidest thing I've ever done was trying to cuddle an attack dog."

"You did what?"

"Well, two attack dogs." He smiled, picturing Blade and Scope. "They ran at us, snapping and snarling, and I dropped to my knees and opened my arms."

"You're crazy."

"Yeah, but it worked. I think it confused them. I must've messed with their heads. They had one goal, one job to do, but a bit of kindness from me flipped their minds."

Troy snorted softly. "You definitely do that. You confuse and disarm people, and dogs too apparently."

"It turned out okay in the end. I took Blade and Scope home, and now they're my boys."

"Jesus, Ranger."

He scrolled the list. "Happiest memory?"

"I'm not a happy guy."

"That's not an answer."

"Fine." Troy huffed. "Probably watching you trying to get out of the bath. You flopped over the side, and I beat your arse cheeks like drums, that was pretty fucking funny, and then afterward, when I stuck my tongue in your—"

"Not funniest or dirtiest."

Yes, Troy had rimmed him senseless while he hung halfway out of the bath while groping his stinging arse cheeks. Ranger got his revenge in the middle of the night by sneaking Gavin into the bed and watching as Troy's arms clamped around him. His scream had woken up the neighbors. Ranger chuckled, then shook his head. "Happiest."

He wanted happiest, and he pouted until Troy gave in with a sigh.

"Cuddling up on the sofa watching Netflix with the dogs around us. Yeah, I'll admit it. I felt happy, or at least content, but it was always in the back of my head that it wasn't going to last."

Ranger nodded. "Yeah, I'd pick that too. The sex was great as well."

Troy hummed. "Without a doubt. Especially when I made you cum down the side of the bath—"

"Saddest memory," Ranger blurted. "I'll go first. When I saw your face on Yates's computer and realized you'd played me. I realized I'd fucked up, and my pursuit of love might have cost Yates his. I was sad for me but sadder for him."

Troy closed his eyes. *Was it genuine guilt?* Ranger couldn't tell.

"Your turn. What's your saddest memory?"

"When your phone went off in the morning and you told me Yates was calling. I knew you'd realize I was an arsehole. I mean, I kept telling you I was, but you didn't believe me. I didn't want that morning to end, but I knew it had to. When the phone went off, it was like someone had dug a blade into my side."

"I'm glad it hurt. It hurts me too."

"My intention was never to hurt you. I swear it, Ranger, I didn't want to hurt you. I tried to push you away, remember?"

"Maybe you should have tried harder." Ranger sighed. "Let's get back on topic. Worst movie you've ever watched?"

Troy tipped his head back and laughed. "That's an easy one. *Wilma's Wedding*. I came into the cinema late and sat behind you and pretty boy. The whole movie he kept gazing at you like he wanted you to kiss him, but you didn't."

"I was too engrossed in the movie."

"Liar. Your cheeks are burning, Ranger."

"Fine, I knew he was looking at me like that, but I didn't want to kiss him. Someone else's kiss was still on my mind."

"You better be talking about me."

Ranger kicked him under the table. "Maybe, maybe not."

"Oh, you are. My turn to ask a question?"

"Okay."

"Hottest blow job you've ever had."

Ranger rolled his eyes. "Down some dirty alley."

"With me, right?"

"Maybe, maybe not." Ranger quirked his eyebrow.

"It was definitely me. I agree, it's the hottest blowjob I've ever had the pleasure of performing."

The alarm on Ranger's phone went off. "Soup's ready."

"How exactly am I gonna eat it?"

"I'll have to spoon feed you."

"Are you serious?"

"Yup."

Ranger fed Troy soup. He slipped it, spilling it down his chin. His face burned, but Ranger only looked at him fondly.

"You know, I wanted to do this…"

"Feed me soup?"

Ranger rolled his eyes. "Look after my poorly boyfriend."

Troy licked his lips, then opened his mouth obediently for the next spoonful. Ranger kept talking.

"I thought about cooking him soup, and wrapping him up in blankets, and making him comfortable. It's a weird thing to want, isn't it? My imaginary boyfriend to get ill just so I can take care of him and make him better again."

"It is weird," Troy whispered. "But it's kinda nice too."

"Eat up," Ranger told him.

Afterward, when he'd finished the soup, Ranger filled up a bowl of cool water and cleaned Troy's sweaty face. He sighed and moved his head in Ranger's direction.

"Why are you being like this?"

"Like what?"

"Nice. I don't deserve it."

Ranger bopped Troy on the nose. "This is me, being me, and I was hoping if I'm nice, you'll tell me where Dylan is."

Troy shook his head. "I'm not gonna."

Ranger stroked the cool cloth over Troy's cheek. "It was worth a try."

"If I told you, I'd be a dead man."

"You're a dead man anyway. No one's coming to save you."

"I know, but I won't betray my father again."

"Okay," Ranger said, cleaning Troy's lips. "I won't ask you to."

Troy frowned.

Ranger dropped the cloth in the bowl and ran his fingers over Troy's hair. He massaged his scalp, taking extra care when he came to a bump. Troy breathed out and leaned even further toward Ranger.

"You confuse me so goddamn much."

Ranger shrugged. "I confuse myself."

Troy rested their heads together.

"If things had been different…"

"Go on," Ranger whispered.

Troy leaned back. He smiled, and his eyes grew shinier. "If things had been different, we would've had that third date." He swallowed. "I think we would've had more after that too."

"Well, you know how persistent I am. I would've made sure of it." Ranger smiled. His chest tightened. "Thank you."

"For what?"

The temptation to kiss Troy's lips one last time was too much. Ranger leaned his mouth closer to meet Troy's. He moved away before kissing back harder. Ranger sucked on Troy's bottom lip and released it with a wet pop that left him gasping.

"For making me feel a slither of happiness among all this pain."

The door burst open. Yates didn't look toward them as he powered over to the counter and snatched up the secateurs.

"Enough of this shit." He growled. "It's time to get serious."

CHAPTER FOURTEEN

"Wait," Ranger said, holding up his hand to Yates.

"What do you mean wait? I've had to listen on the other side of the door while you flirted and laughed with *him*. They've got Dylan somewhere. They could be hurting him, and you're in here giving him a sponge bath."

Yates lashed out at the table, sending the mugs and plates flying. "You told me you'd get a location from him."

"I couldn't, okay?"

Yates kicked Ranger's chair away, flung the table aside, and dragged Troy closer by his chair leg.

"I'm gonna make you scream."

"Whatever you do to me won't compare to what my father would do if I sold him out. Take my fingers, take my toes, pull my teeth, skin me alive. I'm not telling you where your boyfriend is."

Yates shook him. "Donnie! Get in here."

Donnie stepped into the room, followed by a ruffled-haired Elliot.

"I need you to untie his hands. We're gonna start with his fingers."

Ranger stepped in front of Troy. His heart thumped in his chest as his eyes met Yates's. "No."

"Wh—what do you mean no?" Yates's eyebrow twitched with uncertainty.

"I won't let you do it."

Yates took a step back. "You're choosing to save him over saving Dylan, but you said—"

"No, I..." Ranger squeezed his head. "I won't let you hurt him anymore. Just let him go, Yates. He's not gonna tell you anything. Let him go."

"Let. Him. Go? He's the reason Dylan's been taken, he's the reason—"

"The reason Dylan has been taken is because you deceived Marco Russo and took his money."

Yates's breath shook as it came out. His brow twitched with something close to hurt.

Donnie widened his eyes. "What the hell, Ranger?"

Ranger pointed at him. "And the reason Yates chose to deceive Marco Russo was because you refused to kill Elliot. That is why we are in this situation, because of you two. Your selfish decisions led us here. I want to let Troy go—"

"Cayden," Elliot interrupted.

"Troy, Cayden, whatever. I want to let him go. I want him to live. That's my selfish decision, okay? You've both made one. Now let me."

"We're not letting him go," Yates growled. "Not until he tells us where they've taken Dylan."

He shoved Ranger, who fell onto Troy. "Don't push me around."

"Stop acting like an idiot. Ever since that bullet to your brain."

Ranger surged to his feet and pushed Yates into the counter. He struck it hard and cursed, holding his hip.

"Motherfucker."

"Hey! Hey!" Donnie shouted; he kept hold of Yates. "Let's not turn on each other."

"It's not me that's turned."

"I'm done here," Ranger snapped. He reached around Troy to get to his wrists. "I'll help you get Dylan back, I'll make sure no harm comes to Elliot, and in return, you'll let Troy go."

"Ranger," Troy hissed. "What the hell are you doing?"

"Disappointing some fish, I imagine."

Troy's lips moved into an unsure smile, "You can't be serious?"

Ranger brushed Troy's cheek with the back of his fingers. "I am."

Before Ranger could smile, Yates's fist met the side of his face and sent him tumbling to the floor. Pain flared in his shoulder, and his jaw clicked as it met the hard floor. The room spun. His eyelashes fluttered before closing as he slumped into the tiles.

Yates stooped over him. "I think he's out… Donnie, chair."

"What…what are you doing?" Troy asked.

Ranger didn't open his eyes. Yates picked him off the floor and dumped him onto the chair. It screeched across the floor as Yates moved him. His neck flung back as he came to a stop, even with his eyes shut the room still felt like it was spinning.

"Donnie tape his legs and *one* of his arms."

"Yates…"

"Don't argue, just do it!"

"Right or left?" Donnie asked.

"Secure the left one."

"Why?" Troy asked. He didn't mask the worry in his voice. "What are you going to do?"

"He's that desperate to stop you from being hurt that I'm gonna let him. For a little while." Yates spread Ranger's fingers apart. Cold metal pressed against his skin.

"This is going to be one hell of a wake-up," Yates mumbled. "But he deserves it."

The secateurs clicked, a crunch followed. Ranger threw himself back into the chair as he screamed, struggling against his restraints. His throat ached when his painful cry came to an end. A soft thud hit the floor as he breathed in frantic gasps.

Yates waved the bloody secateurs at him. "It's not my fault, it's not Donnie's fault, it's yours for running that fucking mouth of yours and telling him everything."

"Stop it!" Troy shouted. "He's your friend. He's your fucking friend."

"No friend of ours would take your side," Yates spat. "The old Ranger would've ripped your throat out for deceiving him. He would've cut your skull open and searched for that location in your goddamn brain."

"He's not the old Ranger."

Ranger took a deep breath, heaving. When he opened his eyes, he found himself back to back with Troy, their chairs pressed together. He peered over and spotted the small nub of his finger on the floor.

"Yates," Ranger's eyes burned. "Please don't—"

"Shut up." Yates slapped him across the mouth. "You care so much about this piece of shit; you can die with him."

Donnie and Yates fought to hold on to his free arm. The sharp blades ran down the sides of his finger.

Click. Crunch. Thud. Ranger yelled through his clenched teeth, fighting to free himself from Donnie's and Yates's grip.

Another finger dripped a puddle onto the floor.

"Stop it!" Troy shouted. He shook his chair, jumping the legs off the floor. "I said, stop it!"

"Elliot gag Troy," Yates growled.

"What?"

"You heard me!"

Donnie nodded. "Do it, Elliot."

"On it."

Troy flung himself back, thumping into Ranger who grunted. "Don't you touch me! Ranger fight, get angry, get out of here."

Another click. Another snap. Another thud. Ranger's scream tapered off into a painful moan. His feet shook against the floor. His body trembled.

"Christ," Troy gasped. "What the fuck are you doing to him?"

"Sit back so I can put the gag back in," Elliot told him, wrestling Troy into behaving.

"He's your friend. He's gonna risk his life for your happiness, you mean more to him than his own goddamn life, and you're chopping bits off him."

Ranger breathed out an even breath and met Yates's glare.

"Troy... if they want to do this, let them do this. It won't bring Dylan back, but if it makes them feel better, it's okay."

"It's not goddamn okay! None of this is okay. You're the one person in this room who doesn't have to be involved in all this shit. Fuck. He loves you guys so much."

"Not as much as you," Yates snapped. "I'm done hearing your voice. Sit back in your seat so Elliot can gag you."

Ranger flung his head back into Troy's and slurred, "We're gonna make a lot of fishes very happy."

"Leave Ranger alone. Cut my fingers off, not his. He's a good guy."

Yates stepped away with the splattered secateurs. He waved them for Troy to see. "Don't worry, they're sharp enough to last the both of yours. Just got to do your little finger, Ranger, then we're moving on to your other hand."

"Ascope industrial park!" Troy screamed at the top of his lungs. He panted. "It's a warehouse. That's where they would've taken Dylan."

"Ascope industrial park?"

"Yes, now stop, just stop."

Yates dropped the secateurs to the floor. "I've got to hand it to you, Ranger, that worked like a charm."

Ranger ripped himself out of Donnie's feeble bindings and stood up. "Told you."

"What?" Troy struggled to lean his neck back far enough to see. Ranger stepped in front of him and wriggled his fingers. "Carrots and ketchup."

From the angle Troy had been able to see, the bloody stumps looked quite effective. Ranger put his hand on his heart. "I'm not gonna lie, it made me happy when you screamed for me like that. It made me feel good, right here." He pressed his palm over his heart.

"You...you played me?"

"Yes." Ranger rested his hands on Troy's thighs and got in his face. "*I* played you. It's not nice when someone messes with your feelings, is it?"

Tears shone on Troy's cheeks. His swollen bottom lip trembled. "No, it's not."

He pushed off from Troy's thighs. "Now we're gonna go save Dylan."

Yates hurried Donnie and Elliot from the room. "Come on, we've got to get to Ascope."

"Shouldn't we untie him?" Elliot asked.

"It's up to Ranger."

Ranger grabbed a knife off the counter and cut Troy free. "And just so we're clear, I don't think we should date anymore. This relationship isn't working out for me. I can do better."

Troy snorted. "I told you so."

****

"All the times I've threatened to hit you," Yates mumbled, dropping his head into his hands. "Never ask me to do that again."

"Never is an awfully long time." Ranger squeezed Yates's shoulder. "And it worked."

"How's your head?"

In all honesty, it ached, but not from Yates's punch. It hurt being him.

"No different than normal."

Yates lifted his head and fixed his gaze on Donnie and Elliot in the front.

Donnie glanced at him in the mirror. "What's the plan when we get there?"

"There are guns in the back."

Ranger frowned. "That doesn't sound like much of a plan."

"I can't think of plans anymore." Yates tapped his temple. "My mind is chaos. If they've hurt him…"

"Don't think about it. Think about killing the guys that took him."

Yates growled through his gritted teeth, "I wanna rip their heads off."

Ranger patted his shoulder. "Yeah, focus on that."

"Gut them alive."

"Good."

"I'm not letting Dylan out of my sight ever again."

Ranger tilted his head. "Creepy or romantic, I can't tell…"

"We're here," Donnie said, pulling up on the curb.

The building beside them didn't scream out it was a hideout. The smashed windows and rusty fence around it put Ranger on edge.

He leaned forward between the seats. "You sure?"

Donnie nodded. "Yeah, this is it. Ascope Industrial Park."

Yates didn't wait around. He reached over the seats into the trunk and snatched up a gun. Before Ranger could even unfasten his belt, he was gone. The gate in front of the building whined as Yates kicked it open. It didn't even have a padlock or a chain around it. Ranger grabbed a gun and went after Yates. Donnie and Elliot took the rear, checking they were well covered. There were no men, no cars—the only sound came from the wind whistling through broken windows.

Ranger studied the ground. No tire marks whatsoever. Not even a discarded bottle or a crisp packet. The unsettling silence grew like a cancer in his gut. He grabbed himself as he stooped over.

"You okay?" Donnie patted his back.

"I thought I was going to be sick."

It was the second time one of Troy's lies had almost floored him.

Yates kicked open the main door to the building. Ranger watched him go inside but didn't dare follow. He winced at Yates's roar. It broke off, cut short as his outrage turned to despair. The place was empty, nothing but a shell of rust and broken glass.

"Start her up." Donnie threw the keys at Elliot, who caught them against his chest, then helped Ranger over to the fence. "Easy does it."

He crouched against the rusty gate post and closed his eyes.

"I need a minute."

"Take as many as you need."

Ranger swallowed. "He fucking played me *again*. I was so sure, Donnie."

"He's convincing. I'll give him that."

"Sometimes when I look into his eyes, I feel like there's a different side to him. One that cares, but it's all wishful thinking, isn't it? I'm so desperate for him to give a shit about me that I convince myself he does."

"The panic in his voice… He convinced me too."

"He's a shark, he's a shark, and I'm a…" He turned his frown to Donnie and opened his eyes. "What do sharks eat?"

"Fish."

Ranger waved the insult away. "I'm higher up than a fish."

"A squid?"

"Yeah, a squid…the cuddliest of earth's creatures."

Donnie grimaced. "I wouldn't describe a squid as cuddly."

Yates released another roar, and something crashed inside the building.

"Can you go…" Ranger gripped his hair before finally pointing toward the noise. "I can't face Yates right now. Not when I've let him down."

"You haven't."

"He trusted me to get Dylan's location."

"This isn't your fault, Ranger. It's like you said. The blame lies with me and Yates. I'll go get him," Donnie said, jogging in the direction of another smash.

Ranger slid his back up the post and trudged back to Elliot waiting in the car.

Elliot drummed his fingers against the wheel, darting glances back at Ranger slumped on the backseat.

"He lied. He fucking lied even when he thought my fingers were being cut off."

"The fear on his face looked pretty damn real to me."

Ranger gestured to Elliot. "Then he tricked the untrickable."

"Maybe he didn't lie."

"Look out the window. Nobody's been here for—"

"But they might have been once. Remember, Ranger, he's not sitting at the top table anymore. He only gets the crumbs. Maybe our father used this place once. Maybe Troy hasn't even been told where they've taken Dylan."

"Then why not just say that?"

Elliot snorted. "He's stubborn and proud and a pain in the arse."

"Yates will kill him for giving him false hope like that. As soon as he's done trashing the place, he'll get in here and demand we find Troy and slit his throat."

"Do you want my brother to die?"

Ranger met Elliot's eyes in the mirror. "No."

"Then what do you say to confronting him alone? Just you and me."

"What?"

"You heard me. One last chance to make my brother see sense."

Ranger climbed into the passenger seat beside him. "I think that's a great idea."

"Thought you might."

Elliot slammed his foot down on the gas.

****

Ranger's phone buzzed on the backseat, and Elliot's pumped out a clubbing track from his pocket. Neither of them answered.

"What do you know about your father?"

Elliot gave him a sharp look. "He's toxic. He'll kill anyone who wrongs him."

"That's stuff I know already."

"He's got various money-laundering operations. His gang is violent and intimidates local businesses into paying protection money. If you can't pay, he'll burn the place down and he won't care who's inside."

"Yates said Troy's gym burned down."

"Two people died." Elliot nodded. "My father's doing."

"I don't understand why Troy would want his father's forgiveness."

"If you're born into that life, it's a hard mentality to break. Loyalty, honor, respect. He wants them back. Our father probably dangles enough of a carrot to make him think he can get it. Cayden would've taken over for him eventually, but then he let me live. He disappeared after that, I didn't hear anything about him, thought he was dead, but there he was on Yates's laptop, still alive, clinging to the hope of forgiveness."

"Even if we gave you up, you don't think he would be forgiven?"

"No." Elliot glanced at Ranger. "You know the expression love is blind?"

"Yeah."

"Well, it's deaf, stupid, and ugly too."

"Nice to see you and Donnie are keeping romance alive…"

Elliot went on, "Cayden won't allow himself to see it. My father hates him as much as he hates me, but sometimes we choose to be blind to something right in front of us. Cayden's set his heart on my father. Love isn't always kind, or rational, or worth it."

Ranger turned to the window and the crumbling house Troy lived in. He sighed as Elliot pulled up beside it.

"Let's make him see the truth."

"We can try. As I said, he's stubborn and a pain in the arse."

"I used to think that about you."

Elliot made a sound of disappointment. "What changed?"

Ranger opened the door and jumped out. He didn't wait for Elliot but raced down the cracked path. He spied shadows through the slats of the window and stepped into the dirt to peek inside.

His jaw dropped open, and stifling anger filled his head. It was red, and hot, and so thick.

"What is it?" Elliot whispered.

Ranger barely heard him. Out of the corner of his eye he could see that Elliot had grabbed his shoulder, but he didn't feel it. Numbness swamped him as he continued to stare at the scene through the window. He couldn't feel the wind or the texture of the ground beneath his feet.

Elliot's sharp gasp broke through the fog in Ranger's head. He could see what the men inside the room were doing too. They hadn't noticed they had an audience, too engrossed in their task.

"Stay outside."

Ranger's voice was alien to his own ears. Growly and feral.

"What?"

Ranger pushed Elliot away as he reached for his gun. He screwed on his silencer, breathing harder and faster through his nose.

"Trust me, you don't want to be in there when I lose it."

He struggled to contain himself as he stepped toward the door. The last thing he was aware of was the door clicking shut as he closed it on Elliot's gaping face.

****

Each breath filled his mouth with the taste of blood. An irony tang Ranger had once enjoyed. Blood ran down the walls and soaked into the carpet. It had sprayed the torn-up sofa and the cracked blinds where two wide eyes watched.

Ranger had been fast and brutal; he was good at that. He was good at shooting and moving, never hitting the same target at the same trajectory. It made the blood splatters appear from all different angles. The room was a masterpiece that depicted his rage, and as he slowly moved in a circle to admire it, he smiled.

The headache was gone, but so was everything else. He couldn't remember why he'd stepped into the room, why he'd loaded his gun twice to make sure five bullets went in both of the men's skulls. He didn't even know who the man was watching from the window, or where he was, or what day of the week it was, but why did that matter when he wasn't in pain and his brain felt free?

A laugh bubbled out of him, but he didn't know whether it was savage or joyous.

He waited for the fog to clear and his mind to snap together again. A sound halted his laugh. He scrunched his face at a whimpering noise. It was muffled and wet. The sound of someone dying. He huffed, loaded his gun, and stepped around the sofa to put whoever it was out of their misery.

His gaze connected with the man on the floor, and reality delivered a slap to his face.

Ranger dropped his gun just as Elliot burst into the room. "Ranger!"

"Yeah," he said, dropping to his knees next to Troy. "I'm back."

Disjointed and numb, but back.

Troy struggled to keep his eyes open. He whimpered beneath his bloodied gag, twitching and shaking. Ranger took it from his mouth and cradled his face. His eyebrow piercing had been ripped off, and blood poured down his torn cheek.

Ranger spied bloodied pliers on the carpet and fought off a wave of pain in his head. They were already dead; Ranger couldn't bring them back to life and kill them all over again, no matter how much he wanted to.

Elliot crouched at the other side of Troy. "Do you see now; do you see how little he cares about you?"

Troy scrunched his face and turned away from his brother. Blood had soaked his T-shirt, and there was a growing patch on his open jeans.

"I'll...I'll get some towels."

Elliot jumped up and left the room. Ranger had no idea where to touch him and not cause him pain. He stroked Troy's face, but it was wet from blood and sweat, and so tight and swollen he was certain a feather against it must have been agony.

"We got here just in time," Ranger murmured.

Troy only managed to open one of his eyes. "You got here too soon." Ranger had to lean his ear over Troy's mouth to hear him. "You should've let them kill me."

"Did you not hear me earlier? You living is my selfish decision. Everyone else has made there's, and this is mine. You're not dying today, you hear me?"

Elliot returned with a couple of towels and pressed one to Troy's chest. He hissed in a breath that morphed into a rattling sob.

"Ranger..." Troy's eyebrows twitched, making more blood run down.

"Shush. Don't speak. We're gonna get you help."

Ranger got his arms beneath Troy and ignored his sharp cry when he lifted him. Elliot tripped over the fallen punching bag in his rush to get to the door.

"We're gonna get you to the hospital," Ranger told Troy, "and when they ask, we'll say we found you like this behind the bookies, and they'll fix you up and while you're lying there getting better, you'll realize your father needs to die."

"Ranger—"

Troy winced, and his focus drifted away.

"I told you to shush. Save your energy."

"They ripped out my piercings." Troy spluttered blood onto Ranger's chest, then he whispered against his heart, "They ripped out *all* my piercings."

Ranger felt those words go through him. They reawakened the inferno inside his head, but it didn't swamp him like he feared it would. It prickled, ready to unleash at a moment's notice.

Marco Russo was going to pay.

CHAPTER FIFTEEN

"Look." Ranger squeezed the bridge of his nose. "I just want to know if the guy that came in earlier is okay."

"You'll have to be more specific."

"More specific?"

"It's been a busy night for the A&E department."

Elliot snatched the phone from Ranger's hand. "He had a chunk missing from his cock. Is that specific enough for you?"

He handed the phone back to Ranger.

"That guy," Ranger whispered.

"He's stable. He had some horrendous injuries. The doctor has stitched his wounds, but the reconstructive surgeon won't be in until morning."

Ranger winced. "Reconstructive surgeon…"

"Yes. Cayden is sleeping now. Visiting hours are closed until seven—"

"I don't want to visit, I…" He ran his hand through his hair. "I just want to know he's gonna be alright."

"He's been given pain relief and a blood transfusion. He's as alright as he can be in his current state."

"Thank you."

"Who should I say was calling to check on him?"

Ranger swallowed the lump in his throat. "No one."

He hung up and tossed his phone on the sofa beside Blade. Scope whined by his feet, thinking only of his empty stomach.

Elliot caught his eye. "Well?"

"Surgeon's gonna sort him out."

"Good. Good." Elliot hummed. "So, this might come at an odd time, but I've got to ask. What the hell is that?"

Ranger followed Elliot's finger pointing at the corner of the room. Gavin stared at him with a black expression, slumped on the floor with his legs spread wide.

"Not a what, a who. That's Gavin the Gay sexbot."

Donnie stepped into the room, rubbing the back of his neck. He laughed when he found them staring at the sex toy.

"I can't believe Yates actually gave that to you."

"Neither can I."

Elliot tilted his head, studying the doll. "Why are there wires sticking out of it?"

"*Him*." Ranger sighed. "He's charging."

"Why?"

"Because…Because I was going to scare the shit out of Troy with him. He's not a fan, and he's got the highest pitched scream ever."

"Me and my brother don't agree on much, but I'd say that's the creepiest thing I've ever seen."

"Shush," Ranger said, pressing his finger to his lips. "Gavin can hear you."

Elliot took a step back. "You're not helping with the creepiness. Where's Yates?"

"He's crashing in the spare room," Donnie said.

Ranger frowned. "How the hell did you get him to sleep?"

"Zopiclone. Your bathroom cabinet is like a pharmacy. I've never seen so many painkillers and sleeping pills in all my life."

Donnie folded his arms, staring at Ranger for an explanation.

"He's gonna be pissed at you when he wakes up."

"He's always pissed at me." Donnie checked his watch. "We're always pissed at each other. I'm pissed at you for kidnapping my boyfriend."

"If anything, I kidnapped, Ranger."

Donnie grabbed Elliot by the back of the neck. "I'm not happy with you either. Yates was so angry I thought he was gonna kill me and the taxi driver." He looked at Ranger. "What did the hospital say about Cayden?"

"Troy," Ranger muttered.

"But his name is Cayden."

"I want to call him Troy."

Donnie bit his lip. "Okay, Troy it is then. How is he?"

"He's stable. They're waiting on a surgeon to fix him up."

"How bad was it?"

Ranger flared his nostrils. "He had a Prince Albert piercing. Now imagine someone ripping it out with pliers."

"Christ," Donnie hissed, shifting from foot to foot. He cupped himself. "Did you recognize the guys?"

"They were a mess when I came to."

Donnie popped his lips. "When you stopped *raging*?"

Elliot shuddered and couldn't meet Ranger's eye. "I recognized them. Darren Trice and Matt Gear."

Ranger tried to pull the image of their faces up in his head but couldn't. It was nothing but violent flashes and the faint taste of blood in the back of his throat. That was all that was left of them.

"That's two less arseholes to deal with," Donnie said.

"My father has many more… What if I—"

"Don't think about it."

"This is between me and my father. I don't want you getting—"

Donnie pressed his hand over Elliot's mouth. "We've gone over this."

"Gone over what?" Ranger asked.

"Elliot's stupid idea of offering himself up on a plate. I'll never let that happen. I'm not losing you, okay?"

"Okay," Elliot sighed. "I'm tired, that's all. I think I need some sleep."

Donnie checked his watch. "You're right. It's two in the morning."

"You and Elliot can take my bed."

Elliot shook his head. "We can crash down here—"

"No, I insist." Ranger pointed at the sofa. "I want to stay down here with my boys." He cracked a small smile. Blade and Scope were watching his every move. Anna had offered to have them for another night, but Ranger wanted them with him—he needed them.

"Bitches sleep upstairs, and boys sleep down."

Donnie squeezed the back of Elliot's neck. "I'm still mad at you for taking off like that."

"I said I'm sorry."

"But you sure as hell don't mean it."

Elliot wrinkled his nose. "I don't."

They looked as if they were about to kiss. Ranger cleared his throat.

"So, there's spare toothbrushes in the drawer by the sink."

"Thank you." Donnie smiled softly. "Night, Ranger."

He sighed. "Later, bitches."

The door clicked shut behind them, and Ranger flopped onto the sofa. Blade rearranged himself around him and shoved his wet nose into Ranger's neck.

"Is that a goodnight kiss?" Ranger asked.

Scope climbed up and collapsed on Ranger's chest. He licked Ranger's face until Ranger groaned and pushed him away.

"You smell like cheese." He scratched Scope's ear. "You've got to stop breaking into the fridge. A whole Camembert? I'm surprised you're not dead."

Scope whined sharply and buried his head down the back of the sofa.

"I'm gonna need you guys tomorrow…cheese permitting." He stroked Blade's ear. "And I won't make you hold back like I do with the ducks; I swear it."

Blade stared deep into Ranger's eyes as if he understood what he was saying, then lowered his head to sleep.

****

Blade slid from beneath Ranger's arm. His feet clicked along the floor as he stalked across the living room. Ranger tried to creep after him, but Scope pinned his legs, snoring noisily, masking the rustling from outside the room.

Ranger pushed him, and Scope's head jerked up. He grabbed Scope's muzzle before he could yelp.

"Shush."

Ranger listened. A car engine rumbled outside.

"Stay."

He let go of Scope and tiptoed across the room to Blade waiting at the door. The lock on the front door clanked. Gently at first, then harder. Someone was trying to get out, not in.

Ranger swung open the door and caught Elliot in the act. He jumped and crashed back against the wall.

"Ranger!"

He folded his arms. "Elliot?"

"What's with all the locks?"

"They stop people getting in and getting out."

Elliot rolled his shoulders and glanced at the stairs. "Let me out."

"Why?"

"I wanna go to the shop, get something for breakfast—"

"I've got a well-stocked fridge."

"Ranger—"

"I know what you're doing. Don't take me for an idiot. I won't let it happen. No one's getting sacrificed today." He waved his hand at the door. "Call the taxi, tell him to go."

Elliot's brow creased. "I didn't call any taxi."

A frantic fist beat on the door. Blade growled, and the hair along his spine stood up.

"Elliot, get back." Ranger waved him closer, and once he was within reach, he stepped in front of him. Elliot moved to the stairs and gripped on to the banister.

"Hey, you in there? Open up!"

"Who's that?" Elliot asked.

Ranger narrowed his eyes. "Haven't got a clue. Blade."

Blade click-clacked over to the door and sniffed. He darted a look back at Ranger before resuming sniffing. A weaker fist knocked on the door, followed by a hoarse voice, "It's me."

Ranger shared a look with Elliot. "What the hell?"

He stepped up to Blade and started on the bolts and locks. "There's no way…"

Ranger spied Troy through a crack in the door, barely being held up by the sweating taxi driver.

"You should be in the hospital." He opened the door wider but didn't assist the man crumbling under Troy's weight.

"I told him that on the drive here, but he insisted."

"Hospital isn't safe," Troy mumbled.

The taxi driver lost his grip and let Troy slip down the doorway, and he landed with a pained whimper. Ranger winced for him but stopped himself from helping him into the house.

"You're getting back in that taxi."

"I can't move."

"Then I'm putting you back in that taxi—"

Troy's brow knitted together. He didn't pull his gaze from Ranger's feet. "Please, Ranger. I have nowhere else to go."

"The morgue would've been better."

Ranger startled at Yates's voice, thick with sleep. His footsteps boomed down the stairs. "Get out of here."

Troy shuffled closer and closed his hand around Ranger's ankle. He dragged himself along the path before resting his cheek on Ranger's bare foot. "I know you hate me right now. I deserve it, okay, but I didn't know where else to go. I don't have anyone else. I'm sorry, Ranger, I really am."

"Look at me," Ranger whispered.

Troy took a deep breath and lifted his head. Battered and bruised. Ranger stared down at a broken man, one with tears in his eyes and pain rattling his body with shivers. He leaned down, grabbed Troy's arm, and hoisted it over his shoulder.

Yates blocked the way. "You can't be serious."

"This is my house; I decide who's welcome and who isn't. Elliot…"

"Hello, big brother."

"Don't."

Elliot snorted and grabbed Troy's other arm. They dragged him into the living room. Scope made room for Troy before trying to climb onto his lap.

Ranger stopped him.

"Hey, bud," Troy murmured, scratching Scope's ear.

"How's the pain?" Ranger asked.

"Horrific. I cried my eyes out when I tried to have a piss. It burned like you wouldn't believe. I thought I was gonna pass out or be sick. Instead, it was a little of both, and it wasn't pretty."

"I've got pills—"

Troy smirked. "I doubt over-the-counter medicine are gonna touch this."

"It's not over the counter. It's prescription, and it's strong." Ranger touched Troy's forehead. "Jesus, you're burning up. I'll get you some ice too."

"Did…did you get Dylan back?"

Ranger narrowed his eyes. "He wasn't there."

Troy averted his gaze. "That's where they used to—I thought he'd be there, I swear."

"Well, he wasn't."

Troy tried to grab Ranger's hand, but he moved it away and glared at Troy until he lowered his trembling arm back onto Scope.

Yates confronted him in the kitchen by bumping their chests together. "What the fuck do you think you're doing?"

"I couldn't leave him out on the street."

"He used you, Ranger."

"I know," he snapped, rubbing his temples.

"I don't trust him."

"And neither do I, but he's here, and he's staying, Yates. The drugs I'm gonna give him will knock him out. They'd knock out a horse."

"Wait," Yates said, searching Ranger's eyes. "Did you slip me something last night?"

"Guilty," Donnie said from the doorway. He raised his hand with a small smile. "You needed to sleep."

"I didn't want to—"

"But you needed to." Donnie snagged Elliot by the wrist and pulled him close. "Feeling nostalgic?"

"What?"

"You left a note on the pillow. Bye, baby?"

"Oh," Elliot swallowed. "That…"

"Damn near gave me a heart attack." Donnie grabbed him by the chin and gave him a quick peck on the lips. "Now's not the time for jokes or trips down memory lane."

"Sorry…"

"If you two are gonna tongue fuck each other, can you do it in another room?" Yates growled. "I can't tolerate it right now." His phone buzzed, and he pulled it from his pocket.

"What is it?" Ranger asked.

"A time. Two o'clock."

"A location?"

Yates shook his head. "Not yet. How are we supposed to make a plan if we don't know where we're supposed to meet?"

"They'll kill you all!" Troy shouted.

Donnie whipped around. "Why the hell is he here?"

"He's still got his claws in Ranger's heart," Yates muttered. "If you'd let me cut off his fingers, it wouldn't be a problem."

Ranger folded his arms. "I invited him in, and I'm in the process of getting him ice and pills to knock him out."

"They'll have guns! Lots of guns!"

Yates pinched the bridge of his nose. "Ranger, if you don't do it quickly, I'm gonna go in there and snap his neck."

"I'm going, I'm going."

Ranger rocketed upstairs to get to the bathroom and snatched the bottle off the top shelf of the cabinet. He returned just in time to see Yates slink into the living room, brandishing a rolling pin.

"I've got him something, okay?"

Ranger pushed past Yates and stopped at the sight of Troy biting into a cushion. He wriggled and fidgeted, face covered in a fresh sheen of sweat.

"Why the hell did you leave the hospital?"

Troy released the cushion from his teeth. "They'll have guns."

"Yeah, you said." Ranger tapped two pills out onto his palm.

"No, listen, they'll have guns. They'll kill you all."

Ranger took a pill and inched it closer to Troy's mouth. "Here comes the drug-induced Cho-Cho train—"

"No." Troy turned his head. "The meeting place will be somewhere secluded, out in the open where no one can hear gunshots."

Yates stepped closer. "Where?"

"There's an old airport in Waymirth. It hasn't been used for decades, cracked, and overgrown. That's where they used to conduct this kind of business."

"Waymirth?" Yates got his phone out of his pocket.

"They will park one side of the airstrip and get you to stop on the other, then they'll ask you to walk Elliot into the middle, and they'll bring Dylan. The second they've got Elliot back, and Dylan is in your arms, they'll open fire from the trees flanking the airstrip."

"How do you know so much?" Yates asked.

Troy clacked his tongue. "I used to be involved in this kind of thing."

"There are woods on either side?" Ranger asked.

"There used to be."

Yates showed Ranger the phone. "There still are if he's telling the truth."

"That's where they'll wait. You won't get out of there alive. It's a death trap. They'll kill you and bury you in the woods." Troy looked away. "That's probably what they're doing right now, digging your graves."

Yates's phone buzzed. He frowned as he read the message. "I'll show you mine, then you show me yours... I don't understand—"

His phone pinged again, and Ranger winced at the video of Dylan. Blood ran down from his nostrils, and his eyes were half-closed as if they'd drugged him.

"Smile for the camera."

Dylan's eyes widened at that. He swallowed. "Don't... Yates, please don't put yourself at risk to save me. Please." His voice hitched. "I've fucked up. I've made mistakes. I'm not worth it, and it's...it's okay. I'm okay with it. Call it karma, call it deserved. I just need you and the others to be okay."

Ranger peeled the phone from Yates's iron grip before he crushed it.

"And Ranger...don't let him." Ranger side-eyed Yates. "You're the one person who can stop him coming after me. Do whatever you have to and keep Yates from danger." Dylan's eyes shifted away to someone off camera. He pressed back in his chair, trying his best to keep his distance, but the figure marched straight up to him and backhanded him around the face. Dylan spluttered blood down himself. "Please, Ranger, promise me you'll keep Yates safe. That's all that matters. I *need* him to be all right. Promise me."

The video cut out, and Ranger met Yates's red-rimmed eyes. They glared at each other.

"Sorry, my freckled friend, but that's a promise I can't make."

Yates deflated, giving Ranger a nod. The phone vibrated; Ranger checked the message. "Now show me yours." He gestured to Elliot. "Tie him up."

"What?" Donnie said, strolling forward.

"They've shown us a video of Dylan. Yates has to prove he's got Elliot. Tie his wrists."

"And hit him," Troy added.

Donnie whirled around to face him, squirming on the sofa. "That better be the painkillers talking."

Ranger showed him the two in his fist. "Not yet."

"Cay—Troy's right," Elliot whispered. "If it's supposed to look real, I've got to be scared. I've got to be bleeding."

Yates ran his hands through his hair and pulled it. "Like Dylan is."

"Exactly," Elliot said. He moved in front of Donnie. "Punch me."

"There's absolutely no way in hell I'm doing that."

"Baby, punch me, pretty please."

Donnie's nostrils flared. "No."

"Fine." He turned to Yates. "Punch me."

Yates threw a punch at him. It caught his nose and knocked Elliot to the floor. Donnie's cheeks reddened, and he leaped at Yates cursing, and growling.

"Take the picture," Elliot said.

Ranger ignored Donnie and Yates rolling around on the floor and took a picture of Elliot. Blood flowed freely from his nose, and he kept his arms behind his back as if they were bound.

"I've sent it," Ranger said.

Elliot rushed over to grab Donnie and pull him aside. "I'm fine."

"He goddamn hit you!"

"I asked him to."

Troy growled as he bit into the cushion again. "Pills," Ranger remembered. He pushed them at Troy's mouth, but he dodged them.

"Now, you need to take Elliot's clothes off."

Ranger frowned. "Now's not the time for us all to get kinky. Elliot's clothes stay on. Swallow the damn pills."

"What are they?"

"Oxymorphone hydrochloride."

Yates straightened his shirt as he got to his feet. "They're strong, right? For chronic pain? What are you doing with them?"

"Your head," Troy sighed. "The rage you try to contain."

Ranger's hand trembled. "I'm clinging on to it right now. Take the pills."

Troy opened his lips and allowed Ranger to push them inside.

Ranger handed him a glass of water. "Swallow."

Troy did and even showed his tongue afterward. "Let me help you."

"Look at you, barely conscious. You're no help."

"Put Elliot's clothes on Gavin."

Ranger glanced at Gavin in the corner. "What?"

"You heard me. First, you need to gut him."

"Lie down," Ranger told him. "You're talking crazy—"

"I want to hear him out," Yates said, crouching down. "Go on."

"Gut him, fill him with explosives, and put Elliot's clothes on him. Put a pillowcase over his head and blow them all to pieces."

Yates's phone pinged, and Ranger checked it. "It's a location. Waymirth airstrip…"

CHAPTER SIXTEEN

Ranger's brow pinched with sympathy. "I'm sorry it had to end like this."

Emotionless eyes stared back at him. Ranger pouted as the blade dug in deep, tearing a hole from his belly button to his throat. "I want you to know I enjoyed our dates; I'll hold those special moments dear to me."

Where he expected to see red and pulsating organs, he locked eyes with white plastic and wires. Yates huffed from his nose and glared at Ranger. "It's really disconcerting when you talk to it."

"Him. He's Gavin the Gaybot. Dylan named him, remember?"

Pain flickered in Yates's eyes. "I remember."

"And now Gavin's gonna sacrifice himself to save Dylan. What a hero."

Yates dropped the knife to the carpet and ripped Gavin's chest cavity open with his hands. "I don't think Gavin has much choice in the matter."

He began stuffing Gavin's chest full of small bags of gunpowder.

Donnie watched over them, breathing steadily. "You'll have to judge the situation," Yates told him. "If what Troy says is true, they'll shoot me and Dylan within seconds of the exchange. I'll try and get him clear, but if it looks as if they're about to shoot, beat them to it."

"You sure it'll go off?"

"The impact should set it off."

Donnie looked away. "Should…"

"I'll protect Dylan with my life. I'll take shots, I'll take explosions, anything they throw at me. My goal is to get Dylan behind the car. The rest is up to you and Ranger."

Ranger snapped his fingers. "And Blade and Scope."

"Only one of them is useful." Yates gave Blade a sure look. He grimaced at Scope.

"Scope's coming along for moral support."

"What about me?" Elliot asked.

Ranger snorted. The clothes he'd given Elliot hung off his body, and he'd used an elastic band to draw in the T-shirt's waist. Donnie's belt just about held up the jeans, but they were folded over at the bottom so he couldn't trip over.

"What about you?" Ranger snorted. "I'm sure the fashion police will want to speak to you."

"They're your clothes."

Yates sat back on his heels. "Donnie will give you a gun, don't start firing until he does, and please don't shoot yourself in the foot."

"Like I would…"

"Ranger." Yates bit his lip. "I'm gonna need you—"

"Raging, I know."

Yates shook his head. "I need that level of skill, but you need to be aware of what's going on. I need you in control. Otherwise, you could hurt one of us."

No pressure then.

Ranger eased out a breath. "I'll be okay."

Yates leaned back against the sofa and checked his watch for the hundredth time. "You better get ready."

Ranger nodded and left the room. Black combat pants with plenty of knives and a black vest with a two-gun holder strapped to his shoulders. Ranger slid his shades over his eyes as he admired himself in the mirror, but something was wrong, something was missing.

"Donnie!"

He stroked his hair as he waited for Donnie to shout back up the stairs to him.

"What is it?"

"Come up and bring the scissors from the kitchen."

"I'm on it."

Ranger grabbed his shaving foam off the side for when they were ready. Donnie didn't need instructions; he strolled straight over to Ranger by the sink and fisted a section of hair. The colors started to appear as Donnie snipped away. "I don't know why you grew your hair out in the first place."

"I wasn't getting any dates."

"If guys take one look at your tattoo and don't want to get to know you, fuck 'em. They don't deserve to know you."

"That's easy for you to say when you've got Elliot. Tell me, what's it like?"

"What?"

"Being in love and having that person love you back."

Donnie squirted shaving cream into his hand, lathered it up, and stroked it onto Ranger's head.

"Elliot is everything. Home isn't a building, or a town, or a country. It's one person, and I was really lucky to have found him."

"I wanted a home too."

"You've got one, with Blade and Scope."

Ranger smiled. "Yeah, I guess you're right, they're my boys, but I was hoping for a guy too."

"There's one downstairs on the sofa." Donnie met Ranger's eyes in the mirror. "He came here—"

"He had nowhere else to go, he said so himself."

"And he collapsed outside your door, and you brought him in. I saw genuine fear in his face when he thought Yates was hurting you. That wasn't a lie."

"What are you suggesting, Donnie? That I give Troy another chance?"

"All I'm saying is love hasn't run smoothly for any of us."

Ranger tilted his head to give Donnie a better angle. "All I wanted was a sweet boyfriend to settle down with it."

"You don't want that."

"I do—"

"Then why did you end up dating a guy like Troy, huh?"

"No sweet guy would have me."

"You like them rough around the edges, always have. Troy, or Cayden, is exactly your type, chip on his shoulder, prickly, but deep down rejected, lost, confused. Expresses himself with anger but occasionally a slither of genuine feeling. He's just like you used to be before your accident." Donnie finished up and dabbed Ranger's head with a towel.

"You said I used to be terrifying."

"Without a doubt the scariest guy I've ever known. You were angry at the world, could never keep a boyfriend, but would try to convince yourself you didn't want one anyway. You've always been searching for a home, Ranger."

"A stable relationship needs trust, and I don't trust him, Donnie. Who's to say he's not leading us into a trap? He could've arranged all this with his father, a double bluff. A trap within a trap."

"Do you really think that?"

Ranger's head throbbed. "I don't know."

"Either way, we're walking into it. We have no choice." Donnie squeezed his shoulder. "Come on, it's almost time."

Ranger followed Donnie out of the bathroom and downstairs. Yates waited by the front door with Gavin slung over his shoulder. A pillowcase covered his head, but Elliot's clothes were visible, bleached blue jeans, a red hoodie, and yellow sneakers. The ones he wore for the photograph.

"You're wearing the present from Dylan," Ranger said.

Yates glanced down at his shirt, black with yellow lilies. "I found it hidden away, couldn't help but open it."

"It looks…" He stopped himself. "It suits you."

Donnie nodded. "It does."

"I have to get him back."

"We will." Donnie squeezed his shoulder.

Ranger poked his head into the living room and found Elliot crouching by Troy. They spoke in hushed whispers before Elliot realized they were being watched. He stood up and toed a bucket closer to Troy sprawled out on the sofa.

"For when you need to piss."

Troy groaned and adjusted the icepack on his groin. "I'm never pissing again."

Elliot passed Ranger in the doorway. "Your turn."

Ranger cleared his throat and addressed Troy without looking at him.

"There's plenty of pills on the coffee table. The phone's there for when you come to your senses and realize you need to be in hospital… Yeah, see ya later." He cringed at his parting words, but Troy called out after him, and he paused in the entrance hall. Donnie, Elliot, and Yates looked at him, then averted their gazes.

They were giving him a moment with Troy, even Yates, who clutched Gavin like he was a lifeline, was permitting him to make peace.

"Fine," Ranger huffed. He trudged into the living room and crouched on the floor beside Troy. His eyes fluttered open and fixed on Ranger's head.

"There she is, my sexy cobra."

"It's a boy."

"You look badass."

Ranger leaned back and glanced at himself. Dressed all in black with guns and knives strapped to him.

He nodded. "I do."

"Fuck," Troy hissed, curling up. He squeezed his eyes shut. "I can't get aroused."

Ranger snorted.

"I missed eyeballing your tattoo from the bar."

"It had to go when my dates kept running out on me."

"Only half of your dates ran out on you."

Ranger frowned. "What?"

"The other half I scared out of the bathroom window." Troy snorted. "I told you I wasn't a nice person."

"You chased my dates away, why?"

He shrugged. "I wouldn't have seen you anymore. I wouldn't have watched you time after time, undeterred by rejection. Always smiling, always happy. I admired and hated your spirit and wanted to see it pushed to the limit."

"All those rejections, and it was you that broke me."

"No." Troy scrunched his face up. "Don't say that. You're not broken."

"I think I've been broken for a long time, long before I got shot. You just made me realize it."

"Promise me you won't die."

Ranger whistled. "No can do."

"Don't die."

"What's my incentive to live?"

"Me making it up to you. I will. I'll do whatever you want. I'll prove to you I'm sorry. We'll go on a third date, anywhere you want to go. We'll take the dogs, buy them ice cream, sit by an even bigger duck pond."

"Blade would hate you for that."

"He hated me from the start."

Ranger clacked his tongue. "He is the clever one. Scope took to you right away; he's an idiot, like me."

"You're not an idiot." Troy snorted. "Are you fishing for compliments?"

"Maybe a few."

"You're kind, and loving, and lovable." Troy shifted and bit the cushion before growling out, "And so fucking hot thinking about you is pure agony."

"It's karma, bitch."

"It's time we get moving," Donnie said from the doorway.

"Okay." He looked down at Troy squirming. "I'm off to avenge that beautiful cock of yours. Wish me luck."

****

"Ranger, can you hear me?"

He adjusted his earpiece. "I hear you, Donnie."

He crept his way through the woods, seeing nothing but foliage and greenery. Blade and Scope walked with him. In his eagerness Blade kept inching forward, desperate to reach their prize first. Ranger stopped and waved the dogs toward him. They stood by his side as he scanned the trees with binoculars.

He, Donnie, and Elliot arrived long before Yates and Gavin. They trekked on foot using the trees and abandoned buildings as cover. Ranger and Elliot went left, and Ranger and the dogs went right. It was a standard pincer movement, but the key was to keep it slow, keep it steady, keep it silent, or as close to silent as they could.

Blade huffed from his nose and flicked Ranger an unimpressed look. Ranger ignored him and spied through the trees. Low voices carried, and Ranger's nose pulsed with the smell of cigarette smoke.

He kept moving, treading on the side of his feet to limit his sound. The dogs had the advantage with their soft pads, leading Ranger down a quieter path. Through the trees, he could see the airstrip and three gleaming black 4x4s.

"Yates is on the way," Donnie murmured.

Ranger crouched down, drawing the dogs toward him. He couldn't see Yates approaching, but he heard the rumble of a car.

"Tell me what's happening," Ranger whispered.

"He's driving along the airstrip. I've counted five men outside the cars, three more in them."

"There are men in the trees too."

They'd gone silent, but Blade stared ahead, locked onto a target Ranger couldn't yet see.

"Do you know how many?"

"No. I haven't seen."

"Yates is getting out. He's got Gavin slung over his shoulder. I...I can see Dylan."

Ranger swallowed. The blood in his veins felt thicker.

"Jesus, Donnie, keep talking to me. The suspense is too much."

"They're meeting in the middle. Yates has put Gavin on the ground and is beckoning for Dylan to go to him."

Ranger eased out a slow breath, trying to keep calm.

"Are you ready?" Donnie whispered.

"As I'll ever be."

Ranger leaned forward, desperate to see. He made out Yates through the trees, encouraging Dylan to him, within reach. A gun raised behind Dylan's back, and Ranger's gut clenched.

The explosion blasted heat across Ranger's face and took off his eyebrows. The trees whipped back, and blinding white lingered in his vision. Shots were being fired, and an agonized roar filled the air.

"Now," he yelled at Blade, who took off through the trees. He ran after him with Scope glued to his side.

Specks moved in the distance, but they fast became men, rushing and shouting, using the trees as cover as Donnie kept shooting. Bullets popped and pinged against Yates's car. Ranger prayed he'd managed to get Dylan behind it.

The knowledge was freeing in a sense. No one on the airstrip would get close to them with Donnie firing like a madman, but the men in the trees would have the perfect shot.

Donnie and Yates had both played their part, and now it was up to him.

Ranger gritted his teeth and followed the sound of Blade's growl. He burst through the trees, took a deep breath, and let the red fog of anger swamp him.

He shot the closest man with ease. There was a squelch of parting flesh followed by a dull thud as the bullet passed through and into the tree behind. The man flung his arms out in dramatic fashion as he fell to the ground. Just like the violent action movies Yates loved.

One down.

Blade chased the men from out of their tree cover into the shooting zone. The sun sneaking through the gaps in the leaves caught a polished-up shoe poking out from behind the base of a tree. Ranger blasted a chunk out of the top of the man's foot.

He screamed, falling forward where Ranger shot him again through the chest, then head.

Two men down.

Ranger's pounding heart warped in his ears. The voices and screams faded; he couldn't feel the gun in his grip, nor the crunch of twigs beneath his feet. He was lost in the haze, seeing only snippets. Dead eyes looking up at him. A mouth opened in a forever scream. Sharp teeth and snapping jaws. Chaos and panic, and blood, not a color but a taste in the air.

A scream cut the fog in half, and it opened with clarity on the woods. Not a person's scream, but a dog whose cry tapered off into a whimper of distress. Blade stopped mauling a man and ran to his brother lying on the ground. Scope whimpered and thrashed, stretching out his long legs before falling limp.

"No, bud, no." Ranger ran over and skidded to his knees. Scope's coat was soaked in blood, and Ranger pulled him into his lap. "Hey, bud, it's all right."

He stroked the side of Scope's face. "I'm here; Blade's here."

"Ranger, get onto the airstrip—they're driving away."

He ignored Donnie's frantic shouts and searched for Scope's wound. Blood had soaked his fur, but Ranger couldn't locate the gaping hole. Scope whimpered, holding his front paw up to his face. He licked at it, one tentative swipe. Ranger frowned and inspected his pad.

A twig stuck out from between his toes.

"You've got to be shitting me."

He pulled it out, and Scope wagged his tail and sprung back to his feet.

"Stupid dog."

Scope licked the blood and sweat off his face.

"Ranger!" Donnie shouted down his ear.

"I'm on it," he said, rushing through the trees. Wheels squealed nearby; he broke through the tree line just in time to see the car roaring away. He took a deep breath, held out his gun, and fired.

The car reared violently to the right and crashed into the trees.

"Jesus," Ranger said, looking at his gun. "Did you see that, Donnie?"

"I saw."

"And you always told me you were the better shot."

Donnie snorted. "I lied."

"What?"

"You've always been the better shot."

Ranger strolled up to the smoking 4x4 with Blade and a limping Scope at his sides. His shot had sailed through the back windscreen and splattered the driver's head inside the car. The windows dripped, running down like a horror movie.

Blade grumbled at the movement in the car and stopped rigid beside Ranger. The passenger door opened, and a man slipped out onto the dirt. The blood spray from the driver had seeped into the cracks and crevices on his face. He was old, despite the thick brown hair on his head, and he drew his top lip back in a snarl as he stared at Ranger.

Blade matched his snarl with his own threatening rumble. The man pressed his back against the car, no longer eyeing Ranger but the dog with the red-stained teeth and demonic eyes.

"Marco Russo, I presume." Ranger took a step closer and crouched down. "It's so nice to meet you."

Ranger held out his hand. He didn't know whether it was shock or arrogance that made Marco shake his hand, but he punished him by snapping his wrist in one smooth motion.

Marco flailed and cursed, cradling his wounded hand.

"As much as I want to kill you for what your men did to Troy—"

"Who the fuck is Troy?"

Ranger huffed. "Cayden." He stamped on Marco's ankle and broke that too. He waited until Marco had stopped howling before continuing. "As much as I want to kill you for what your men did to *Cayden*, it's not my place."

He turned around and pointed at Elliot strolling closer. "It's his."

CHAPTER SEVENTEEN

Elliot stopped in front of his father. His arm hung by his side, but his grip on his gun turned his knuckles white. Ranger noticed they had the same eyes, frosty blue.

"Never thought you'd be the one who survived." Marco shuffled his back against the smoking car, still holding his wrist.

"You underestimated me," Elliot whispered. "If you'd just let me and my mother go, it wouldn't have led to this."

Bodies lay along the strip, a team effort from Gavin and Donnie. Ranger couldn't see Yates and Dylan and hoped they were okay, or as okay as they could be having been so close to Gavin when he'd exploded.

"*Your mother* wouldn't let me go," Marco seethed. "She wrote love letters and sent pictures of you, so desperate to be loved, for you to be loved, but you're not."

"Not by you."

"You're a mistake, an accident, nothing but your mother tricking me into getting her pregnant. You weren't made out of love, just sex—meaningless, empty sex. A whore in a nightclub who was greedy. Nothing special about her, nothing memorable."

"Shut up," Elliot growled, raising his gun. His hand trembled as he aimed at his smirking father.

"Look at you…" Marco laughed. "What are you waiting for?"

Elliot blinked back tears. "I don't know."

His hand shook worse, and he bit his lip.

"You can't do it, can you?"

Ranger thought about taking the burden from Elliot or touching his shoulder to ground him, but Donnie appeared in his peripheral vision, coming to Elliot's aid.

"He can," Donnie said. He pressed his front to Elliot's back and reached around him to steady the trembling gun. "If he wants to, he can, and if he doesn't want to, I'm here to do it for him."

Elliot eased out a slow breath. "I want to. For me, my mother, and for Cayden."

"Cayden," Marco smirked. "I told them to cut out his heart, to make him feel how I did when I found out he let you live."

"Well, they didn't," Ranger said. He waved his gun at Marco. "I got there first."

"I'm not talking about yesterday." Marco's smile narrowed his eyes. "I'm talking about today. Do you really think I'd let him live?"

"You don't even know where he is—"

"He's been watching you, and we've been watching him. I took an educated guess and sent a man to your house."

Ranger swallowed, taking a step back. "Liar."

"You think I wouldn't clean up after myself?"

"Shut up," Donnie growled. "Elliot, whenever you're ready."

Ranger turned away and spotted Dylan and Yates. Dylan looked as if he was trying to burrow into Yates's chest cavity, and Yates looked seconds away from ripping his ribcage open to let him. They were wrapped up in their own world, and when he spun back to look at Elliot, him and Donnie were the same. Donnie whispered into Elliot's ear, steadying the trembling gun. The shot rang out with a finality that set Ranger off in a run.

He needed to get home. He needed to save Troy.

****

Blade got to the car before Ranger and Scope. He'd launched through the left open door and climbed into the passenger seat.

"If only I'd taught you to drive."

Ranger closed the door after Scope and rushed around to the front. He pressed his phone to his ear, but Troy didn't pick up.

"Damn it!"

The drive home went by in a blur, too fast and too slow all at once. He wanted to get there, but he didn't want to know if he was too late. Would he find Troy with a hole in his chest and his heart on the table? He shuddered, pushing the thought away.

He pulled up beside his house and launched out of the driver's side. Blade barked and clambered out after him. Ranger didn't dare peek through the living room curtains. He slammed up to the front door and battled to get the key in the lock, but it swung open before he could, already busted by *someone* else.

The smell of blood filled the hallway. He held his breath to avoid it and pressed on into the living room, where he sucked in a breath and froze. A bloodied white sheet covered Troy on the sofa. A veil to keep Ranger from his gory wounds. It was too late. *He* was too late.

"Shit."

He faltered, knocking into Blade.

"I don't think I can…"

He pinched the corner of the sheet between his thumb and forefinger and eased it back as his heart slammed over and over into his ribcage. It felt as if it was swelling in his chest, so big and fast it risked choking him. The sheet inched back over brown hair, a blood-covered forehead, a tattoo by his temple.

Ranger frowned and ripped the cover away completely.

"That gets you back for all the times you freaked me out with Gavin."

He spun around, still holding the sheet, and glared at Troy sitting on the floor. His legs were splayed wide, and a cushion was held to his groin. Despite the pain twisting his lips and pulling at his brow, he still managed a shaky smile.

Ranger stalked toward him, so angry his head felt on fire. He flexed his hands at his sides and crouched down to Troy, getting eye to eye.

"I could kill you."

Troy swallowed, staring back into the abyss of Ranger's eyes. "I can handle you, Ranger."

"Not right now, you can't. That wasn't funny."

Troy chuckled. "It was, just a bit."

"No." Ranger held on to Troy's shoulders. "I thought you were dead."

"Did you feel relieved?"

"Not even for a second."

Troy licked his dry lips and spluttered out, "Good. Ranger…"

"Yes?"

"I don't feel so good." He drifted to the side. "I'm gonna be sick."

"Let me get you back to the hospital."

"Okay." He removed the cushion, and Ranger hissed at the fresh blood soaking his hospital gown.

"Are you determined to lose your cock?"

Troy was so far gone he laughed. "Only in your arse."

Despite the situation, Ranger laughed too. "You're an idiot."

"How…how is everyone?" Troy asked.

Scope staggered into the room and collapsed dramatically onto the carpet. He lifted his injured paw in Ranger's direction, like he was reaching, then let it drop.

"What the…"

Ranger rolled his eyes. "Everyone will be fine."

"My father?"

"Is dead."

Troy squeezed his eyes shut. Ranger couldn't tell whether he closed them in sadness or relief, but when they opened, they were wet.

"Come on, let's get you fixed up."

He heaved Troy to his feet and walked him to the door. Blade pushed past and got into the passenger seat and growled Scope into the back of the people carrier when he tried to follow.

"We'll drop them off at Anna's on the way."

Troy pressed his face into Ranger's neck. "Suddenly my cock comes second best to your boys…"

Ranger nodded. "That's exactly how it should be."

****

Ranger watched as Troy was wheeled away before wandering the hospital. He found Yates with ease, the biggest complainer, he hooted and howled as the nurses applied bandages to his burns. The back of his neck and a strip across his lower back where his clothing hadn't been covered were the worst.

Ranger reached down and grabbed a shred of his ruined shirt. "I'd say this is an improvement."

"Ranger!" Dylan jumped up from his seat. Ranger took his chin in his hand and studied the nasty bruise under his eye and his split lip. "That's a good 'un."

Yates struggled upright and reached for Dylan. "Let me see."

"Stop," Dylan took his hand. "You've already seen it."

"I wanna see it again."

"Every time you move, it hurts you. Please, *please* stay still." There were tears in his eyes. "I'm all right, I promise."

Ranger looked at Yates. "How are you feeling?"

"I'm covered in blisters and burns. How do you think I'm feeling?"

"Don't be so dramatic. No one's ever died from burns and blisters."

Yates stared at Ranger before closing his eyes and muttering something inaudible.

Ranger sighed. "Guess that tango lesson will have to be put on hold."

Yates's eyes peeled open. He spoke through his teeth, "What a shame."

"Yeah," Dylan said, scratching the back of his head. "I was looking forward to it."

Ranger burst out laughing. "No, you weren't."

Dylan widened his eyes. "Yes, I was. If Yates wants to try it, I'm more than happy to—"

"I didn't want to—wait..." He flared his nostrils. "Goddammit, Ranger."

"I'm sorry, it was too easy."

Yates's hand tightened into a fist on the bed. Dylan grabbed it in both hands.

"Although..." The edges of his lips pulled up in a coy smile, tugging the cut. "I told my friend at university about it, and she said she wanted to design the outfit as her final project. I've seen her sketches. Lots of flowers on the shirt and pants, maybe even the shoes."

Yates's eyebrows lifted up his head. "Shoes?"

"Yeah," Dylan grinned. "Shoes."

Yate's eyes glazed over. Ranger hoped it was the morphine.

"Shoes...with flowers on them."

Ranger scrunched up his face. "Dylan, I think your friend is gonna fail fashion design, big time."

"I want to see the designs."

Dylan beamed. "Thought you would, and you can model it too."

"Hardly model material, am I?"

"You're perfect."

Ranger snorted. "Is he?"

Yates sighed. "I've hit my Ranger limit." He shifted over as much as he could on the hospital bed before patting the spare space on the bed.

"Cuddles. For me?" Ranger asked.

"Not on your life."

Dylan laid down, pressing his forehead to Yates's.

"I'm sorry," Yates murmured.

"You've said that a hundred times."

"It'll never be enough." He slung his heavy arm over Dylan's side and pinned him to the bed. He groaned like a dying animal.

"Hurts?" Dylan asked.

"No, the painkillers are pulling me under."

"Finally," Dylan whispered. "I'm not going anywhere. I'll be here when you wake up. I swear it."

"If you don't move in with me after this, I'll go insane."

"Is that you asking?"

"Yes."

Dylan hummed. "I guess I'll think about it."

"Motherfucker."

"Shouldn't that be daddyfucker?"

Yates laughed as he drifted, but his eyes fluttered open and found Ranger's again. He lifted his hand, and Ranger took it.

"Thank you."

"Anytime."

He squeezed, Yates squeezed back, then Ranger lifted Yate's hand and kissed the back of it.

"What the fuck, Ranger?" Yates yanked his hand back. "Why did you have to make it weird?"

He darted out of the room, laughing, and went in search of Donnie and Elliot.

Ranger found them in the hospital canteen; Elliot sat on Donnie's lap, letting his shaky hands be massaged. Elliot glanced up at Ranger's approach.

"Is Cayden alright?"

"Yeah, he's back in the hospital but left a mess in my house."

Elliot frowned until Donnie whispered something into his ear. "Oh, right."

"How're you doing?"

"I'm fine, good, great." Elliot's eyebrows slanted together. He nipped his lip. "Maybe not."

"You will be, though," Donnie insisted, still touching Elliot's fingers. "I'll make sure of it."

"We don't have to hide anymore."

"No, we don't have to run and hide anymore, Elliot," Donnie whispered. "Drink some coffee. The caffeine will help."

Elliot reached for it, but his hand still shook, and Donnie steadied him with that too.

"It's just shock. It'll wear off soon." He took the cup from Elliot and placed it back on the table. "I was thinking, we could get away for a few weeks, sand, sea, sun…"

Ranger reached for Elliot's shoulder and gave him a reassuring squeeze. "I hear the Maldives is nice."

Donnie snorted. "It is."

Elliot looked back at him. "I've always wanted to go there."

"Then we'll go. I'll book it right now, and we can get out of here, just me and you."

He slumped into Donnie's chest. "That sounds really good actually."

Donnie reached for Ranger's hand and squeezed his fingers. "Thank you."

He grinned, pulled Donnie's hand up to his lips and kissed it. Donnie didn't snatch his hand back like Yates. He raised his eyebrow. "Okay…"

"Excuse me?"

Ranger turned to the nurse and smiled. "What can I help you with?"

"You brought Cayden in. Ranger, right?"

"That's right."

"Do you know him well?"

"Cayden? Not at all."

She smiled. "Well, you've made an impression on him. He's sent me to find you, refuses to let his dressing be changed until you're there."

He shot Elliot and Donnie a parting smile.

"Later, bitches."

****

Troy flashed him a guilty look when Ranger stepped into the room.

"I hope you don't mind that I asked for you."

Troy held up his hand. Ranger took it and sat down in the chair beside the bed.

"This is gonna be painful."

The nurse wrinkled her nose. "I'll go as gently as I can. We managed to get the catheter back in."

Troy shuddered. "Yeah, that was a barrel of laughs."

"Have you remembered anything about what happened?"

"No. I woke up here—"

"And called a taxi to leave." She shook her head in disapproval. "It's a good job your boyfriend was at hand to talk some sense into you."

Troy didn't correct her, and Ranger didn't either. How he'd longed for someone to describe him as a boyfriend, but it hit him as bittersweet.

"It's like childbirth." Troy snorted, glancing down at his groin. "If you look, you'll never be the same again."

"Nine out of ten people enjoy watching their children coming into the world."

"What magazine did you get that from?"

"Mother and Toddler."

Troy tilted his head, studying Ranger.

"What? I thought it might have some tips for dealing with Blade and Scope."

"Surely a dog magazine would be more suitable."

Ranger shrugged. "They're my boys, my babies. I tried to toilet train them at one point."

"Did that work out well?"

"No." Ranger popped his lips. "No. It did not."

Troy pointedly didn't look down when the nurse began unwrapping his cock. The bandage had turned dark brown from dried blood.

"You really shouldn't have been walking around—"

Troy crushed Ranger's hand. "Yep, I'm feeling that now."

Ranger didn't speak while Troy's bandages were changed. His cock, his nipples, and finally the chunk missing from his eyebrow. It was slow and painful, but Ranger held his hand the whole time until they were both slippery with sweat.

"The plastic surgeon will be in soon."

She smiled at them both, then left the room.

"I think you should ask the surgeon for a few extra inches."

"You're an arsehole, you know that?"

"Oh, I know. One *heck* of an arsehole."

Cayden snorted. "You once said you only found me hot because of my cock."

"I still find you hot." Ranger looked him over. "Even when you're beaten down and high on morphine."

"The morphine is the only thing stopping me from screaming the place down. Is your head hurting? I can pull my drip out and sneak you some."

"My head's okay. I let my aggression out in a controlled burst, and I feel better for it."

Troy raised his good eyebrow. "Controlled burst?"

"As controlled as I get."

"I can handle you," Troy whispered. "I can if you'll let me."

"Not at the moment you can't."

"No, not right now, but one day I'll be able to. I want to."

Ranger pulsed their fingers together. "What you're saying is you want to fight me again?"

"No, not just that, I want to fight you and fuck you, but all the rest of it too."

"Elaborate."

"Really?"

"Yup, my ego demands it."

Troy groaned. "Fine. I want the lazy Netflix nights on the sofa, the dog walks at the park, the dinners, the dates. I want to feel happy. I don't even think I know what it feels like. The only times I think I felt it is when we were together, and even then there was something niggling away at me."

"That niggling was probably the fact you were lying and using me."

Troy winced. "Lying to you, yes, but using you, no. I like you, Ranger. I like you a lot."

"Cayden." Ranger tried out the name again. "Cayden...tell me about yourself."

"I'm an arsehole."

"As long as you're not a shark."

"Huh?"

"Never mind." He looked at Cayden. Cayden. The beaten guy, bloodied and bruised, with sad eyes and a frown that was hard to shift. "So...Cayden. Tell me about your dad."

Ranger heard him swallow.

"My father was a mean arsehole, meaner than me, but it was better to be on his good side than bad. I'd have done anything to be on his good side, to make him proud, to make him happy. I disappointed him once, and he never let me forget it. He didn't let me move on and have my own life either. My only option was to make amends."

"And how did you do that?"

"By listening to rumors, by putting myself in the right place to hear them, but they were always just rumors. I gave up, and instead, I watched a guy go on dates again and again. I watched him fail, again and again, but he didn't give up. He always had a smile on his face. Even when I began scaring his dates away, he still was happy, and an ugly part of me hated him for that. The rejection didn't deter him. Ever."

"Oh, it did. Yates and Dylan in the flower shop and Blade and Scope at home got the brunt of it. Whole afternoons I spent on the sofa eating ice cream with the dogs around me."

"I never saw that part. I found myself feeling more and more bitter over my father's rejection, and there you were, seemingly unbothered by yours. Always chirpy and polite."

"The night I punched you, did you scare my date away?"

Cayden shook his head. "No, he was scared of you the second he stepped inside, but your reaction intrigued me."

"How?"

"Not many guys gaze up at the ceiling after I've punched them and smile, but you did. You smiled like you received my punch as a gift. You became fascinating after that, not because of my father, but because I found you curious. I thought it was a sex thing, but I wanted more than sex with you."

"Despite repeatedly telling me you didn't."

"Then I heard you speaking about Donnie and Elliot, and I had to make a choice, pursue you or get my father's forgiveness. I chose wrong. I knew it that morning we woke up together, but things happened so fast, and I had to go along with my choice, try to convince myself it had been the right one. My head and heart were being tugged all over the place." Cayden shook his head. "It was a mean trick making me think Yates was hacking your fingers off."

"You deserved it."

"I did, but Christ, Ranger." He shuddered. "That hurt more than when my cock piercing was ripped out."

"That shouldn't make me happy, but it does."

"When I sleep, it's a mishmash of the past twenty-four hours, a horror story. So much happened."

"Elliot's still alive, we've got Dylan back, and the doctors are gonna fix you up. That's a pretty good ending for a horror story."

"Ranger..." Cayden wrestled with his words before blurting, "I'd love it if we could start over."

"From date one?"

Cayden nodded. "Yeah."

"You've got a lot of making up to do."

"I know. I'm fully prepared for that, even if we've got to discuss hummus or what dog breed we're most like."

"Yates says I'm a cocker spaniel."

"You know what? I can see it too."

Ranger snorted. "Ya know, they say you shouldn't put out on the first date."

"There's no danger of that happening. I'm not gonna be up for much for months."

"Holding out on sex for the first time is supposed to strengthen a relationship too."

Cayden's brow creased. "Really? Where did you read that?"

"I made it up to make you feel better."

"Oh." Cayden laughed, gripping Ranger's hand tighter. Ranger's heart stopped in his chest when Cayden lifted his hand and pressed a slow kiss to it. "Will you go on a date with me?"

Ranger thumped his chest, reminding his heart to beat. "All *this* because you wanted to ask me out…"

"Is that a yes or no?"

"It's a yes."

EPILOGUE
Four months later

"Taste," Ranger said, bringing the spoon to Cayden's lips.

"I swear to God if you keep doing that, I'll shove the spoon up your arse."

Ranger winked and insisted. Cayden gave in and let the spoon part his lips. He slurped before nodding. "Gravy tastes great. Everything tastes great."

"I want it to be perfect."

"A dinner party," Cayden huffed. "We're not dinner party kinda people. None of us are."

"We're all gonna sit and eat a meal together. No punches will be thrown, no kicks beneath the table. No shots fired or knives thrown. We're all gonna get along just fine."

Ranger clutched his head at the sudden spike of pain. Cayden brushed his fingers aside and started rubbing. "Here was me thinking ten rounds in the ring with me would've sorted you out enough for today."

It had helped. Being in Cayden's newly renovated gym had helped, but the fizzling in his brain persisted.

"I just want everything to be perfect."

"Nothing ever is *perfect*, but we make do. We get by, we enjoy. We're happy." Cayden flicked his eyes away. "I mean, you and me are happy. Blade's furious."

Ranger turned to Blade. He'd ripped up his bow tie collar and sat evil-eyeing them across the room.

"I wanted him to look smart."

"He's not a bow tie sort of dog. He needs a black leather collar with metal studs. Don't ya, bud?"

Blade continued to stare.

"His brother's not fussed about wearing his."

Cayden snorted. "That's because Scope's an idiot."

Scope sat a few meters away from Blade, wearing a pink bowtie and a pair of flower-shaped sunglasses. Not once had he attempted to remove them.

"Don't call him an idiot."

"We threw that towel over his head to test his intelligence. Blade throws it off his head within seconds, Scope sits there for thirty minutes and whimpers to be let out of the dark."

"Is that intelligence, or does he just trust us not to keep him in the dark?"

"The dog magazine said intelligence."

Ranger shrugged. "Magazines aren't always right."

Cayden gaped. "No way." His face cracked with a grin, and he gave Ranger a playful push.

"Don't distract me." He turned back to the stove. The bruschetta was ready to be served, the roast dinner was being kept hot in the oven, and the chocolate mousse was setting in the fridge.

Ranger turned his attention to the table. Six places were set. He kept Yates and Cayden as far away from each other as he could. The glasses sparkled, the cutlery gleamed, and he'd folded the napkins into heart shapes.

"It looks good," Ranger whispered.

Cayden rolled his eyes. "It looks great."

A fist struck the front door. Ranger whipped his apron off and hurried to welcome his guests. Dylan had to push Yates through the door. They were sandwiched so closely together it was hard to tell where one ended and the other began. Dylan grinned, so big and bright, any lift of lips from Yates could only be described as a sneer in comparison.

"Thanks for the invite." Dylan gave Ranger a quick hug but reglued himself to Yates's side when Cayden came closer. He shot him a wary look, taking a fistful of Yates's shirt. Scope bounded forward and greeted Dylan by slobbering all over his jeans.

"Yeah," Yates muttered. "Thank you for inviting us round. We brought wine."

"And dog treats," Dylan added.

Cayden lifted his scarred eyebrow. "That's one hell of a hideous outfit."

Yates looked down at himself, his face turned the same red shade as the tulips printed all over his shirt.

"You're passing judgment on me?"

Cayden snorted. "Point taken."

Ranger pouted and ran his hand down Cayden's T-shirt. A picture of Blade and Scope, with Cayden in the middle. The top of the T-shirt had the words Ranger's boys.

"How's the cock?" Yates asked.

Dylan elbowed him in the side and hissed something Ranger didn't catch.

"I'm only asking."

"The cock is fine." Cayden smiled tightly. "Thanks for the concern."

"Can you seat Yates and Dylan at the table?"

Yates frowned and threw Ranger an unsettled glance. "Who are you, and what have you done with Ranger?"

"This way," Cayden sighed. "And he's been reading far too many dinner party magazines."

Ranger checked his watch and waited in the doorway for Elliot and Donnie.

Elliot appeared first, running up the street.

Out of breath, he stooped over in front of Ranger.

"Is Donnie here yet?"

"Not yet."

"Yes." Elliot punched the air. "I beat him."

He stepped inside the house. "When he gets here, say I've been here for ten minutes."

"Why?"

Elliot begged with his hands. "Please, Ranger."

"Fine."

Cayden appeared in the kitchen doorway. Elliot turned to him and held his arms out wide. "There's my big brother."

"Stop calling me that."

"Sure thing, brother dearest."

Cayden pointed at the kitchen. "Get in there and sit down."

"Spoken like a true big brother."

"You are so irritating."

"I've got to pack as much irritating as I can into our relationship. We're years behind." He pinched Cayden's cheek. "Come on, call me it."

"Call you what?"

"Little brother. Just once."

"No."

Elliot pouted. "Spoilsport."

Ranger caught Cayden's smile before he could hide it.

"What?" Cayden asked.

Ranger darted looks between Elliot and Cayden, no longer glaring and snarling at each other. "It's nice to see you getting on."

Cayden rolled his eyes, but the small smile came back. "Don't get ahead of yourself."

Elliot darted inside the kitchen at the rumble of an engine.

Donnie jumped out of his car and slammed the door shut. "Please say I beat him."

"Sorry, he's been here ten minutes."

"Ten minutes?" Donnie scuffed his shoe on the ground. "How is that even possible?"

Donnie crushed Ranger in a hug. He lifted the carrier bag he was holding. "I've bought beer and snacks."

"Snacks?"

"Just in case…ya know."

Ranger narrowed his eyes. The pressure in his temples began to rise. "In case what?"

"Your food isn't—"

"The oven breaks," Cayden interrupted. "In case the oven breaks."

"Yeah," Donnie nodded. "Exactly that."

Ranger smiled and tipped his head back. "Go on in."

Cayden shifted to allow Donnie room to pass, then came up behind Ranger. He planted a noisy kiss on the side of Ranger's face.

He took a few minutes just to watch the scene in the kitchen. Donnie and Yates talking, Elliot searching around the kitchen in his impatience, and Dylan kneeling down being slobbered on by Scope. Even Blade's tail twitched with something that resembled happiness.

"Ready?"

He nodded. "I've done the food, I've got conversation starters, and after dinner games, coffee, a fucking cheese board, unless Scope's gotten into the fridge."

"He hasn't." Cayden chuckled.

"I just want everything to go—"

"Perfectly, I know, but nothing will ever be as close to perfect as a room full of people and dogs who love you very much."

Cayden wrapped his arm around Ranger's back and pulled him in the direction of the kitchen.

Ranger let out a pleased sigh and pressed his face into the side of Cayden's neck. "My bitches, my boys, and my boyfriend. That's the definition of happiness right there."

****

Ranger waited on the bed; the list unfolded on his thigh. Cayden came out of the bathroom after showering and brushing his teeth. A towel covered his midriff but left his scared nipples visible. The rosette of his nipple was paler, and the shape was no longer a smooth circle.

He sat down beside Ranger and gave him a quick peck on the lips. "Tonight was a success."

"Yeah, Yates only threatened to kill you twice. That's progress."

Cayden snorted and jabbed his finger at Ranger's leg.

"Why've you got that out?"

"One more thing on the list."

"A massage."

"I'd like to try."

Cayden swallowed. "What you mean is you'd like to try sex."

"I wanna get you nice and relaxed, and we'll go from there."

"Ranger, I…"

Ranger pressed his finger to Cayden's lips. "Let me try. If you get uncomfortable, we'll stop."

"Okay, and only because I trust you, Ranger."

"Trust. It's in the top three requirements for a solid relationship."

Cayden rolled his eyes. "I don't even give a shit what magazine that's from."

"Lie down," Ranger said.

Cayden shuffled up the bed, biting his lips as he watched Ranger lower the lights. He lit incense and a few scentless candles.

"What the hell are you doing?"

"Setting the mood."

"The mood is I'm terrified this is gonna hurt."

"I won't hurt you, I swear it. Trust me."

"I do but…but this is my cock we're talking about."

Ranger shook his head. "We're talking about a massage."

"The second you start touching me, I get turned on."

"Trust me."

"It's hard to associate my cock with anything good anymore. Months of pain and no pleasure."

"Let me change that."

Ranger stalked over to the bed and climbed on top of Cayden. He tugged at his towel until it slipped open, revealing his cock. It was already hard, and Cayden sucked in a shaky breath when he looked at it.

"Relax," Ranger told him, reaching for the oil on the side. He warmed it up in his hands before placing them high on Cayden's chest.

"Close your eyes. The scent of lavender is supposed to be relaxing."

"It's the scent of old ladies."

"And have you ever seen a manic old lady?"

Cayden cracked open one of his eyes. "Yes."

"Close your eyes and enjoy the feel of my hands on your body."

"Fine," Cayden grit out.

Over the course of fifteen minutes, the tension in Cayden's body ebbed away; he sunk into the mattress with a long sigh and let Ranger's hands work their magic. Cayden's cock stayed hard, but the rest of him melted into the sheet. Blissed sighs left his lips, and his forehead relaxed of all creases.

"It feels good?"

"Mhmm."

Ranger leaned down and took Cayden into his mouth. He flinched like he expected pain, and when there wasn't any, he flopped back against the pillow and ran his hands through his hair.

"So fucking good."

Ranger traced the ridge of Cayden's scar with his tongue.

Rougher, and thicker, but still sensitive when he gave him a small suck. His cock still jerked the same and tasted the same. Ranger breathed him in; he smelled the same too. He still had the most beautiful cock Ranger had ever seen, long and wide, a delicious shade of purple frustration. Ranger stopped admiring it and sucked it again.

Cayden's moan sounded more like a sob. He shot a look down and watched with a slack mouth as Ranger fed his length past his lips and into his throat.

They'd gotten that far before. It was the next part that scared Cayden the most. He feared cumming like he'd feared pissing for weeks. It'd hurt, no matter the medication or the advice Ranger found online about making urinating more comfortable. It burned, and left him squirming, and angry.

"Ranger..." Cayden tugged at his hair. A warning he was close, and Ranger should ease off or stop. Ranger latched onto him, always gentle, always slow. Cayden stiffened all over, fear twisting his rope of muscles tighter and tighter.

"Oh God, oh God, it's gonna…"

His voice trailed away in a strangled groan as his cock spilled across Ranger's tongue. He fought the urge to go at Cayden's cock harder, and force more pleasure from it, and eased off, cleaning him up with long slow strokes.

Cayden panted with an expression of awe. His shiny eyes fixed on Ranger.

"See." Ranger grinned. "Told you I'd take care of you."

Cayden pulled him up the bed. "And I told you I can handle you, in every way. Now get your cock inside me."

"What a bossy boyfriend you are."

"And you love it."

"Can you at least wait long enough for me to get lube up there?"

"Get on with it."

Ranger snorted and set himself the task of prepping Cayden as slowly as he could. In no time he was withering, cursing, and bashing Ranger with his knees.

"Okay, okay."

Ranger sunk himself into Cayden's hole. His eyes fluttered as he was welcomed home by a vice-like grip and heels digging into his back. He rocked forward and hoisted Cayden's legs higher to get a better angle.

"Show me," Ranger begged, nudging Cayden's face with his nose. Cayden smiled. It reached up to his eyes and ended with his rumbly laugh. He wetted his lips, then poked out his tongue.

Ranger gazed at the stud, Cayden's new piercing he loved to tease with. He crunched it between his teeth, and the metallic grind left Ranger shivering all over.

"Come get it," Cayden whispered.

Ranger chased his mouth, finding his prize inside. Cayden was good at avoiding him, all until Ranger hit the right spot and his mouth opened on a gasp. He licked at the piercing, tangling his tongue with Cayden's as he pushed into his body. Cayden's legs slipped from Ranger's back, and he reached down instead, groping Ranger's arse, driving him deeper and deeper, until he could sneak a finger into Ranger's crack.

Ranger whimpered at his hole being stroked, losing his rhythm.

"I can't wait until I can fuck you again," Cayden murmured. "Thinking about fucking you while you're fucking me is driving me crazy."

He groaned. "I wanna slip my cock in here."

He pushed his finger inside, leaving Ranger powerless to the sensation in his cock.

"Maybe I don't have to use my cock to get you to come like this."

Ranger snorted. Cayden's fingers had brought him to the brink, and he was seconds away from coming inside Cayden's arse.

"Maybe I can use my tongue."

Ranger shivered from his head to his toes. Cayden chuckled and pushed him away. "You like the sound of that, huh?"

"Your...your tongue?"

Cayden hummed, shifting down the bed. Ranger's brain had slowed, and he jolted when he realized where Cayden was heading. He flashed Ranger a glance of his tongue piercing from between his legs.

"Fuck," Ranger mumbled, flinging his arm over his eyes.

He let Cayden position his feet and force his hands underneath Ranger to grip his arse. He kneaded the flesh while muttering dirty words at his exposed hole.

Ranger closed his eyes and fisted the sheets. Cayden's tongue stud rubbed against him, and he damn near lost it. His control almost slipped when Cayden wiggled his tongue inside.

His brain cleared of everything but pleasure as Cayden fluttered his tongue and slipped it in and out. He moaned as he feasted on Ranger's arse, and when he added two fingers to the mix, Ranger was a goner. Cum slapped onto his stomach. His knees trembled, and his toes twisted into the sheet. Ranger exhaled, sated and tingly.

"Do you know how hot it gets me that I'm the first one to fuck you?"

"First," Ranger breathed, "And hopefully last."

Cayden hummed. "Without a doubt last." He bit Ranger's arse. "Like I'm ever gonna let this go."

"I think you only love me for my arse."

Cayden came back up the bed, tipped Ranger's chin up, and slipped his tongue that had just made Ranger orgasm into his mouth. Ranger sighed at the stud, knowing it had just been inside him made it all the dirtier, more erotic. He battled to keep it in his mouth.

Cayden drew back and smiled. "I love you for *you*. You're pretty damn amazing."

"And you," he poked Cayden on the nose, "are average."

Cayden jabbed his fingers into Ranger's sides until he squirmed away laughing.

"You know... All good romances should end like this."

"What?" Cayden raised his scarred eyebrow. "With the protagonist being tongue fucked in the arse?"

"Yes. Exactly like that." Ranger sighed in bliss with love brimming in his heart and a pleasant tingle deep inside. He lifted his head and whispered by Cayden's ear, "*The end.*"

FLOWERSHOP ASSASSINS

LOUISE COLLINS

The Viper

A FLOWERSHOP ASSASSINS SHORT

CHAPTER ONE

The bell rang. A happy chirp of a noise. Yates already despised it despite only installing the damn thing days before. His shop needed a more fitting bell. A crazed cackle or the cock of a pistol.

Something altogether more *him*.

His day got worse when he came out of the back office and caught sight of his visitors.

Not customers, visitors, and unwelcome ones. Police officers.

PS Waymirth and PC Aster.

One short and stubby, one tall and lean, stood side by side they looked almost comical, emphasizing the other's height and width.

"Isn't that a friendly smile?" Waymirth removed his hat, revealing a bald head that glowed under the lights. It was an unconscious cue for Aster to remove his own, unleashing a mop of messy hair. He tried to brush it back with his fingers, but his hair had a mind of its own, sticking upright.

Yates folded his arms. "What do you want?"

Waymirth shrugged. "Maybe I just fancied looking at some flowers."

"The flowers in here are shit."

Dead leaves and petals covered the aisles, and the shop had an earthy scent of decay no matter what spray Yates used to mask it. Several times a day he asked himself why the hell he chose a flower shop. He knew the answer, but still.

"And yet you're still in business…isn't that curious."

"I don't see you harassing anyone else on this street."

"No one else on this street acts suspicious."

"What about them?"

He pointed at the bakery opposite. The air on the street reeked of new paint and the sign above the shop had only recently been revealed.

"Anyone who calls their bakery Stud Muffins needs to be investigated."

Aster lifted his chin and gave Yates a studious look. "They've only just opened up."

"They've got to be dodgy. Who in their right mind would move here?"

"You did."

Yates glared at him. "Exactly."

"Look." Waymirth took a step closer. "I'm going to keep this short and sweet."

Yates narrowed his eyes as he smiled. "That's probably best for you…"

"The Viper…"

"Who?"

"Don't play dumb with me. The Viper," Waymirth repeated. "We're going door to door for any information. He's dangerous, and the quicker he's caught, the better for everyone. People want to feel safe again. They want to go out without the fear they might be his next victim."

"You better catch him then."

Waymirth's lips thinned. "Yes, and we will but we can't do that without the cooperation of the locals. You've now been here long enough to qualify as a local."

"Lucky me."

"Don't you want to help your community and find this guy?"

"That's your job." Yates smiled tightly. "My job is to sell flowers."

Waymirth snorted. "They're the worst flowers I've ever seen."

"And you're the worst police officers I've seen. If you catch him, I'll personally give you a round of applause."

"I'll hold you to that."

Yates flared his nostrils. "Now. If that's all, kindly leave my shop."

And go fuck yourself.

"There will be a bigger police presence around the area," Aster added. "Just to let you know."

Yates waited until they were gone before opening the news app on his phone.

The Viper this, and The Viper that. It was all anyone was talking, writing, and even singing about. A song had been released about him. The Vile Viper.

Ranger was using it as his goddamn ring tone.

He used snake venom as his murder weapon and soon ended up with the nickname The Viper. His method had even acquired a nickname.

If you were killed by him, you were said to have been *vipered*.

None of his victims were linked. Not as far as anyone could tell anyway, but Yates knew different. Yates knew that his three victims were linked, and he was the common denominator.

They were hits, and he knew they were hits because they'd been contracted out to him first. Specifically, they were Donnie's hits that he had to cancel when he decided Donnie's drinking and partying had become a liability.

The Viper was an assassin, a good one, but he tended to drum up a lot of press, and suspicion, and generally, cause Yates a massive headache.

He swiped the news article about The Viper's latest victim away and brought up Ranger's number.

"It's me…be at the shop at three."

****

Blood filled out the vein above Yates's left temple. He paced, back and forth between the aisles of the flower shop with his arms crossed, elbows brushing the drooping flowers. He hated waiting, and wherever he walked, he kept his gaze fixed on the door, pulse steadily increasing, throbbing in his overfilled blood vessel, all until—

"Got here as soon as I could."

Yates raised his eyebrow at Ranger, unimpressed. They'd agreed to meet at three. It was three-thirty, and Yates glowered. His biceps ached from how hard he tensed them. If that wasn't the biggest giveaway of how angry he was, his nostrils were. He flared them, flushing air through them like a rabid animal ready to tear out Ranger's throat.

"Bitch, I'm sorry."

Ranger ran his hands over his head, right over his freshly done snake tattoo. It hid the scar from surgery. The design, the colors, the pose of the cobra, most days made Yates seethe with jealousy, but not that day.

He ground his teeth together. "Don't call me bitch. Why are you late?"

"Well," Ranger wagged his finger before backing out of the shop. The vein in Yates's head teetered on the edge of explosion. Ranger disappeared, before returning, dragging a corpse with him.

"What the actual—"

Not a corpse. It groaned.

"I was getting the other bitch." Ranger announced, pulling a tatty-haired Donnie into the shop. Donnie slumped forward, his head lolled, and Yates was pretty sure he was asleep on his feet.

"Where the hell have you been?" Yates snapped.

Donnie shrugged. "You know…partying."

"Partying," Yates rolled his forefingers into his tempers, doing his best to calm his temper. He needed to focus, not throttle Donnie.

"Yeah, I'm Donnie King, haven't you heard? I fuck like a wild thing."

Ranger nodded. "Yeah, you do. If that wild thing has been knocked down repeatedly and scraped off the road."

"Arsehole." Donnie took a swing, missed, and crashed into a table.

"Where did you find him?" Yates asked.

Ranger tilted his head, watching Donnie. "His place. There's not much there."

"What do you mean?"

"I think he's been robbed and hasn't noticed."

Donnie slipped down to the floor. He looked ten times worse since the last time time Yates saw him. His *parting* was clearly killing him.

Donnie's head flopped back. Leaked out dribble stuck his hair to his face, and the puffy red skin beneath his eyes made him hard to look at. Yates averted his gaze. What a waste to be that handsome and let it go so spectacularly. What a waste to have it *all* and lose it. Good looks, confidence, swagger, an unworldly reputation between the sheets.

"Why the hell did you bring him?"

"Ya know," Ranger glanced down at their pitiful friend. "In case we need him."

Yates nudged Donnie with his foot. He collapsed into a table with a groan. Then rubbed his head feverishly against the metal leg, as if the cold offered him salvation from the obvious hangover trying to kill him.

"We're not going to need him. He needs rehab. I told you last time, Donnie, get yourself to a rehab."

"I don't need rehab." Donnie snapped. He tried to focus on Yates, but his head drifted back, and he slumped into the table leg again. "I've been parting. It's your fault, anyway."

"My fault?"

"I wouldn't be partying so much if you hadn't stopped my hits."

"I stopped your hits because you're drinking too much and I don't think you're capable."

"What's the point of being the best, and hottest assassin out there if you don't reap the rewards."

"You're certainly not the most modest one." Ranger said, kicking Donnie's foot.

"Stop looking at me like that, Yates, I'm fine, fresh as a daisy."

"Don't insult daisies by comparing them to you."

The words had left Yates before he could stop them. Ranger raised his eyebrow before running his eyes around the shop. "You like…daisies?"

Yates didn't answer. It was inevitable really. He was surrounded by flowers and had chosen a flower shop for a sentimental reason, it was natural to favor one flower over another. He liked daisies, but daisies were no match for huge red roses, which he currently didn't sell.

"Huh." Ranger mused. "Hopefully not too much."

"I don't plan on inserting one up my arse if that's what you're worried about."

"No." Ranger raised his hand in a pacifying gesture. "As long as you don't start wearing them."

Yates narrowed his eyes. "You think I'd walk around dressed as a daisy?"

"I didn't mean that, but I find them—flowery patterns I mean, a little taxing on the eye, that's all. They wouldn't suit you."

"Wouldn't they…"

Donnie mashed his face against the leg of the table. His eyes shut, and he slurred out, "Is that why we're here? Yates wants to dress up like a daisy."

"Christ," Yates growled. "You've only been in here thirty seconds, and my gun is calling me in the office to take you out."

"Not my fault your daisy costume sucks."

"Right. I'm getting my gun."

Ranger rushed forward and grabbed Yates's hand before he could disappear into the back. He squeezed Yates's fingers, drawing his attention. "Sorry, we're sorry, aren't we, Donnie?"

"No," Donnie's eyes peeled open. "It is a shit costume."

Yates pulled away from Ranger and gripped the bottom of his shirt. "It's not a costume, it's a plain white shirt, that's all it is like I wear every goddamn day."

"Mix it up a bit." Donnie waved his finger in the air. "Add a yellow dot in the middle and it's a daisy, right?"

"I'm going to kill him."

"No, you're not," Ranger said, leaning all his weight against Yates to keep him at bay. "Now tell us, why are we here?"

Yates stopped trying to walk through Ranger and retreated to the counter. "The Viper."

"Ah, The Viper," Ranger repeated.

Donnie lifted his face from the table leg, and murmured, "The Viper."

Yates nodded. "I wanted to have a civilized conversation about what we're going to do about him."

"That's a good idea," Ranger said. He chomped on his bottom lip before looking at Yates with wide eyes. "Did you know snakes have two penises?"

Yates glared at him. The vein in his temple filled up with blood all over again. It surprised him it hadn't grown to egg-sized proportions and blocked out his left eye.

"Two?" Donnie said from the floor. "God, think of the fun you could have with two."

Ranger twisted around to look at him. "I know right—"

"We need to kill him!" Yates shouted.

He could pick out his pulse in the resulting silence.

Donnie shuffled into a more upright position, and Ranger took a cautious step back.

Yates sighed. "He's taking our business, not only that, but he's also so blatant about it, the police and press are all over him. It's all anyone talks about when they come in here."

"Well, your flowers are shit, who can blame them," Ranger muttered.

"My flowers are not shit."

A drooping bouquet took the opportunity to fall over, and sprinkle dirt, and dead petals all over the floor.

"Need I say more," Ranger said.

"They're just flowers."

Ranger's mouth dropped open. "That's blasphemy in a flower shop."

"You're not here about the flowers!"

Yates needed a rest from Ranger grinning moronically and looked at Donnie instead. He'd scrapped his hair back from his face, and his eyes had sobered. This was Donnie. The old Donnie. Yates caught a glimpse of him and was determined to hold onto it. He stepped closer, keeping eye contact. "The Viper needs to go."

Donnie let loose a long sigh. "I don't like how he goes about it. His method. It's…inhumane, but Yates, are you sure you want to go down this route. Assassin against assassin."

Yates had spent the whole day thinking it over, assassin against assassin, an unspoken code, but this was business, and with Donnie not at his best, Ranger no longer psychotic, and The Viper becoming the go-to nightmare assassin, he needed to act fast.

"We need to take this seriously."

Yates blinked in surprise at Ranger's statement. He turned back to him, and they nodded to each other. "We do."

Ranger licked his lips. A crease appeared between his eyebrows. "He might have friends."

Yates took in a deep breath. He thought about that too, the chance of retaliation. An out, out territory war. He didn't want to put Ranger or Donnie at risk, but he needed to protect the business.

Their business.

"He might…"

Ranger's gaze roamed the shop. "Like…I dunno…Lizard-Man or Gecko-Girl."

Yates turned his face to the ceiling, and yelled loud enough the lights dimmed, "Christ Ranger!"

"What?"

Donnie's laugh morphed into a retch, and the retch proceeded into a coughing fit. He banged his own back, clearing his throat.

If there was sick on the shop floor, Yates was going to lose it, no doubt about it. He squeezed the bridge of his nose, and inwardly counted to ten.

Ranger pushed Yates lightly on the shoulder. "So, let's do it."

Wait…what?

"Yeah?"

Yates glanced back at Donnie who struggled to his feet. He adjusted his jacket and scrapped back his hair with his fingers. "Yeah. The three of us."

Ranger rubbed his hands together. "Bitches, let's go snake wrangling."

CHAPTER TWO

Yates had sent them home, under orders to shower and dress as smartly as possible. Ranger came out of his house in a white vest and jeans until Yates threatened to run him down with his car.

"Fine." Ranger huffed. "But I'm wearing my shades."

He retreated inside and slipped on a suit Yates was unaware he owned.

"You look…good."

Ranger lifted his glass just to show Yates he was rolling his eyes. "Don't sound so surprised."

"Let's hope Donnie has managed to dress himself." Yates shook his head. "I still don't think it's a great idea for him to come."

Ranger chuckled, "Give him a chance."

"Why? I can see a fuck up on the horizon and had to cancel his hits. I don't know what they hell is wrong with him."

"You could ask…"

"And he'll say he's fine. If he fucks up tonight—"

"If he fucks up you get one free punch to my face. No retaliation."

Yates narrowed his eyes. "You can't make that promise. You might have one of your…moments."

"That's a risk you'll have to take."

"I'd prefer not to," Yates put his foot down, flinging Ranger back. He winced as he clutched his neck, and Yates saw it. The flash of rage in his eyes. It was gone as quickly as it had appeared.

"That was mean."

"I'm a mean guy."

Yates pulled up outside Donnie's apartment and punched the horn until he strode out of the front doors of the block.

"See," Ranger said, nudging Yates in the ribs. "He's fine."

"He's not fine, but he's at least managed to dress himself."

He approached the car brimming with his usual confidence and circled to get to the passenger side. That's when Yates noticed the creased shirt, the askew buttons and the stain that he guessed was whiskey.

Ranger wound down the window. "I don't fucking think so."

"I always get the front seat."

"That was until I became Yates's favorite."

Donnie wrinkled up his nose. "You're not Yates's favorite."

"You both equally irritate me," Yates said. "Now get in the bloody car, Donnie."

He conceded and flung himself across the backseats instead.

"You good?" Yates asked.

"'m fine."

Donnie rested his cheek against Yates's seat. "Why have I been demoted to the back?"

"You're a waste of space right now, and Ranger was first on the way, is that enough of a reason?" Yates put his foot down, flinging Donnie out of sight.

He glanced at the clock. "We don't have long to get there."

Donnie groaned, "Your driving sucks."

Yates curled his fingers around the wheel. "I'm a good driver."

"It's too jerky, too stop and start. Nauseating."

Yates gestured to the windscreen. "There's a lot of traffic lights along here, what do you want me to do, run every red light?"

"I was only saying, be a bit gentler with the gas, treat the car like you'd treat a lover."

Yates throttled the wheel, cursing under his breath. "This *is* how I treat my lovers."

Ranger twisted to face him. "Donnie has a point."

"What?"

"You are a bad driver."

"I wasn't after a critique."

"We're only trying to help," Donnie said, with Ranger nodding along.

Yates slammed his foot on the brake, sending Ranger and Donnie flying forward. Donnie whimpered and clutched his head. Ranger's eyes flashed with anger, a warning not to push it, and Yates eased out a small sigh.

"Let's concentrate on the task at hand."

"Lay it on us," Ranger said. "I want to know what we're up against."

"The Viper has been given a hit for tonight. Mr. Quentin Bells. He's attending a charity auction at the Somerton House, and has to die before the last item goes up for sale."

"What's the last item?" Ranger asked.

"Does it matter?"

"I was curious, that's all."

Donnie's face appeared between the seats again. "Are we trying to save Quentin?"

Yates shook his head. "Doesn't matter either way. The Viper's target is Quentin, but ours is The Viper."

"How do you know where they'll be?"

Yates sighed. "Originally, I was contacted over the hit. They requested you, but I cancelled it."

Donnie shook Yates's seat. "What? Why?"

"I haven't been able to get in touch with you for weeks Donnie!"

"You know what it's like, one party rolls into another. Maybe if you hadn't have banned me from hits."

"This would've been your comeback if you'd bothered to answer my calls. I was willing to give you a chance."

"Hold up," Ranger said, slamming his hand to Yates's chest. "We have a cancellation policy."

"Yes, twenty-four hours. I told the client Donnie wasn't up for it."

"Fucking great," Donnie muttered. "Why did you tell him that!"

"Because you're not. I thought you might be, but I couldn't contact you, and the risk you'd fuck up was too great."

"I wouldn't have fucked up."

"You've lost it, and until you've proved to me you've *got it* again, no more hits."

He folded his arms. "I've still got it."

Yates gritted his teeth. "Kill The Viper, then we'll talk."

"Fine. I will," Donnie snapped his finegrs. "Lets here the details."

"I haven't found out much about him, other than he calls himself The Viper, his specialty is venom, and he leaves behind a calling card with a snake."

Ranger hummed. "Did you know some snakes can see in the dark?"

"How does that help us?"

"You shared some useless information, so I thought I'd share some too."

"Mine wasn't useless."

"You've got no idea what The Viper looks like, how are we supposed to pick him out in a crowd."

Donnie snorted. "He's got you there, Yates. Not to mention, I don't want to wither on the floor with snake venom turning my blood to jelly. That's not the way I want to go."

Ranger hummed. "What's your favorite flavor?"

"What?"

"Jelly."

Donnie and Yates shared a look. Ranger huffed and folded his arms. "I was only trying to lighten the mood. Mines strawberry in case you're wondering."

"He uses venom," Yates said, "So let's assume he isn't carrying a snake around with him at all times, he must have it on him, a container, or a bottle or something."

"How's it administered?" Donnie asked.

"The press says it's injected. The Viper is quick and efficient. He only needs to get close enough to the victim, stab them, and then he leaves. Only takes a few seconds to take effect, and a few minutes to turn fatal, by that point he's gone, and he leaves behind his calling card near the scene."

"A calling card you say." Ranger drummed his fingers against his chin. "I want one."

Donnie brushed his face against Ranger's seat. "What would it be?"

"Hearts and a rainbow or something pretty. We're assassins, but it doesn't all have to be doom and gloom."

Yates's clenched teeth ached and he shook the wheel. "Can you two concentrate! I need this done tonight. It's the only time I'm going to know where he is, The Viper is evasive."

Ranger twiddled an invisible moustache. "You could say he's a slippery character."

"Right," Yates said, reaching over and grabbing the handle. "Out you go."

"But we're on the motorway."

Yate's eyes almost popped out. "I don't give a shit!"

"Yates…"

He met Donnie's eyes in the mirror, noting they were more alert than they'd been ten minutes ago. Donnie looked as if the cogs in his brain were turning. He blinked, clearing even more of his hangover glaze. "Somerton House is that huge estate just outside of town, there's a massive gate around it. They're not going to let anyone in."

"No, you're right. You've got to be on the guest list, which you are, well not Donnie King, but Noah Spears. You would've known all this if you had bothered to answer my calls."

"I told you, I've been busy…"

"Yes, I imagine you've gotten quite dizzy with that downward spiral you're on."

"Hold up," Ranger said, raising his hands. "That's one of us, what about the other two?"

"Well, when we get close enough, I'll change places with Donnie, and me and you will climb in the back, and cover ourselves with a sheet."

"Cozy."

"Not cozy, necessary. We're both suited, I'm sure we'll blend in at the auction."

"Noah," Donnie said. "You'll have to call me Noah."

"Not going to happen," Ranger said with a smile. "You're still bitch to me. Bitch one and bitch two, but collectively, my bitches…and what am I to you?"

Yates glared at him. "A massive pain in my arse."

****

"I've always wondered what it would be like to snuggle with you beneath the sheets."

Yates shook with anger, and it only got worse when Ranger shifted closer and kissed him on the nose. "It's definitely cozy."

"I'm gonna kill you."

Ranger just smiled. "That your bedroom talk?"

"Very. Slowly."

It took a few goes for the guard on the gate to recognize Donnie as the Noah on their list. Photo IDs were great when they matched, but Donnie looked worlds away from how he did months three months before.

Yates heard the guard mumble, "I think it's you."

"That's what I've been saying for the last ten minutes, now look what you've done, there's a huge queue behind me backing up down the road."

Yates could hear the engines revving and the impatient car horns. He sighed when the car began moving again, wheels crunching over loose gravel as Donnie drove what felt like a mile away from the gate.

"We're in," Donnie said.

Yates flung off the sheet and sat up. "Thank fuck."

"Well, I was enjoying myself," Ranger said, righting himself.

Yates ignored him and looked out the window. His mouth dropped open at the other guests. He'd assumed the auction would have a black-tie dress code, but from the sparkles, patterns, feathers, and glitter he'd been wrong.

"I am awake, right?" Donnie said.

Ranger rubbed his eyes and took another look. "Yes, either that or we are *all* asleep."

Bright colors, feathers, lace, mesh, satin, silk. Yates's gaze settled on the guy closest to him, wearing a shirt covered in huge red roses. He swallowed and gripped his head. "What are we doing here again?"

Ranger pushed him. "The Viper, remember?"

"Yes." Yates hissed, "Of course." He reached in his pocket and pulled out a photograph of Quentin Bells. He passed it to Ranger who took a long hard look, then passed it to Donnie in the front. "That's Quentin. If we keep him in our sights, then we're bound to find The Viper."

Donnie handed the photograph back and flung open his door. "Let's get this over with."

Chapter Three

Yates had never seen so many flowery shirts in all his life. They weren't ghastly Hawaiian print, but stunning, and when he subtle brushed the back of his hand against the red-rose shirt, his knees weakened at the smooth fabric. He wanted that on his chest. He wanted to run his hands down it throughout the day, and catch the reflection of it in his shop windows.

"Our best bet is to split up, right?"

He glanced at Donnie. "Huh?"

"I said should we split up?"

Yates nodded. "That's our best bet."

Donnie gave him a strange look and then disappeared into the house.

Ranger gestured to the gardens. "I'll go see if I can spot Quentin over there."

"Good idea. I'll find the auction room. Quentin might already be seated."

Every room of the mansion was packed, and as Yates squeezed his way through the crowds, he realized there was more than one auction going on at a time. More than one room with hundreds of seated people holding numbered paddles. They all faced the auctioneer which made spotting Quentin impossible.

"Fuck," he retreated outside to search for backup. He found Ranger in a circle of guests. "Shit," he said, squeezing in next to him. Yates expected to see a body on the floor, but instead, it was a guy dropping down on bended knee.

"Any luck?" Yates whispered.

"I'm wishing them all my luck. Hannah and Stu seem like such a cute couple."

"Who the fuck—"

"Shush." Ranger slapped his hand to Yate's mouth. "Don't ruin it. I want to listen."

Yates rolled his eyes at the cliché "Will you marry me?"

Ranger gasped and pulled Yates closer in an anxious clutch.

"Yes!"

The circle of guests cheered and clapped. Yates struggle out of Ranger's hold and whirled to face him. Tears were glistening in his eyes. "Wasn't that the most romantic thing."

"I don't know what's going on with you, but sort it out. I'm going to find Donnie."

He left Ranger to congratulate the happy couple and went in search of Donnie, but he'd vanished. He strode through every room on his quest, but couldn't find him.

"Champagne?"

Even the waiter had a flamboyant outfit. Vibrant pink. He smiled at Yates, and he took a flute of champagne off his tray, only to curse, and grab the waiter by the shoulder before he could leave. "Hey, you see a guy in a suit like mine, with long tatty hair and red eyes, don't give him any."

"Such a person has already mobbed me for my first tray. Literally. He launched at me, I tripped and dropped it all. It caused quite the commotion."

"Shit." Yates hissed, releasing his hold on the waiter. "I'm sorry about that."

He leaned up on his tiptoes, trying to spot Donnie.

"If you're looking for him, he's upstairs."

"What?"

"Yes. He vanished with another tray, and triplets I believe."

"Triplets..."

"Yes. Handsome young men. I don't know what possessed them to go off with him."

"He has a reputation."

"As a caveman?"

Yates squeezed the waiter on the shoulder before making his way past. "Thank you for letting me know."

Donnie and Ranger were utterly useless.

When a job was worth doing, it was worth doing himself.

It was in the moment he saw him. Not Donnie, not even Quentin, but The Viper. It could only be the Viper. Face covered in a snake print tattoo, with a matching snake print suit. His eyes glowed green with slits for pupils. He was huge, muscular, taking up two seats, and sitting two rows in front of him was Quentin.

The Viper was in his sights, lounging casually, casting his fake eyes around the room. Yates couldn't kill him outright in front of everyone. He had to lead him out, somewhere quieter so he could pop him between the eyes and leave in a hurry.

Yates stopped beside him. "What item are you after tonight?"

The Viper turned to him slowly, attaching his striking green eyes to Yates. The chairs he was sitting on creaked as he turned to face Yates fully. "Who wants to know?"

"Just making conversation. Getting to know you."

"And why would you want to know me?" The Viper slowly rubbed his thighs, back and forth, back and forth. "You want to sit on my lap, big guy?"

Yates recoiled. "What!"

"Want to lean over my legs so I can spank you good?"

Yates surged forward and grabbed The Viper by the collar of his shirt. "No. I want to put a bullet between your eyes."

The Viper smirked in Yates's face before slipping out his tongue, it broke the seal of his lips and split down the middle.

"You take your persona to the next level, don't you?"

"Sure do, sweetheart."

Yates scrunched up his face. "Sweetheart?"

They broke apart at a scream. Yates looked over to see Quentin thrashing back and forth in his seat, gurgling, and choking. Everyone began rushing around and shouting for someone to help.

The waiter dropped his tray and hurried past. "I'll call an ambulance."

Yates could see at least ten guests on their phones, all calling for one, and a few asking for the police. "Shit," he hissed, flapping his hands. "Don't call the police," The guests closest to him glared, Yates faltered, "I mean yes, call the police. Lock the place down, and call the police. That's what I meant to say."

When he turned back to find The Viper, he'd gone, exiting the row of chairs on the other side. Yates tried to go after him, but the guests swarmed and surged, and somehow he lost sight of the guy in the snake skin suit.

"Motherfucker." He hissed, elbowing his way from the room.

He needed Donnie and Ranger to help find him.

Yates found Ranger outside, playing with a dog in a handbag.

Of fucking course he was.

"Christ," he hissed, marching over and snagging Ranger by the top of his ear.

"Ouch, Yates, that hurts."

"You're supposed to be concentrating."

"I'm sorry okay, but did you see that dog in the handbag? There was a dog in a handbag."

"I swear to God, Ranger!"

Yates shifted his jaw from side to side, trying to stay calm.

"Okay, okay," Ranger frowned at the guests rushing from the front door. "What happened in there?"

"Quentin's dead. The place is getting locked down. We've got to find The Viper."

"Small problem with that, none of us know what he looks like."

Yates pinched the bridge of his nose. "Funnily enough, he looks like a viper."

"What?"

"Snakeskin suit, snake tattoos, snake eyes, snake tongue."

"Wow."

"Yeah." Yates nodded. "Shouldn't be hard to find him."

"Where's Donnie?"

"Searching for the viper in a very specific place."

Ranger frowned. "Which is?"

"Up some triplets arseholes."

****

Yates expected one police car, and one ambulance to turn up at the property. Five of each screeched onto the scene. Police offices were everywhere, walking in every direction, asking for names, checking them off against the guest list.

He even recognized Waymirth and Aster.

They were getting harder and harder to avoid, and The Viper had vanished. Him and Ranger hid around the side of the house, in one of the many gardens. A fountain sprayed water into the air in the center.

Ranger shrugged. "Well, we tried."

"I'm not admitting defeat, yet."

"What's your plan?"

Yates snorted. "I need you to be a distraction, cause a scene, draw everyone's attention."

Ranger bit his lip, nodding, before tilting his head towards Yates and asking, "On a scale of one to ten—"

"A cast-iron ten. I want you to go for it. Full. On. Dramatic."

"Got it." Ranger pushed off from the wall, and walked a few meters away from Yates, softly clearing his throat, before breaking out in a run, and screaming at the top of his lungs.

"That's my father in there!"

"What the actual fuck." Yates muttered under his breath.

He gaped but kept his out-of-sight position against the wall as Ranger ran towards the house, shouting that his father was inside, his father was Quentin Bells. He wailed, sobbed, and screamed. The police officers rushed his way, as did all the guests, eager to see Ranger break down at the sight of his poisoned body in the auction room B.

The police were preoccupied, now all Yates had to do was find The Viper.

"Now we're alone, we can begin the spanking."

Yates froze, but before he could turn around, he fell forward under a brutal shove. An arm wrapped around his neck, strangling the air out of him until he dropped to his knees.

"Or choking. I prefer choking to spanking," The Viper said, tightening his arm, and tensing his bicep into Yates's throat. He clawed at the arm, but it had no effect. Darkness pressed in at the edges of his vision. The Viper applied more weight to his back, pressing into him until Yates couldn't support himself on his arms, and flattened to the ground with the arm still around his neck, suffocating him. "Bullet between the eyes. I don't take kindly to being threatened like that."

The pressure on Yates's neck vanished. He turned on his side, gasping in air, as he watched Donnie drive a champagne flute into his attacker's eye. He screeched and swung his fist, catching Donnie in the gut. He staggered, clutching himself. Donnie aborted his attempt to follow The Viper and fell to his knees a few meters from Yates.

He turned his head and found Yates wheezing with his hand massaging his throat. "You alright?"

Yates nodded. "Thanks to you."

Donnie's lips twitched with the start of a smile, his handsome smile, and for a second Yates thought he might be okay. Donnie would get better, smile that smile, and swagger into the flower shop eager for his next hit, and Yates would allow him a contract, and all would be good in the world again.

But Donnie's smile failed, and he pitched forward, vomiting onto the ground.

So much vomit.

He collapsed onto his hands and crawled over to Yates. "You don't think he poisoned me, do you?"

"No, I think you drank too much and he punched you in the gut."

"Well, that's okay then…"

Yates rolled onto his back and stared at the stars. "This is not the night I imagined."

"Out of curiosity, what part didn't match up for you?"

Yates snorted, and Donnie smiled, patting him on the shoulder.

"I think I've had enough humiliation for one night, shall we go?"

"Great idea." Donnie sighed. "We've just got to find Ranger."

He staggered up and offered his hand out to Yates.

"How were the triplets?" Yates asked as he got to his feet.

"They got annoyed."

"Why?"

"I struggled to tell them apart."

Yates smirked. "I guess that's a flaw with being identical."

"They weren't identical."

"Oh."

"How's your neck?"

"Fine, just feeling a little light-headed that's all."

Donnie swung Yates's arm over his shoulder and helped him to walk.

"You know what…"

"What?" Donnie asked.

"I think flowers on a shirt look good."

"Nah," Donnie shook his head.

"That one for instance." Yates pointed at the guy wearing the huge roses, earning himself a scared glance.

"I'm admiring the shirt, not you." Yates snapped.

"I think The Viper might have squeezed your neck a little too hard."

Ranger waved at them across the parking lot.

"Is that lack of oxygen or is Ranger really in the back of an ambulance."

Donnie sighed. "He's really in the back of an ambulance."

Ranger tucked a shock blanket around his shoulders and flapped the magazine on his lap. An oxygen mask covered his mouth, and When Yates got to him, he promptly stole it.

"I found out what the last item was," Ranger said.

Donnie waved, encouraging the answer. "And?"

"A stuffed eagle."

"Random."

"This whole place is random. You'll never guess what I saw in a handbag."

Yates glanced over to the house and groaned when he spotted Aster and Waymirth.

"Time to go." He croaked.

"You got The Viper?"

"Nope, but I'm done for tonight. I want to leave."

"Me too," Donnie said. "My guts killing me."

Ranger stabbed his finger at the magazine and pouted. "But I just found the problem page."

"Now." Yates winced, grabbing his aching throat.

"Okay, okay." Ranger threw the mask aside, and let the blanket drop from his shoulders. "Thought this place was locked down?"

"Only for those that haven't made a statement," Donnie said. "And luckily for you two, Noah made his so let's get the hell out of here and go drown our sorrows."

"No more alcohol for you," Yates growled.

"Aww Yates," Ranger lifted his eyebrow. "We get to snuggle under the sheet again."

"I'll strangle you with the sheet if you keep looking at me like that."

Ranger blew him a kiss. "How erotic."

CHAPTER FOUR

They'd failed. Spectacularly failed. Yates held open the door to the flower shop for Ranger and Donnie, both grim-faced, and hanging their heads as they trudged inside.

Not for the first time, Yates wondered, why the hell them?

Why did he want to set up this business venture with these two clowns?

Except, when this all started, they weren't clowns.

Ranger had a reputation of being a crazed-psychotic killer, and Donnie was a master assassin, matched with his plotting and contacts, they seemed a match made in a sadistic part of heaven.

Donnie sunk to the floor, clutching his gut. "Well, that went well."

"It would've gone a lot better if you hadn't gotten distracted by the free booze, and the triplets."

"I don't have a drinking problem."

"You most certainly do."

Ranger lifted himself onto the counter, knocking over a stack of bills. Yates whirled on him, shaking a finger. "And you…where were you?"

"I was looking—

"At a couple getting engaged and a dog in a handbag."

Ranger folded his arms. "What about you?"

"Me? I'm the one who found our target."

"Found him, but didn't finish him. From what you told me on the way back, you needed Donnie to save your arse. A wasted Donnie who had just been knee-deep in triplets."

"Fine." Yates snapped. "I didn't handle it. I let him get away. Is that what you want to hear?"

"I'm just saying, none of us were on our A-game tonight?"

Donnie pressed his face against the metal table leg. "What letter were we all on exactly?"

"Let's hope and pray that was our Z game," Yates said. "I don't wanna know if we can get worse than that performance."

Yates looked at all the dying flowers in his shop, the wilting leaves, the curled up petals on the floor. The place was a mess.

He sighed and pointed at Donnie. "What's eating you?"

"Apart from getting distracted by champagne and triplets."

"Yeah…apart from that."

"I should have been able to kill that guy."

"You took out his eye."

Donnie knocked his forehead against the table leg. It clanged. "But I should've been able to kill him. I should've been able to go after him, punch to the gut or not. What's happened to me?"

"You know what's happened. You need help. You've lost it…but that doesn't mean you've lost it forever, but first, you've got to admit it to yourself."

"Admit what?"

"You've got a drinking problem."

"I do not. If I've got a problem, it's a partying one."

"No." Yates pressed his teeth together and counted to ten. "It's drink, and you've lost your edge."

"Huh?" Donnie peeled his face from the table leg. "I've still got it. Give me a hit and I'll prove it."

"You said you'd kill the Viper."

"Are you forgetting I saved your life tonight."

"I'm grateful—

"You don't sound it, maybe I shouldn't have bothered."

Yates rolled his eyes and turned his attention towards Ranger. "And what's wrong with you?"

"I'm grand. I got to see a dog in a bag and a couple get engaged."

"Ranger…"

He shook his head. "Nothing, it doesn't matter."

"Tell me."

"It's just," Ranger clacked his tongue to the roof of his mouth. "I'd finally found the problem page, ya know…"

"Christ, Ranger!" Yates tugged his hair and moved to the door. He yanked it open, and not looking back, he stepped out and slammed it shut in his wake.

"Fucking idiots," Yates yelled, hurrying up the street. "I should put a damn bullet in both of them, or spare myself and put one in me."

He raved and growled until he reached the corner shop, and shoulder barged the door open.

"Can't believe I scouted them out." He snatched a packet of paracetamol off the side.

His muttering earned him a few concerned glances, but he ignored them, in favor of muttering some more. "Can't believe I thought this would work."

He stalked the shop, yanked open the freezer door, and reached for the peas. "I should cut them off."

Yates shifted the peas and paracetamol to one hand and stopped by the magazine rack. "That's what I should do, ditch them, start again."

He selected a women's mag that promised a juicy problem page and then dumped his items in front of the cashier.

He pointed at the cool cabinet behind her. "And a bottle of water."

"Right."

She cast her gaze over them. "This…this is what you needed. Paracetamol, peas, water and a magazine."

Yates snapped open his wallet. "I don't need them, some other idiots do and before I cast them out, I thought they could do with a few treats to soften the blow."

"So you thought…peas, paracetamol and a magazine."

"Look." Yates squeezed the bridge of his nose. "I'm tired, grouchy, and I'm struggling to stay polite."

"This is you polite?"

He cracked his knuckles. "Can you just put the items through so I can leave?"

"Sure."

It took a twenty-minute stroll and a trip to the shop for him to calm down enough to return to the flower shop.

Ranger and Donnie were exactly where he left them, still drooping under the weight of sadness.

Yates strolled up to Ranger and dropped a magazine on his thigh. "There ya go."

Ranger lit up. "Aww, you shouldn't have."

"I know." Yates snapped. He trudged over to Donnie and crouched down.

"Here." He popped out two paracetamol from the foil packet.

"For the gut," Donnie said.

"No, for the hangover."

Yates forced them into Donnie's mouth and then handed over the water.

He gulped them down. "What's with the peas?"

"They're for you?"

"The gut?"

"No. The hangover. Put them on the back of your neck, it'll help."

Donnie narrowed his eyes slightly but did as Yates told him. He hissed at the cold, before groaning in pleasure. "Hey, that actually feels nice."

Yates stalked away and sat down with a healthy distance between both Ranger, and Donnie. "This is never going to work. It's over. We're over."

Ranger flicked open his magazine. "Stop being so dramatic."

"I'm not being dramatic! We're shit."

"Speak for yourself."

"Can you drop it, Ranger, just for a minute, drop it."

Ranger slipped down from the counter and came to sit by Yates's side. Donnie crawled across the floor, still clutching the bag of peas. He collapsed on his side, with his head on Yates's thigh. A long uncomfortable silence filled the shop, only broken by Donnie repeatedly letting go of the peas. His head got heavier and heavier on Yates's thigh, and he kept jerking back to consciousness.

"Go to sleep."

Donnie groaned, and weakly raised his hand. "I admit it."

"That you've got a problem, you need to talk to someone and you've lost your edge." Ranger guessed.

"No, I admit, I'm hungover, still, and I'm really tired."

Yates sighed and took the peas from Donnie. He held them to the back of his neck.

"That feels nice," Donnie whispered.

"Go to sleep, Donnie."

"I worry what I'll dream about."

His voice came out soft, barely audible.

Yates frowned, about to question him, but Ranger leaned over and murmured by Donnie's ear. "Snakes, you're gonna dream about snakes, and how they turn your blood to jelly."

"Don't whisper that in his ear."

Ranger shrugged. "I'm curious to see if it'll work."

After only a few minutes, Donnie's breathing levelled out, and he snored softly, asleep on Yates's leg.

"We're not over." Ranger said, "Everyone has their ups and downs, this magazine says so, we've just got to get up again, that's all."

"*All?*" Yates smirked.

He looked down at Donnie.

Ranger looked too. "It's just.... some people's *all* is harder than others."

"He's going to kill himself, and I don't think…"

Ranger nudged him. "You don't think?"

Yates's eyes burned. He swallowed the words he was going to say and instead growled out, "I don't think it's good for business."

"Give him a chance to save himself."

"How? He won't go to rehab."

"Give him a hit. He's partying more and more because you stopped them."

"His drinking—look, Ranger. I can see a disaster on the horizon."

"Let him feel like the old Donnie King again."

"What if he fails?"

"He won't."

"It's too much of a risk."

Ranger smirked. "What's life without the risk?"

"He doesn't realize it, but me stopping his hits is a good thing. As soon as he fails…that's his reputation gone."

"Give him an easy one. You must have someone."

Yates sighed. "Hanson Sale."

"Who?"

"An easy hit. I was going to do it myself."

"Give it to Donnie."

"I don't know, my gut is telling me it's a bad idea."

"Listen to your heart."

Yates glanced at Donnie. "My heart is telling me to press a pillow over his face to save myself."

"Fine, don't listen to your heart…listen to mine. He *needs* it, Yates."

Yates sighed and tipped his head back into the table. Something toppled from the other side, no doubt sprinkling spoil everywhere.

"Why a flower shop?" Ranger asked.

"Why not?"

"You don't give a shit about flowers. Well…not physical ones. I think it would've suited you."

"What would have?" Yates asked.

"That shirt," Ranger smiled. "The one with the roses. The one that your eyes went wide for."

"Thought you hated flowery patterns?"

"I do, but surely that's an incentive to wear them."

Yates laughed. "Yes, a very good one. Every day, starting tomorrow."

EPILOGUE

At first, Yates wasn't sure about the daisy-covered shirt, then he'd got it off the hanger, and put it on and everything was right with the world. His eyes bulged at how much he loved it as he admired himself in the mirror. The shop assistant showered him with compliments and said how good it looked on him, and he smiled, agreeing with her every word.

It was a bonus when Ranger came into the shop and retched at the sight of it.

"Nice to see you too," Yates mumbled.

"That's…that's definitely a flowery shirt."

"Doesn't it suit me?"

"It would suit no one, maybe a tablecloth at a wake, but that's about it."

Yates sighed through his nose. "Is there something you wanted?"

"Right," Ranger said, rushing closer. "I wanted to know if you'd heard the news—

The bell chimed out, cutting Ranger off. They both turned and glared at the two visitors, not customers strolling closer. DS Waymirth and DC Aster.

Waymirth slapped a newspaper down on the desk.

"That news," Ranger said.

"The Viper, or Harrison Fox, is no longer an issue."

Yates flicked his gaze from Waymirth, down to the newspaper. He scanned through the article, not taking in a word other than the headline. "He's dead."

"Yes. He died last night at Somerton house. We had multiple calls reporting a suspicious death, and when we attended, we were lucky enough to catch him."

"Um." Ranger raised his finger. "Not to be technical, but you can't catch a dead man. Unless he's falling from the sky…then maybe you can."

"We identified him," Aster said.

"Yeah, but he was already dead so you can't really count it as a police success." Ranger turned to Yates. "Apparently, The Viper was the waiter. Well, he tied up the real waiter and took his place, then he pricked Quentin with a needle inside the auction room, no one suspected a thing."

Not the huge burly guy that almost choked Yates to death. He glared at Ranger until the skin beneath his eye began twitching.

"Hey," Waymirth said, pointing at Ranger. "Weren't you there last night."

"Nah, I've got one of those faces…and haircuts."

"I'd say you look pretty unique." He elbowed Aster. "Isn't he Quentin's son? The guy who wailed his head off?

"Must have been some other guy," Ranger said.

Aster narrowed his eyes. "Yeah, I think the other guy had a beard."

"Really?" Waymirth asked.

"Tell you the truth, I didn't pay him much attention. I was too focused on catching The Viper."

"Yes." Waymirth rubbed his hands together. "Which means a round of applause from you."

"You didn't catch him. He died." His eyebrows tugged together sharply. "How did he die?"

"Yep. That's the best part." Ranger beamed.

Waymirth leaned up on his tiptoes. "The best part is he's no longer terrorizing the area and we can finally put a name and face to him."

Ranger ignored him. "According to the article, he slipped over by the fountain and broke a spare vial of poison in his pocket. He vipered himself."

"Slipped over? On what?"

Ranger hummed. "There's an eyewitness who claims there was a pile of sick by the fountain…"

"Eyewitness," Yates whispered.

Aster snatched the paper off the counter. "There's no mention of an eyewitness suggesting he slipped in sick."

Ranger threw his hands up in the air. "That's what I heard."

"From who?" Waymirth snapped.

Yates's phone buzzed in his pocket. He pulled it out, to see a message from Donnie.
I've still got it.

The End

FLOWERSHOP ASSASSINS

Bye Baby
So Pathetic
Raging Ranger

Special thanks to:
Lara and Alba for Beta reading.
Truus for naming Dylan.
Karen for editing.
Books&Moods for the amazing cover.

And huge thank you to everyone that read these ridiculous stories, I hope they distracted you from the real world for a while and made you smile!

If you enjoyed it, please think about leaving a review on amazon or goodreads and spreading the word on social media.

Even the smallest of reviews or a rating is a huge help in getting my books noticed <3

Are you on facebook?

Why not come join the lockup for news, teasers, cover reveals etc. Louise's Lockup

If you enjoy The Flowershop Assassins, you might like some of my other titles:

Self-published titles:
Adrenaline Jake Series
The first in the novella series is free on amazon, and the second is free if you sign up to my mailing list: Sign up

Evernight tiles:
The Freshman
The Psychopath
The Rat
Balls for Breakfast
New Recruit
One for Sorrow
Two for Joy

Happy Reading
Louise <3